FOR I HAVE SINNED

A James Bay Novel

KATHLEEN IRENE PATERKA

DEDICATION

For my dear, sweet St. Linda.

Rest in peace.

.

ACKNOWLEDGMENTS

I am extremely grateful to a multitude of people who were so gracious in lending their assistance when it came to telling Father Greg's story. Special thanks to the following:

Jenna Mindel and Christine Elizabeth Johnson, simply the best friends and critique partners an author could hope to have. Both of them are tremendously talented authors, dedicated and devoted to their craft, and I am so blessed in their friendship. Jenna and Christine, the Queen of Hearts Club rocks!

Catherine Chant and Edie Ramer, for their enduring friendship, valuable feedback, and unwavering support.

Amy Atwell and Therese Walsh, for believing in Father Greg and his story, and encouraging me to go for my dreams.

My beta reader, Peggy Kusina, who after reading the manuscript, told me *"Be not afraid."*

My editor, Anne Victory, who fell in love with Father Greg even as she edited the pages; Karen Duvall, for her inspirational artwork; and Amy Eye, the Queen of Formatting.

And, as always, my husband Steve. Only someone who lives with a writer can understand all that goes into the birth of a novel. Steve is my someone, and always will be. Thank you, sweetheart.

Last, to believers and non-believers everywhere. This novel is not meant to offend. Rather, it is meant to open eyes, ears and hearts to the glory that is God, and belongs to God alone. I was advised time and again not to write this story, but in the end, I had no choice. Once Fr. Greg's voice began rumbling in my head, he was insistent upon being heard. I alone take full responsibility for the contents of this novel. Any mistakes in it are mine.

I will place my law within them, and write it upon their hearts.

~Jeremiah 31:33

CHAPTER ONE

Maybe the nuns lied.

Year after year, with us kids cooped up like prisoners in stuffy, overheated classrooms that smelled like dirty socks, they drilled the rules into our heads about the need to repent. Confession, they warned, and receiving absolution for our sins was the only way to enter heaven and be with God.

So where is everybody?

Every Saturday afternoon for the past two years I've spent as priest in this parish, it's been pretty much the same thing. I sit alone in this tiny afterthought of a room, tucked away in the back of church and wait for someone to show up. From four o'clock to four thirty when my confessional is open, I've got time enough to say one rosary plus count the stained-glass panes adorning the window; two rosaries, if I skip the window. It's my regular routine and I've got it down to a spiritual science.

Obviously, people nowadays have better things to do on Saturday afternoons than visit my confessional.

Or maybe not. There's a creak as the door opens, then a

slight rustle as someone kneels, a shadowy figure behind the linen screen.

"Hello? Father? Are you still here?"

The voice—young, female—comes as a surprise. The occasional penitent tends to be elderly, but she sounds barely out of her teens.

"Go ahead." I shove my rosary in my pocket, shift in my chair as the church bell tolls four thirty. First—and last—customer of the day. Mass starts at five.

"Bless me, Father, for I have sinned. It's been *years* since my last confession." The voice rushes through the screen. "Ohmigod, Mama would kill me if she knew. When I was growing up, she always said you had to confess at least once a year, or it's considered a sin. And she would know. Mama went to Catholic school. She knows all the church rules."

I can't help chuckling to myself. Sounds like her mama and I might know some of the same nuns.

"Let's not worry how long it's been," I suggest. "Instead, give yourself some credit for showing up today. That's a good first step, and I'm sure God agrees."

"You think so?" A sigh filters through the screen. "I don't think He'll like the other part." She hesitates. "Can you go to Hell for hating people? Especially if one of them is a priest?"

Did I hear her correctly? I'm fifty-four years old and thought my hearing was fine.

Until now.

"Could you repeat that?" I lean closer to the screen.

"I know it's a terrible sin to hate someone." Her voice drops, barely above a whisper. "Do you think God will forgive me?"

Forget about God. I'm curious which guy she's talking

about. Our diocese in Northern Michigan has over forty priests, and I can think of a few I don't like either without too much trouble. So, which one is it?

My gut tightens. Good Lord, what if it's me? All those jokes I tell from the pulpit; I should have known they'd get me in trouble someday.

"God forgives everyone if they are truly sorry." I tug at the Roman collar tightening around my neck. When did the room get so stuffy? Who the hell installs a stained-glass window that can't be opened?

"I'm not sure about the being-sorry part, but I'm working on it," she says. "It was hard enough getting up the nerve to come in here and admit the truth to you. I sat in that pew for what seemed like forever. In fact, five minutes ago I nearly lost my nerve and walked out. But then I remembered your sermon from last Sunday, how you laughed all the way through it…"

Oh, God, she *is* talking about me. And I'm guilty as charged. But this is the first time anyone has complained about my jokes. Besides, I've always believed God to have a marvelous sense of humor. Why not bring it along to Sunday Mass?

"But it was your eyes that finally got me out of the pew and in here on my knees. You've got kind eyes, Father, the kind of eyes that smile. You don't seem like all the other priests. That's what made me take the chance and come here today. I thought you would understand. At least, I hope you will."

I blow out a long sigh, stretch out my legs. Okay, obviously we're not talking about me.

"I'm probably doing this all wrong." She hesitates, her voice wistful. "I know the church has rules about the way they like things done, including the way you should make a confession. But I'll admit it, Father. I've never been good at following the rules."

A rebel when it comes to the rules? That makes two of us. I've had enough skirmishes with the diocese about insisting I enforce archaic church rules to last me a lifetime.

Pick your battles with the bishop carefully, I tell myself.

One confrontation at a time, my friend Father Ray tells me.

One day at a time, my program tells me.

"You're doing fine," I assure her, "although some people find it easier talking face to face. Come around the screen, if you like. I have another chair over here."

But I'm not holding my breath. Despite my attempts to convince them otherwise in my two years here as pastor at St. Mary's of the Lakes, parishioners are bent on adhering to tradition.

I blink as she scoots around the panel and suddenly stands in front of me.

"I'm Gina," the young woman says, extending a hand. "Gina VanBrabant."

The firm handshake comes as a surprise, as does the break in anonymity. People who show up for confession don't shake hands, much less introduce themselves.

Nor do the priests.

"I'm Father Greg Kozminski."

"Yes, I know." She sinks into the chair facing me. "I've been coming to Sunday Mass here in James Bay since Joe and I moved to town."

I've noticed her in church for the past several weeks, a silent lone presence in one of the side pews. A tangle of black curls frames her face. A shy smile tugs at one corner of her mouth. I catch the glint of a diamond wedding band on her finger. She's married? In those flip-flops and worn jeans, she looks barely old enough to be out of high school, let alone someone's wife.

But even in the dim glow of the little lamp on the table between us, her face is pale. Dark eyes warn there could be trouble ahead.

"Your sermons are great. People probably think I sleep through them because I always close my eyes. But I learned long ago that's the best way to listen." A high blush rises on her cheeks. "I like to pretend you're talking directly to me," she confesses.

I knock down a quick swell of pride. My ego would love to claim a seat on God's throne, but I'm merely a voice for the words she hears at Mass. He's the One who put them in my heart.

"Glad you decided to forego the kneeler." I settle back in the hard wooden chair, encourage her with a smile. "It gets lonely on this side of the screen. Most people don't bother with confession anymore."

"Do you blame them? Who wants to admit you screwed up, much less tell a priest? It's bad enough knowing you're guilty."

Guilt and grief. In my twenty-five-years-plus as a priest, I've heard countless admissions of fear and loneliness rampant in people's hearts. Marriages destroyed by adultery, promising careers ruined by drinking and drugs, families torn apart by abuse. A priest gathers the darkness that collects in people's souls and hopefully helps them walk toward the light of forgiveness.

Though lately, fewer people seem interested in seeking out my help. What's causing them to lose heart? Am I trying my best? Is it me? The church?

God, help me to help this young woman choose the right direction.

"What brings you here today, Gina?"

Her gaze drops, coming to rest on the purple silk stole draped around my neck. The stole proclaims me God's representative on earth, capable of absolving her sins.

Suddenly the wariness is back in her eyes.

She fingers the wedding band, worrying it back and forth over her knuckle. "Father, do you believe in love at first sight?"

The question is a definite first in my confessional. I swallow down a smile. "I'm not sure I have an answer for that."

"I fell in love with Joe the day I met him. Mama always said that love is the greatest gift of all. And I believe, with all my heart, that's what Joe is… a gift to me, straight from God."

Her mouth twists. "Although my father doesn't think so. He has definite ideas about life and church, and the way things should be. '*How dare you think about dating someone like him?*' he said. '*He's not one of us, and I'll be damned…*'"

She pauses, blushing slightly. "Sorry, Father Greg, excuse my language, but I'm just repeating my father's words. '*…and I'll be damned if I'll let my daughter marry one of them.*'"

Gina's eyes narrow. "You see, Joe's not an American, and he didn't grow up in this country. I don't think he realizes how intolerant some people can be. People like my father. '*He's not one of us….*' " Her face tightens. "I was done listening before he even said that. But then Mama cried and begged me to go see Father Michael, so I made the appointment. There's no way I could ever tell Mama *no*."

"Who's Father Michael?" I ask, though I've got a pretty good idea we're finally talking about the errant priest.

"He's the pastor back home in our parish between

6

Ypsilanti and Ann Arbor." Gina's face scrunches in a scowl. "Joe and I kept the appointment, but I should have known it would end up being a waste of time. Father Michael was as bad as my father. Worse, even; you'd think at least a priest would have some clue about kindness and compassion. Father Michael was horrible when we went to see him. I think he actually enjoyed refusing to marry us."

"Did he give you a reason?" *He's not one of us...* Her father might be a jerk, but this Father Michael is a Catholic priest, trained to be open-minded. Catholic means universal, welcoming to all. No matter what a person's nationality or faith.

"He mentioned something about a six-month rule. Even after I explained that Joe and I had known each other for six months, Father Michael told us it didn't matter, he still wouldn't marry us. He said even if we were a normal couple, there'd be no getting around the rules." Gina rolls her eyes. "He especially seemed to love that part, bringing up the rules."

"I assume he was referring to the premarital counseling sessions," I say gently. "The six-month waiting period is customary."

Mandatory is more like it. When it comes to canonical laws, the Catholic church holds an exclusive copyright.

"Sorry, Father, I guess I didn't make myself clear. Father Michael said that even if Joe and I waited six months, he still wouldn't marry us."

I frown. That doesn't make sense unless there's a religious impediment she's not mentioning.

"He told us we had no business getting married. He said it didn't matter that Joe had already finished his university studies and had a good job or that I was in college, too. Father Michael told me I was too young to understand what I was getting myself into, and that the cultural differences would prove too great. He said that if I did go through with marrying Joe, I'd eventually end up sorry." Her eyes narrow. "Then he threw us out of his office."

I blink. "He did what?"

Gina nods. "Father Michael said if Joe and I were hell-bent on getting married, that's exactly where we would end up… in Hell."

I've stumbled across my share of coldhearted guys wearing the collar throughout the years, but this Father Michael sounds like a holier-than-thou jackass, the kind of priest that gives the rest of us a bad name. And as for cultural differences? No one deserves to be treated the way Gina's described, no matter who they are or where they're from. We've got to be dealing with another faith for her father to be so harsh, her mother so upset, and the priest so adamant in his refusal to marry them.

A radical orthodox faith.

"Joe and I were married two months ago in a civil ceremony in front of a judge. Definitely not the wedding I always dreamed of, but definitely the right man," she says. "I love Joe with all my heart. And I know God was there with us in the courtroom that day, no matter what anyone thinks—including my father or Father Michael. I believe God lives in people's hearts, not in some old church or what some stuffy priest says.

Gina's hand flies to her mouth. "Holy crap! No offense, Father. I didn't mean you."

"No offense taken." I chuckle softly. She's a delight. "Believe it or not, I've bumped into a few of those priests myself."

More than a few.

"Joe is the most positive loving man I've ever met. How anyone could hate him for what he is is beyond me. What makes people think they have the right to judge?"

Religious intolerance. How many wars have been fought throughout history because of that very thing? There's a big Muslim population in downstate Michigan, especially near the university towns. If things were bad before the terrorist attacks in 2001, the fragile truce that now exists between Christianity and Islam barely borders on civility. It's hard to believe the world—even in modern-day America—can be like that, especially tucked away like I am in this small Northern Michigan town. But every visit home I make to see Mom downstate serves as an instant reminder that people haven't let go of their fear or anxiety. You feel it everywhere: restaurants, shopping malls, even in the grocery store. People keep their distance. The distrust and apprehension is there in their eyes, and the quick turn of their heads as they encounter men with swarthy faces and women in head scarves, some shrouded with face veils.

Not one of us.

What the hell does it matter who or what a person is? Muslim, Jewish, Protestant, Catholic. We're not defined by a country or a religion.

One man at a time. One heart at a time.

"Life is short enough as it is," Gina says. "There's no time or room for hatred."

"The world would certainly be a wonderful place if everyone thought that way," I agree. "Unfortunately, hatred exists—so much of it because of religion."

She eyes me carefully. "What do you think, Father?"

Do I tell her the truth? That she's sweet, spirited, and a bit of a rambler? If I was smart, I'd tell her to phone the rectory for an appointment, then send her on her way with a penance to say some prayers for her father, Father Michael, and other priests like him. Gina hasn't done anything wrong except skirt a mere technicality mandated by the church.

Although I'm sure if Bishop Holden heard me label marrying outside the church to be *a mere technicality* he would vehemently disagree.

But this isn't the time or place for a theological discussion about the shortcomings of the Catholic church. That's a topic normally reserved for debate with my good friend Father Ray over a leisurely dinner, not something to discuss with a vivacious young woman in my confessional late on a Saturday afternoon.

Not with Mass starting soon.

"The church teaches—"

"I don't care about the church." Black curls swing as she shakes her head. "I trust you, Father Greg. That's why I'm here. I want to know what you think."

How do I admit the truth? I'm a priest, but I'm still just one man. The Catholic church isn't interested in my opinion, nor what Gina thinks, either.

As a priest, as a Catholic, it's a hard reality for me to accept. Hearing any of it isn't going to help her.

But God help us all if the church and its priests dominate to the point that has people afraid to question authorities or search their own hearts.

"The Catholic church is not a democracy." I weigh each word carefully before I speak. "The rules exist for a reason."

She sits forward in her chair, a little of the snap disappearing from her eyes. "Are you telling me you agree with Father Michael? That Joe and I were wrong? That despite what Father Michael said and did, we shouldn't have broken the rules?"

While I don't know the details of what went on in that office with that particular priest, one thing I do know: the church and its rules are damn good at breaking people's hearts.

"Perhaps it would be easier if I put it this way," I say gently. "Ultimately, God is the only judge."

"But—"

I hold up one hand and she sputters into silence.

"And I believe," I continue, "be it right or wrong, that each of us is called to live our lives in a way so that when we finally stand before Him, we are able to honestly say *I did my best and was guided by love*."

"But that's it exactly!" Her eyes shine with a fierce intensity. "It's all about love, isn't it? I knew you would understand."

Her face loses that battered look, like she's found what she came looking for. But at what expense? My gut twists. Maybe it was a mistake, admitting how I feel. My personal beliefs don't belong in the confessional. But how can I let her walk away without hope?

"I don't care one bit about my father, but I haven't found the courage to tell Mama yet. Bad enough she thinks Joe and I are living together. It will break her heart when she finds out we got married outside of the church."

Gina draws in a deep breath, taking up all the air in the small space between us. "That's the other reason I'm here. I want to have our marriage blessed. In church. Maybe this weekend? After Sunday Mass?"

The look on her face is so determined and the trust she's put in me so complete that I long to say yes.

Even though I know it's impossible.

"I'm afraid it's not that easy. These things take time," I say carefully. "The church law is very specific. Marriage is a sacrament not to be entered into lightly."

"But Joe and I are already married."

"Yes, I know, but—"

"Shouldn't that make things simpler?"

It's easy to understand her frustration. Hell, I get frustrated, too, even after all my years as a priest. I still butt heads on a regular basis with the church hierarchy over rules and laws that no longer make sense. I keep waiting for things to change, but how long is it going to take? The Catholic Church is a marvelous institution for upholding tradition merely for tradition's sake.

But at whose expense? At how much heartbreak?

"What if I told you I'm going to have a baby?" Her chin tilts upward. "Would that make a difference?"

Babies trump all. Is she telling the truth or playing the sympathy card to get what she wants? God knows it would not be the first time I've been drawn in by some parishioner who showed up with a sad story.

"I am pregnant, Father," she says, her eyes softening. "I would never lie about something like that. Though I'll admit finding out about the baby was a surprise. But Joe is so pleased, and so am I. It's like God told us that, in spite of everything that's happened, we made the right decision and that things will be okay. That's why I want to have our marriage blessed in church, and I want our baby baptized. More than anything, Father Greg, I want to make things right with God."

She blinks once, twice, and her eyes lock on mine. What's her story? Is she telling the truth or hiding something from me? I search her face, but all I see is honesty, hope, and a plea for help.

Call me a fool, but I want to help. Ray would call me more than a fool. He thinks I'm a pushover, too easy on people, and in all honesty, he's probably right. I can be naïve and too trusting at times. Over the years, I've oftentimes ended up sorry for the things I've done, and the people I've tried to help.

But doesn't everyone deserve the benefit of the doubt? And there's something about Gina that makes me want to believe she's telling the truth. My gut tells me I can believe her.

And I would do anything to wipe away that dark smudge of pain in her eyes.

"What about your husband? Is he agreeable to all of this?"

"We haven't exactly talked about it," she hedges.

I eye her for a long moment. "Did you tell him you were coming here today?"

She shifts in her chair. "Not exactly."

I sit back, consider the options. It doesn't require a degree in theology to see how much she loves her husband. Gina dredged up the courage to seek me out, despite the damage caused by Father Michael. She's turned to me for guidance and expects me to supply some answers. But I don't want to make matters worse, say the wrong thing, and cause her to bolt.

Priests carry so much on their souls, things whispered under the seal of the confessional. Sometimes I feel like I'm drowning under the weight of the sadness surrendered. People expect me to listen, to give wise counsel. But how do I know I've said the right thing? The church has given me the authority to sit in judgment, to counsel them on what to do. But what if I'm wrong? Who am I to judge?

"Please, Father, can you help us? I promise we'll do whatever you say."

What business do I have instructing someone like this young woman how to live her life? Perhaps if priests were allowed to marry, if I'd been permitted to have a family of my own, things would be different. I've honored my vocation for nearly thirty years, and my love for God has deepened, but so has my frustration with the church. The divisiveness tears at my heart. Perhaps that is the worst of

13

all—the necessity of remaining separate, of withholding myself from the rest of the flock.

Jesus spoke of finding the lost sheep. But what of the shepherd? Who goes searching for him when the shepherd feels lost?

Gina isn't here to hear my truth.

That sometimes I feel like a fraud.

That sometimes I feel like ripping this Roman collar right off my neck.

"Tell Joe I want to meet him." I suddenly decide. "Bring him to Mass. The three of us can chat after that."

"Thank you, Father." The sudden glow on her face reminds me of a radiant Madonna. "I knew coming to see you was the right thing to do. Joe and I belong together; you'll see, once you meet him. He's the right man for me. My father was furious when he found out we were dating, and he threw me out of the house. Mama begged him not to, but he wouldn't listen." Her eyes disappear in tiny black slits. "He never listens."

She blinks fast, and I worry there'll be tears soon. When women cry in the confessional, it's usually because the hurt is too huge to hold inside.

I hand her a box of tissues as the church bell tolls the quarter hour. It's my cue to head up front to the sacristy and begin preparing for five o'clock Mass. I hear muffled sounds as the church fills up. People shuffle in the back door, coughing, chatting with the ushers as they grab bulletins.

But I am not going to abandon Gina. It won't be the first time Mass is five minutes late. Besides, they can't start without me.

"I hate the way he makes me feel—resentful and mean." Her fists ball in hard little knots. "I hate him. I think I've always hated him."

"Hate is a powerful word," I say gently.

"Are you saying it's wrong to feel the way I do?"

"No, of course not. A person has every right to their feelings. All of us are human. Even your father," I add.

"Hate the sin, but love the sinner?"

"Something like that."

"But how is that fair?" Her eyes blaze. "Why should I be the one who has to forgive? My father refuses to accept Joe. He's the one at fault, not me."

"But you're the one who came to confession," I point out. "And like it or not, lots of things in the world aren't fair." I cringe as words I myself hated hearing as a child spout from my own mouth. "And it doesn't sound like your father is interested in changing," I add.

"That's an understatement," she mumbles.

"Then the change will need to start with you. Pity the man he is, Gina. Pity the way he lives his life. But most of all, remember to pray for him."

"Prayers won't do him any good," she predicts. "I could spend all day on my knees and it wouldn't make a difference. He'll never change."

"Never is a long time. People have a way of coming around." I've seen hard-core Catholics crack following the birth of their first grandchild, despite the stigma of an interfaith marriage.

"You don't know my father. He'll never forgive me for marrying Joe. And once he finds out about the baby, he'll figure out some way to keep Mama and Donny out of my life. Besides Joe, Mama and my little brother are the only family I've got."

She balls up a tissue and rolls it around in her hand. "Tell me the truth, Father. Will God forgive me for marrying outside the church? For the way I feel about

Father Michael, and for hating my father? I hate the way he treats Donny and how he ruined Mama's life. But I refuse to let him destroy mine, or Joe's life, either. Maybe it's for the best that we're far away from him. Joe's never met my father. He would never understand if I told him even half of what my father said."

Gina shudders. "That I'd been raised to know better, that people are meant to be with their own kind." She struggles to swallow, like the words are a thick clump in the back of her throat. "He said... that Joe and I being together is a sin against God."

And Gina dared to break the rules.

Poor kid. She's had a rough time of it, brought up in a traditional Catholic family headed up by a bully who used rage and religion to keep his family in line.

"I'll help in any way I can," I promise, "starting with marriage preparations. We'll take it from there, then work on the baptism. Meanwhile, you go home and talk with Joe. Tell him you came to see me today. Bring him along to Mass. Let him see what's involved with the church. And if he's interested in taking instructions, I'll be happy to help with that, too."

Gina blinks. "Instructions?"

"If Joe would like to join the Catholic faith," I explain.

"But..." Two bright spots flame on her cheeks. "I'm sorry, Father, I thought you knew."

Knew what? Something's not right.

"Joe is just as much a Catholic as you or me," Gina says. "The reason my father hates him is because Joe is black."

I trudge across the parking lot after Mass, headed for

the rectory, my thoughts still on Gina. With no black families living in town, and—save for Gina and Joe—no interracial couples, either, the two of them should prove an interesting addition to our summer-resort community. Our country has come a long way, especially now we've witnessed an African American president in the Oval Office. But I'm not foolish enough to think the barriers and bigotry have disappeared. Gina and Joe will need plenty of support.

Especially since her father has disowned her.

Especially with a baby on the way.

Especially after that bumper sticker I saw on a car in downtown James Bay the other night.

Never apologize for being white.

The rectory back door slams behind me, a noisy reminder I promised Mom this morning that I would speak with the janitor about having it fixed. If I don't talk to Vince soon, she'll be sure and remind me.

I glance down the long, narrow kitchen, poke my head in the empty dining room. The massive table wears a snowy white tablecloth and is neatly set for two.

Obviously my plans to take her out for dinner tonight after Mass have changed.

I wander into the front entry. "Mom? Where are you?"

"Upstairs." A voice drifts from above. "I'll be right down."

I hang over the railing, watching as she grips the banister and slowly makes her descent. Despite the quilted pink housecoat, she looks regal as a queen. That glorious cloud of white hair crowning her head still surprises me. Sometime during the past year, she let her hair go. When did that happen? How could I have not noticed? How much happens to those we love while we're too busy worrying about other things?

"Gregory, how many times do I have to tell you not to slump?" she says as she reaches the bottom step. "You'll ruin your posture."

"I think it's a little late to be worrying about that now," I say, straightening to my full height of six foot three.

She gives an affectionate rap on my shoulder. "What did I teach you? *Never say never.* It's never too late for anything."

I plant a soft kiss on her cheek. "I'm fifty-four years old, Mom. Maybe it's time you quit telling me what to do."

"I might be an old lady, but I'm still your mother," she chides. "Remember all those years you spent hunched over the piano, and I would tell you to sit up straight? I don't want to see my effort wasted. You would understand these things, Gregory, if you had children of your own."

I hold back a sigh and a twinge of longing for something I've never had, that will never be. A Catholic priest is a spiritual father to everyone, but a biological father to no one. What do I know about married life or babies either, for that matter? My knowledge of infants comes mainly from the baptismal font, where the vast majority usually dissolve in a fit of red faces and piercing screams while I'm baptizing them. Plus, I'm an only child. There will never be any nieces or nephews for me to cuddle.

"Ever wish you and Pop had had more children?"

She halts in the doorway. "Good Lord, Gregory, where do you come up with these things?"

"Just wondering." I trail her into the kitchen.

"What would I have done with two or three more children? You were bad enough." She opens the cupboard and pulls out a skillet. "Once you learned to walk, you never sat still. I was constantly chasing after you. And after you learned to talk? All those questions. *Why, Mama*? You never stopped. It was always *why, why, why*?"

A faraway look flits over her face. "You asked so many questions, sometimes I was afraid I would run out of answers."

With anyone else the words would be hurtful, but the playful smile and gentle look in her eyes tells me I am loved.

That I have always been loved and cherished as a gift from God.

I lean against the counter, watching as she opens the refrigerator and whips out a bowl of eggs ready for scrambling. "I thought we were going out to dinner."

"I thought so, too. But Mass started late, remember? And now it's already past seven o'clock; I changed my mind."

She whisks the eggs in a deft movement, adds a few drops of milk. Butter sizzles in a slow dance inside the skillet as she adjusts the burner. "What happened tonight, Gregory? You never used to be late with Mass."

Do I admit the truth? I was waylaid by two females; one confession by a wild-eyed beauty named Gina before Mass, and one long chat in the sacristy afterward with a frosted blonde named Lila.

Maybe it's best if I keep my mouth shut.

"I got a little sidetracked."

"And I got a little hungry," she says matter-of-factly, popping slices of bread in the toaster. "Besides, there's nothing wrong with eating in. You should save your money instead of spending it on me. And it's Saturday night. Knowing this town, the restaurants are already crowded. The last thing I want is to sit around waiting for undercooked and overpriced food."

"I was going to take you to Chuck's Tavern and Grill. You seemed to enjoy it the last time you came for a visit."

Mom wrinkles her nose. "That place is fine if you're in the mood for a hamburger or fried fish. Which I am not." She halts, skillet in hand, and peers up at me. "And what's wrong with scrambled eggs? You liked them enough when you were growing up. Or has that changed, too?"

"Never," I assure her as she spoons golden mounds of eggs evenly between our plates, adds toast and fresh tomatoes slices. "You make the best scrambled eggs in the world."

She thumbs my cheek with a quick smile. "That's what I like to hear."

I carry our plates into the dining room and we take our seats at the long table with me at the head and Mom on my right. We bow our heads and I offer a simple prayer. The zesty smell of lemon polish mingles with a sweet whiff of strawberry jam as I slather my toast. "I thought you told me you were going to spend this afternoon resting, not cleaning."

She blinks with innocent eyes. "All I did was dust."

I glance around the room. The chandelier sparkles, the sideboard gleams. I know my mother all too well, but she doesn't know herself. At seventy-eight years old, she has yet to learn her limits.

"I've been thinking maybe I should stay a little longer," she muses. "It might be a good idea. This place needs a woman's touch. And you need someone to take care of you, Gregory."

God help us both. I love my mother, but I need my own space. Space without her constantly in it.

"There's no need for you to worry about me. I'm perfectly capable of fending for myself. I know how to cook. You taught me, remember? Besides, I have a housekeeper."

She sniffs. "I've yet to see evidence of that. What's her name?"

"Martha. She comes in once a week, on Mondays."

"Well, whoever this Martha person is, she could use a lesson in proper household management," she says with a shrewd look. "I'm surprised you haven't already had a fire in the kitchen, the grease on the stove was that thick. I must have spent an hour scrubbing it down."

"Come on, Mom, don't go blaming Martha. Remember, this is a big house. She does the best she can."

Built over a century ago, the rectory originally would have housed two or three priests, plus a few associates. Nowadays, I'm left to ramble alone in this drafty old building.

"I'm lucky to have her," I add. "It wasn't easy getting Martha to come in and clean for what the church can afford to pay her."

"One would assume she'd be grateful for the job. Think of how many people in today's economy are looking for work." Mom nibbles at her toast. "And speaking of grateful, I hope the people in this parish appreciate having you as their priest. You're working too hard, Gregory, and I'm worried about you. Just think of everything you did today. First, that fancy wedding, then confessions, and Mass tonight. Plus, the two you'll say tomorrow. By the way, you did a nice job with your homily this evening. Very effective."

"Thanks, Mom. I try my best."

And try even harder when she's here. Mom plants herself firmly in the front pew every time she visits, just like she did at Mass tonight. And while her presence can be comforting, it's also a distraction.

Sometimes I wonder if it might be easier to connect with my parishioners if Mom sat further back.

Maybe in the last pew?

Not that I would suggest she move. I might be the priest, but she is my mother.

"How was the wedding this afternoon?"

"The usual." I spread jam on a second slice of toast. "The bride's father gave her away. The mother cried. The groom looked nervous."

"I notice they kept some of the flowers on the altar. Those roses must have cost a fortune."

I shrug. "Knowing that family, they can afford it. It was quite the lavish affair."

She eyes me over her cup of tea. "What about the reception?"

"They're having it at the Yacht Club."

Her eyebrows lift. "And you're sitting here in the rectory eating scrambled eggs? You'd think people, especially those with money, would have better manners. Don't they know the priest should always be invited to these sorts of things?"

I swallow down the truth along with a bite of toast. Not only did I receive an invitation, the bride's mother was gracious enough to include my mother, too. But I begged off, pleading a prior engagement. I'm sure Mom would have been thrilled to accompany me to the Yacht Club, but today's wedding was one I was glad to be done with. The lavish church ceremony and reception were two years in the making. The bride's jewel-encrusted dress easily cost thousands.

But despite the premarital counseling and the numerous sessions the three of us spent together, the bride's constant nagging and the groom's blithe disregard soured me months ago on this particular couple. Totally wrapped up in themselves, not in each other.

I give them one year, maybe two, at most. And that is being generous.

Perhaps Gina and Joe did themselves a favor. Not that I'm an advocate for young people running off and getting married outside the church. But somehow I have got to figure out how to get engaged couples to concentrate on what matters most: the love between a man and woman, rather than the pomp and circumstance they think is due the bride and groom.

Especially with the divorce rate in this country hovering near fifty percent.

Mom settles back in her chair. "By the way, what is the name of that little blonde who was up there on the altar with you during Mass?"

I scrape up the rest of my eggs, trying to remember which kids were on the schedule to serve tonight. We've got a full roster, girls and boys alike. Finally I recall the two lanky young brothers, one of whom yawned all the way through Mass. "There weren't any girl altar servers tonight."

"No, I'm talking about that woman who helped during communion."

This time there's no need to think. "That was Lila Carter. She's one of my sacristans."

Thank God for Lila. She was in the sacristy while I was in the confessional with Gina. Lila made sure the wine was poured, the hosts were out, the altar servers weren't goofing off. With Lila around, things always go smoothly.

"That's right, I remember now," she muses. "Lila Carter. She came up after Mass and introduced herself."

The mild smile on my mother's face sends shivers up my neck. I've seen that look before. Suddenly, every instinct I have goes on high alert.

"She certainly knows her way around the altar, doesn't she?" Mom nibbles at her toast. "And it's obvious she wants everyone else to know she knows it, too."

I eye her carefully. "Lila is a very nice woman. I'm sure you'll see that for yourself once you get to know her."

"Really? How interesting you should say that, Gregory, especially since I have no intention of getting to know her. Why should I? Pushy, that's what she is. I know her type. Women like this Lila person are always up to something." She peers at me over her tea cup. "And just so we're clear on the subject, I have no interest in having dinner with her, either."

"What are you talking about?"

"She invited us for dinner tomorrow night. Something about a regular Sunday-night thing between friends." She sniffs. "Can you imagine?"

Actually, I can. I'm a frequent visitor to Lila's home nearly every Sunday night. She's a wonderful cook, gracious hostess, and one of the most generous people I know. Her Sunday evening get-togethers are a highly sought-after invitation in our little town. A priest learns early to be cautious around women, but with Lila there's no need. Our friendship is an easy one, based on similar ages, mutual respect, and devotion to God.

Plus our seats across the table from each other every Thursday night at our weekly AA meeting.

"Don't worry, Gregory. I realize this woman is one of your parishioners. I made sure to be very polite. I thanked her, and said that we were very busy. And I told her that since I would be in James Bay for only a few more days, we had other plans."

Even in her late seventies, Mom, a retired schoolteacher, still relishes being in control. She might not have control of her classroom anymore, but she's still got me.

"Lila does a lot for the church. I find her to be a great help."

"Just be careful you don't allow her to become too much of a help. Granted, she's not as young as some, but she's still an attractive woman, Gregory, and you are a priest. Never forget that. I've seen women like this Lila Carter before. They're always after something. Watch yourself, son. You don't want to end up sorry. Don't give her an opportunity to take advantage."

"Duly noted." Somehow I choke down the last of my toast. The thought of Lila having designs on me is almost too much to swallow. Lila carries a sweet serenity about her, not to mention she is the soul of discretion.

"And hopefully, Gregory, you will not make me out to be a liar. When I told her we had other plans, I meant it. I've already been here two days, and I've barely seen you. First you had that funeral yesterday morning…"

I blow out a sigh. "It's not my fault if someone dies—"

She tsk-tsks me into silence. "And then you spent all Friday afternoon working on your homily, plus that wedding this afternoon and Mass tonight. I know you're busy, Gregory, and your parish only has one priest." She pauses. "But you only have one mother."

Mom's an excellent navigator on the Catholic highway of guilt.

"Let me get through tomorrow's Masses and then we'll spend the rest of the day doing whatever you like," I promise. "Would you like to take a drive? The autumn colors are starting to turn."

"What about Raymond? I was hoping to see him while I'm here."

Father Ray Davis, one of my oldest friends since we roomed together during seminary days, has always been a special favorite of Mom's. With his parish only twenty-five miles away, it's an easy afternoon drive.

"I'll call Ray tonight," I say. "If he's busy, maybe the three of us can do something together Monday."

"Isn't that the day your housekeeper comes?" Mom rises from her chair and stacks our plates. "If you're afraid to have a little chat with her, Gregory, I'll be more than happy to help. I've seen evidence of mice in this rectory, and that is completely unacceptable. I raised you better than that. Don't forget, I'm coming for Christmas. I have no intention of putting up with rodents, even if you are my son." She clucks her tongue. "Just think what your parishioners would say, hearing your mother was here for the holidays and had to stay in a hotel."

I hold back a smile. Guaranteed they wouldn't care. Plus, Mom would enjoy room service, and I'd have the luxury of peace and quiet.

"I'll speak with Martha on Monday morning," I say, "as soon as she gets here." I take the dishes from her hands and place a gentle peck on her cheek.

"Promise?"

"Yes, Mom."

"Good." She nods. "And Gregory? One more thing…"

"What's that?"

"That janitor of yours. Does he work on Mondays, too?"

"Vince?" I eye her carefully. "Yes, he does. Why?"

Smiling sweetly, she turns her head and nods.

My heart sinks as I follow her gaze and spy the faulty kitchen door.

Looks like Monday morning, I'll be having a little chat first with Martha, then Vince.

Unless, God help all three of us, Mom gets to them first.

CHAPTER TWO

"So, Mrs. K., let me get this straight. You fired the rectory housekeeper?" Father Ray settles back in his chair with a sly wink for me.

"Well, of course I didn't fire her," Mom says, blinking innocently. A little too innocently, if you ask me. "Martha quit on her own accord. I merely suggested that she might want to be a little more thorough when she cleaned. Is it my fault she took offense when I mentioned seeing evidence of mice droppings in the kitchen cupboards?"

Her nose wrinkles slightly. "Besides, I would never have taken it upon myself to tell her to leave. That's not my place. And certainly not my job."

I break out in a loud fit of coughing. It's pretty obvious whose job it is she's referring to. Once again, I've come up lacking in the my-son-the-priest-does-a-fine-job-managing-his-staff-BUT department.

"I merely pointed out a few things to her," Mom continues. "How was I supposed to know that Martha would quit? But as Gregory's mother, it's my job to do what I can to make his life easier. And personally, I think he's better off without her. Meanwhile, that rectory he's

27

living in is an utter disgrace." She brushes a few bread crumbs into a neat little pile. "The paint is peeling off the walls, and the carpeting needs to be replaced. You've been there, Raymond. What do you think?"

"Truth, Mrs. K.? The place is a dump." Ray drains his Manhattan and signals the waitress for another drink. "Greg deserves better, but we're dealing with the church, remember? It takes money to make things happen."

"It always comes down to money, doesn't it?" Mom blows a delicate sigh that I know is aimed to raise my spirits. Too bad it can't raise the balance in the parish checkbook. "You'd think people would want to do better by their priests, especially seeing how you boys are responsible for them. They should take care of you. If they don't, what's to guarantee you'll be around to take care of them?"

"You can't blame the parishioners, Mom," I remind her. "The economy's not doing great."

"That's got nothing to do with it," Ray says. "People get wrapped up in their own little world. They see what they want to see, and hear what they want to hear. Give them a little push, Greg, and tell them what you need. Most people are glad to help once they know the situation."

"You're saying that Gregory simply needs to give his parishioners a little nudge?" Mom muses.

"Whoa, come on now—" I sputter.

"You know, Mrs. K., you might have something there." Ray eyes me over the table as the waitress serves his drink and provides us with dessert menus. "Greg's not much for entertaining, and I doubt anyone's been inside the rectory lately. Maybe if people had a chance to tour the place, they'd see how bad it is and do something about it."

Mom's eyes brighten. "Raymond, that is a wonderful idea."

I squirm in my chair. The look on her face scares the hell out of me. It's one of those why-didn't-I-think-of-this-sooner? expressions I learned to dread growing up. Like when I was nine and she bought me the cowboy outfit for Halloween when what I really wanted was an astronaut suit. Or when she volunteered to chaperone the St. Francis Eighth Grade Winter Dance when I'd already made up my mind I wasn't going.

Me, dance with a girl? No way.

Especially with my mother watching from the sidelines.

"I've just had the most marvelous idea." She beams at both of us. "I'll host an open house at the rectory. Doesn't that sound perfect? We'll serve coffee, fresh fruit, and pastries. And with the rectory right next door to church, everyone will come. Especially if we have it after Sunday Mass."

If I don't stop her, she'll be off on another of her tangents. "Mom, you know I love you, and I appreciate you wanting to help, but I don't think—"

"But that's the beauty of it, Gregory," she says, stopping me with one of those withering schoolteacher glances that come from years of dealing with recalcitrant students. "You don't have to think. In fact, you don't have to do anything except show up. I will take care of everything."

Mom in charge? The thought scares the hell out of me. I turn to Ray for help, but he merely winks.

Some hell of a friend he's turned out to be. My mother would never be running with this whole invite-the-parish-to-breakfast idea if he hadn't encouraged her by opening his big mouth.

"Mom, please, I'm telling you it won't work. You don't understand—"

"What I don't understand is why you think this will be such a problem," she primly announces.

She'd understand plenty if the situations were reversed. Mom loves her privacy, but mine vanished the day I was ordained. With a priest on call twenty-four seven and a faulty lock on the kitchen door, I'm continually clueless as to who's going to drop by next. I come in after morning Mass, there's a casserole waiting on the kitchen counter. I go out for groceries and an irate parishioner gives me holy hell at the checkout counter because we called another plumber rather than him when a church toilet needed repair. I sit down to watch the evening news only to hear the doorbell ring and find a parent sobbing at the front door, begging me to help get his daughter into rehab again.

I have no privacy, no life of my own. What I do have, according to Mom, are mice scampering through my kitchen cabinets.

"I don't understand why you're being like this. Then again, you always were a stubborn little boy. Why can't you just say *thank you* and let it be?"

I look to Ray for help but he merely shrugs, and sips his drink.

I'm on my own.

"Mom, I don't mean to seem ungrateful. But it's not right."

"What's not right?" she demands. "I don't understand."

I blow out a deep breath. If there was an easier, softer way, I'd take it. "You just can't walk in and take over like this."

"And why not?" Her face and voice are stony. She is not used to being challenged.

And I'm not used to challenging her. It's the stigma of an only child.

"For one thing, we're talking about the rectory, not the church," I say gently. "How do you think it would look if my mother is the one asking for money to fix up the place where her son lives?"

She sits back, hand to her throat, and pauses. "Why, I never thought of that," she says after a moment. "You're absolutely right, Gregory. Appearance is everything. Especially when it comes to asking for money." Her face softens and she pats my hand. "I'm sorry, sweetheart."

"No apology necessary. I know you only want what's best for me." I swallow down the shame over having foiled her scheme.

Then her eyebrows knit together and my heart kicks into overdrive.

"I don't know why I didn't think of this in the first place," she abruptly announces. "It's the perfect solution. Your parish has an active Rosary Altar Society. All I have to do is contact the right women. They'll be more than happy to host the event."

It's worse than I thought. Sixty ladies in the RAS, most of them retired, with every good intention of helping me out. And Mom directing from the sidelines.

It's all I can do not to bury my head in my hands.

"When do they hold their meetings?" she asks.

Ray grins, eyeballs me over his drink. We both know if I don't tell her, she'll discover it for herself easily enough. The information is listed on the cover of our Sunday bulletin.

"The first Monday of every month."

"I had planned on going home after this weekend, but this changes everything," she decides. "There's nothing on my schedule that can't be moved. My pinochle club doesn't start up again until mid-October, and the hospital guild should be able to manage without me for the next few weeks." She nods, her mind made up. "I'll plan on staying until I make sure everything is organized."

Thanksgiving is still more than a month away, but I feel like a trussed-up turkey ready to be popped in the oven. Guaranteed once the RAS ladies get wind of her idea, they'll be all over the rectory and they'll eat me alive.

My mother will be the one wielding the carving knife.

She rises with a regal smile. "Would you boys excuse me? I need to powder my nose. And if that waitress comes back, please order me an orange sherbet."

I grab Ray's arm as soon as her back is turned. "What the hell do you think you're doing, encouraging her like that? You know I couldn't care less about new carpet or furniture."

"Whoa, easy there, Greg." He raises a hand in protest. "She's only trying to help."

"Trying to ruin my life, you mean." I rake my fingers through my hair, wait as the waitress clears the remains of our dinners, takes our dessert orders. "What am I going to do? God knows I love her, but she's driving me crazy. I can't get any work done with her around. I was counting on her being gone by the end of the week, but after tonight..." I shake my head. "Obviously that's not going to happen."

"At least not until you get the carpet replaced or hire a new housekeeper." Ray prods me with a grin. "Did she really fire Martha?"

"Don't remind me," I mutter.

"Your mom's got moxie, I'll give her that. Still, Greg, I'd count my blessings if I were you. She's got your best interests at heart. We should all be so lucky."

"I know," I mumble as the guilt sets in. Ray's parents have been dead for years, and his relationship with his two younger brothers isn't what you'd term the best. They've been estranged for years—from Ray, as well as the church.

"Okay, I get it. And you're probably right about Mom,

too. But this crazy idea of hers about hosting a fundraiser to fix up the rectory is a waste of time. Why spend the money on carpet and paint when we've got tree roots clogging the sewer lines? Most of the windows need to be replaced. And as for the electrical wiring..." I roll my eyes. "I said a Hail Mary every time I turned on the bedroom air conditioner last summer."

"Praying it would work?"

"Praying I wouldn't fry in my sleep." I throw him a gloomy smile. "The garage door opener has been broke for months. I have to get out of the car and open the door if I want to park inside. And I haven't used the fireplace since I moved in. It's in such bad shape, I don't dare. If we had the money, I'd get it fixed or block it off. Every winter we lose heat straight up the chimney."

It's not my imagination, either. I've kept a close eye on the utility bills, despite Cynthia Whitman's best efforts to guard her turf. Our parish secretary has bleached-blond hair, beady brown eyes, and a holier-than-thou attitude that told me from the get-go she believes I'm clueless about everything except how to find my way around the altar.

No doubt Cynthia would be surprised by how much I do know. She's a nosy gossip, not to mention a snoop, and reports on a regular basis to her old boss, Father "Mac" MacAfferty, about the happenings at his former parish.

Plus, grouses to him about the shortcomings of her current boss.

Me.

"Renovating the rectory could end up costing us six figures," I say. "The church doesn't have that kind of money. That crazy MacAfferty put the place in debt with his remodeling project a few years ago."

God's house deserves the best, and I suppose I should be

grateful. The renovations are stunning, befitting a landmark such as Our Lady's, a Gothic beauty over one hundred years old. With a soaring ceiling, painted murals, gleaming wooden pews, and glorious stained-glass windows, Our Lady's is a showcase for Catholics, pre-and-post Vatican II. But Father Mac didn't do us any favors by sinking our parish over a million in debt.

And with the lousy economy, business leaving town, jobs disappearing, and houses falling into foreclosure, I'm the one responsible for coming up with the funds to make the mortgage payments. With a monthly price tag of ten thousand dollars, it's a struggle.

"Even if Mom does somehow manage to raise a few thousand dollars, why should I spend it patching some holes? What that rectory needs is a bulldozer razing it straight into the ground."

Then a wild thought suddenly bulldozes its way straight to the front of my brain. "What if we tear down the rectory and turn it into a parking lot?"

Ray stares at me like I've announced I've decided to run for Pope.

I lean forward, charged with an energy I haven't felt in months.

"Think about it. It makes total sense. The diocese keeps talking about consolidating parishes. We don't have enough priests and soon they won't have a choice. Our Lady's is one of the largest churches in the diocese. I can't see them closing us down." I feel the grin spreading across my face. "And with more parishioners, naturally we'll need more room for parking. With the rectory gone, we connect the space to the existing parking lot. Voila, all our problems solved."

"And where exactly do you intend to live?" he calmly asks.

"Who cares? I don't need much—just a small apartment where I can store my books, eat, and sleep."

Ray chuckles. "Good luck convincing the bishop to buy into that one."

"You think Holden won't go for the idea?"

"It's not the bishop I'm worried about," he says. "That's the original rectory, correct?"

"Yes, but—"

"Forget it, Greg." He eyes me over his empty glass. "You're living in a shrine."

"What's that supposed to mean?"

"Your parishioners' grandfathers and great-grandfathers built that house. Any of them get wind you're thinking about tearing the place down, you can kiss your Sunday collections good-bye. Not to mention, they'll go straight to the bishop. And guaranteed, Holden will back them one hundred percent. He's not going to expose himself to controversy, not when he's only two years away from retirement."

Much as I hate to admit it, Ray's analysis is probably dead-on. Bishop Holden runs a tight diocese and doesn't put up with anything that causes storm clouds in a parish. His priests are under orders to deliver sunshine and blue skies, no matter what the cost to their parishes or them personally.

For me, that means more mice taking up residence in the rectory.

Unless I plan to increase the budget, seal the cracks, and call in an exterminator.

"Maybe you could talk to Holden," I suggest. "You're good at schmoozing."

"Sorry, Greg, but I can't help you. I've been out of his good graces since I did that live television interview about Lenten practices without first clearing it with his office.

Christ, for all the grief Holden gave me, you'd think I'd been on the national news instead of some local station nobody watches.

"Ah, well, no great loss." Ray lifts a shoulder, rattles the ice cubes in his glass. "The less Holden and the diocese see of me, and me of them, the better off we'll all be." He grins. "Maybe you should send your mom over to argue your case. Women like her—devoted, diehard Catholics—are hard to resist."

"I'm sure she'd do it, but I don't need the grief," I mutter. "Holden would either canonize her or throw her out."

Ray leans across the table. "What's got you in such a sour mood tonight? And don't give me that crap about your mom staying for a few extra days. You're blessed to have her, and we both know it."

I ponder my friend across the table. Thank God—thank God! for Ray Davis. We've been best friends since hooking up as roommates our freshmen year in high school seminary, and our weekly Monday-night get-togethers have been a bright spot in my life for years. Lately, one of the few bright spots. I would trust him with my life.

But even Ray would probably find it difficult to grasp something I barely understand myself.

The vague restlessness. The sense that something isn't quite right. The longing for something I can't name. I've experienced feelings like this before, but normally the melancholy dissolves like an early morning mist in the wake of brilliant sunshine. Except this time. I can't even blame it on the weather, for we've experienced a glorious Indian summer for the past several weeks. There's no hint yet of a biting wind that precipitates the plummet from the glory of autumn into the dead of winter.

But there's already a winter chill settling in my heart.

I try to shake off the gloom and doom and focus on my friend, but it's hard to gather my thoughts. They scatter like the dry autumn leaves racing around the foundation of the rectory. Which reminds me, Vince the janitor and I need to have a little talk. If he doesn't get at those leaves before the snow falls, they'll end up in moldy piles rotting against the basement windows. Come spring, we'll have a mess.

"Greg, my friend, I think you need a vacation. How about we take a trip to Las Vegas? Prices are pretty reasonable right now; we could snag a couple of hotel rooms, do some gambling, play a few rounds of golf."

"I don't golf," I remind him. "And Vegas is a little rich for my blood."

"You'd be surprised how cheap it is."

"You'd be surprised how broke I am."

I don't carry the sin of envy on my soul, but I don't have the options Ray was born with. He comes from family money and can tap into unlimited resources whenever the spirit moves him. Ray is a trust-fund baby, but I'm on my own. There'll be no *mother house* like the nuns have, welcoming me home upon retirement. And God help the priest who hasn't seen fit to fund his 401K or sock away enough to buy himself a little condo. He'll end up at the mercy of some young upstart with a righteous-ring-around-the-Roman-collar attitude. Mandatory retirement and no place to retire means Senior Priest status, qualifying you for nothing more than a spare bedroom in a drafty rectory and the not-so-welcome privilege of being assigned the early Mass on Sunday mornings.

"Greg, you can't let this stuff get to you. Screw the rectory. For that matter, screw the bishop, too. Holden's a blowhard. What do they tell you in that twelve-step program of yours? *Easy does it.* Good advice. Let's take some time off, the two of us, and plan that getaway. It doesn't have to be Las Vegas. We'll go someplace warm. Wherever you like. My treat," he adds.

I catch sight of Mom slowly weaving her way back between the tables. Ray catches my look, grabs my arm. "We'll even invite your mom," he offers.

As usual, Ray is being his usual generous self. Somehow I manage a smile for my old friend.

"Thanks, but I'm not sure bringing Mom along qualifies as a vacation. Besides, I can't get away right now. Not with the holidays coming."

"Your mom's a gem, and we both know it," he reminds me. "Though you're probably right about the timing."

With the leaves already off the trees, Advent isn't far off. Normally I enjoy the four weeks the church spends in joyous preparation anticipating the Lord's birth. But this year even the mere thought of putting up a Christmas tree sounds like major work.

Then again, maybe if I string enough lights, the circuits will overload and the rectory might catch fire. All my problems would be solved in one big blaze.

Merry Christmas, me.

"We'll take that vacation, Greg, sooner or later. Meanwhile, try to relax. Let your mom help you out. And if you're looking for an angel to kick in some funds, why not hit up that girl in your parish who won the lottery? What was her name?"

"Lucy Carter," I mumble as Mom reaches the table.

"What are you boys whispering about?" she says as Ray and I both stand.

I keep quiet. One mention about Ray's vacation idea and Mom would have the three of us booked on a Caribbean cruise before tonight.

"Just a little gossip between friends." He gives me a quick wink as he holds out her chair.

"Anyone I know?" she inquires brightly.

"Lucy Carter," he says.

"Bishop Holden," I counter simultaneously, wishing Ray would learn to keep his mouth shut.

She eyes him as he pushes in her chair. "Is this Lucy Carter any relation to Lila Carter?"

"You've met the mysterious Lila?" His eyebrows lift. "Wow, Mrs. K., I'm impressed."

It's all I can do not to give him a good swift kick under the table.

"Oh, I've met her," she says, her lips pursing in a thin line. "Not that I had much choice, seeing how she came up and introduced herself after Mass last weekend." She frowns. "And what exactly do you mean, *mysterious*?"

I shoot Ray a say-one-more-word-and-you're-a-dead-man glare.

"*Mysterious* in that I've never met her," he say smoothly. "I was beginning to think she didn't exist."

"Oh, she's real enough," Mom says with a slight sniff. "And attractive, too... not that you boys would be interested, of course. But I know her type. Very forward, very pushy. She's the type of woman who thinks highly of herself and thinks everyone else should, too."

I sputter over my water glass. Pushy? Lila is anything but. Attractive, yes; anyone with eyes could see that. God created man, then in His wisdom gave us women to add beauty to our lives. Lila Carter is beautiful, but she's also a good friend, a trusted volunteer, and the soul of discretion. She's the type of woman anyone—including a priest, including me—would feel comfortable with. I would trust her with anything. Lila is beautiful, compassionate...

Maybe it's better not to trust her.

"She might be pushy, but she also has plenty of money," Ray advises. "Her daughter Lucy won seventy million dollars in the lottery. They both belong to Greg's parish."

"I remember you mentioning something about that." Mom turns to me. "Perhaps I should contact this Lucy and see if she might be interested in donating…"

"No," I state flat-out. "You are not to ask Lucy for money. She's been more than generous as it is. She just bought new Advent vestments for our parish."

Ray throws me a sharp stare. "The ones you were drooling over in that little shop in Rome? Those vestments cost five thousand dollars."

The pilgrimage we shared last spring seemed far removed from the reality of everyday life until last week when the unexpected shipment arrived. Unzipping the vestments from the thick, protective bag was like unearthing shrouded memories of the narrow, bustling streets of Rome crowding in the shelter of the Vatican walls. The soaring ceilings of the Basilica Major, the smell of incense, the church bells tolling.

I swallowed down a lump in my throat as I slipped the rich, embroidered vestments over my shoulders.

I am the Alpha and Omega… He who believes in me will never die.

But do I believe anymore?

Have I lost faith in God? In church?

Or faith in myself?

"I'll give you credit, Greg," Ray says. "You know how to make things happen. Bravo, for asking Lucy to pick up the tab."

"But I never asked," I protest. "They simply showed up on the FedEx truck one day. Somehow she knew what I wanted. It was like a miracle." I think a long minute. "I guess it *was* a miracle."

"Miracles don't just happen," Ray scoffs. "At least, not in my parish."

"Lila might have mentioned something," I admit. I remember flipping through the church catalogue with Lila one day, pointing out the vestments shortly after my return from Rome. Did I lament the cost? Somehow Lila must have known, but it's hard to remember. We chat about so many things. Lila has frosted blond hair, peaceful blue eyes, and a fragrant serenity that drifts around her like a heavenly cloud.

"Well, if Lucy Carter bought those vestments, there is no reason that you can't ask her to buy new carpet for the rectory," Mom states firmly. "Meanwhile, what is all this talk about the bishop? The grief the two of you have given that man over the years, you're lucky he hasn't fired you both."

"I'm sure the thought has occurred to him," Ray says.

"And replace us with what? There aren't enough priests to go around. Besides," I add, "we don't work for Holden."

"And who exactly do you think we work for?" Ray asks with a smirk.

"I thought we were working for God."

He slaps his hand on the table and barks with laughter. "Good one, Greg. I'd love to be around when you inform Holden you've got a new boss."

The waitress is back with Mom's sherbet, more coffee for me, pie and another drink for Ray. Mom eyes my coffee cup as she spoons her sherbet. "All that caffeine isn't good for you. You won't sleep tonight."

You should have ordered dessert instead," Ray says.

"I don't need the extra calories." I pat my stomach. "I'm trying to lose a few pounds."

"You still jogging?" He grabs his fork and attacks the thick slab of apple pie in front of him.

"Not as much as I would like. The older I get, the easier it is to slough off, especially once the cold weather sets in. Besides, I seem to have misplaced my running shoes."

I cup my hands around my mug, watching as Ray makes quick work devouring the pie guaranteed to add another notch to his already ample girth. With all the boozing and eating he does, he's a heart attack waiting to happen.

I sip my coffee, keep my mouth shut. It's Ray's business how he chooses to live his life.

"Don't worry, Gregory, I'll find your shoes," Mom says. "What about you, Raymond? Are you into this jogging craze, too?"

He chuckles. "Are you kidding, Mrs. K.? Do I look like a health nut?"

"Well, I just wondered," she says. "Gregory always says it helps him relax."

Ray fingers his glass. "Let's just say I relax with a little help from my friends."

Jim Beam and Jack Daniels—exactly the kind of friends I don't need. I did my time slumming with the best of them. When I moved on to washing down my lunch every day with straight vodka in a coffee cup, I figured it was time to find some new friends.

Mom finishes her sherbet in silence, but I can guess the conversation going on in her head. *My son, the priest; my son, the alcoholic.* She's always been ashamed of me. Mom does not like me broadcasting the fact that I'm an alcoholic. But it is what it is, and I am who I am. I am in recovery and a better person for it.

And hopefully a better priest.

Our bill paid, we're in the lobby walking toward the

door when a woman's voice, friendly and familiar, floats over my shoulder.

"Father Greg?"

I halt, turn, and see Gina VanBrabant beaming up at me.

"I almost didn't recognize you." Her words spin through the air in a dizzy rat-a-tat. "You know how you see someone you know, only you can't remember how or where you know them because they're not dressed?"

Her face immediately reddens. "I mean, you're in regular clothes. You're not wearing your Roman collar."

I can't help grinning. "Even priests take a break from the uniform now and then. Mondays are my day off."

"It's funny to see you dressed in regular clothes, just like me." Gina glances down at the skirt skimming just above her knees and grimaces. "Then again, I guess not."

"Good thing. I'd look pretty stupid in a skirt. I've got horrible-looking knees."

Gina giggles. "Father Greg, you're too funny."

She is as pretty and vivacious as I remember from in the confessional the other day. Long dark curls encircle her head like a crown. Her skin shines in a honey-colored light that puts me in mind of a golden Madonna.

"I'm so glad we bumped into you tonight. Now I can introduce you to Joe."

She pulls forward a tall, slender man with handsome features, dark hair cropped close to his head, and rich, brown skin that puts me in mind of cocoa mixed with bittersweet chocolate. "He actually accused me of making you up, seeing how I've talked about you so much."

"My wife likes to tease, but I assure you Gina has said only good things." Joe extends his hand. "It is my pleasure to meet you, Father."

"Likewise." His accent puts a decidedly European twist to the King's English.

I turn to Mom and Ray and make the round of introductions. For once, they're both reserved, unlike Joe and Gina, whose happiness is contagious. To be young and in love; what a blessing. Marriage is a vocation, a gift from God between two people who choose to love, honor, and respect each other all the days of their lives.

More than twenty-five years ago, I made a choice, too, dedicating myself to the service of God through vocation to the priesthood. I chose the church, and I thought it would be enough. For years, it has been.

But is it anymore?

"You two look like you're out celebrating something special," I say.

Joe and Gina trade simultaneous smiles more brilliant than the luminous beams from the overhead chandeliers.

"Congratulations," I offer. "What's the occasion?"

Gina smiles shyly, and the swift intimate look that passes between them nearly brings me to my knees.

Love between two people needs no occasion.

"I've been telling Joe about everything you and I discussed," she says. "We're very anxious to get started with our marriage preparations."

Mom pats my arm. "Raymond and I will wait outside."

I nod absently, watching them go. "Phone the rectory and talk to Cynthia. She keeps my appointment book. Tell her I said to make it sometime this week."

Gina's face falls. "I was hoping we could do it sooner, with the baby and all."

Her eyes are so trusting, as if she believes I can work miracles. But we're dealing with the church. The Vatican hasn't changed much in two thousand years, and no matter what I do, there'll be no miraculous intervention for Gina and Joe.

Yet something about this young couple stirs something inside me. A whisper of hope, a faint remembrance of something that touched me long ago.

"All right, let's shoot for tomorrow," I suddenly decide. "Normally I try and keep Tuesdays free. I've got hospital calls in the morning, then Mass at the nursing home. But I'll make time for you in the afternoon. How does three o'clock sound?"

Joe glances at Gina. "I would have no problem leaving work early."

"I'll pencil it in the calendar as soon as I get back to the rectory," I promise.

"We appreciate you making time for us, Father," he says.

Gina beams. "I knew coming to see you was the right thing to do. You made all the difference."

I push aside a warm rush of pleasure. "I haven't done anything."

"That's for us to decide, don't you think?" Gina leans over and catches me in a brief hug. "Thank you, Father."

They head into the dining room and I stroll out the door. A trace of her perfume lingers on my jacket, and I sniff it, hug it closer. Is this how other men feel—proud, happy, content, with daughters of their own? Gina is old enough to be my daughter. What a blessing she is, this young, vivacious woman who is a delight to all.

But the faint fragrance fades as I step out on the sidewalk and squint against the setting sun. Who am I kidding? I'm not Gina's father, nowhere close.

"That was quite the cozy little picture," Ray says as I join him and Mom in the parking lot.

His comment annoys me for some odd reason. "Knock it off, Ray."

"Pretty girl. Someone from your parish?"

"New in town." I zip my jacket against the cool night air. "Newlyweds, both Catholic, married outside the church. They want to have their marriage blessed."

"Good luck with that one."

"And what is that exactly supposed to mean?" I ask as I open the passenger door for Mom.

He shrugs. "I wouldn't exactly call them the All-American couple."

I eye Ray carefully. "Right. Her husband is from Belgium."

"That's not what I meant."

I've known Ray since we were teenagers, but suddenly the man in front of me seems like a stranger. "When did you become a bigot?"

Mom wags a finger at both of us. "Now, boys, no fighting."

"Just an observation, Mrs. K.," Ray says with a faint smile for my mother and a meaningful look for me. "Look, Greg, I don't mean to cause trouble. But in case you haven't noticed, James Bay is a white-bread kind of town. In fact, I would venture to say that goes ditto for Northern Michigan."

"Raymond, it's been lovely seeing you again. Take care of yourself." Mom kisses him on the cheek and slides into the passenger seat.

I struggle not to slam the door. Ray's comments irritate the hell out of me. He's never been one to hold back his opinions, but normally his observations on church, clergy, and controversy coincide with my own.

But not tonight.

Why should it matter if Joe is black and Gina is white? It's no one's business—Ray's, mine, or even the church's—

whom people choose to love or marry. Each of us is free to make our own choice. Isn't that what free will is all about?

Ray slides behind the wheel of his luxury sedan. "Let's get together for dinner next week," he calls through the open window as he backs up.

I turn the nose of the car around and follow him out of the parking lot. Mom sits beside me, hands folded in her lap.

"And what about you? You're awfully quiet." I finally grind out. My voice is harsh, and I know she's probably offended. But after my unexpected exchange with Ray, it's all I can do to keep my temper in check. "Anything you'd care to add?"

"About what?" She blinks in the shadow of twilight.

"Don't play games with me, Mom. You know what I'm talking about." I grip the wheel so tightly my fingers go numb.

She slips against her seatbelt, turning toward me. Her eyes are hooded in the growing darkness, but I know she's watching. Probably trying to figure out the best way to broach exactly how she feels without making me mad.

Or making me madder than I already am.

"They seem like a nice couple," she finally says, "especially the girl. Very sweet. But Raymond is right. An interracial couple in James Bay? It won't be easy for them. You know how people are. There aren't any black people in this town."

"What's that got to do with anything?" My anger erupts without understanding. "Don't tell me you've become a bigot, too?"

"You asked what I thought, and I am trying to tell you," she says in a stiff voice. "But I will not sit here and be insulted by my own son. If that is the way you intend to act, we might as well stop this conversation right now."

Fine. Let her stew. But if she thinks I'm apologizing, she's got another think coming.

We drive another few miles. The green glow of the dashboard and dim light from the overhead streetlamps casts an eerie silence between us.

"I don't think you realize what having a couple like that in your parish will mean," she finally says. "There are going to be problems, Gregory."

"Why should there be problems? Joe and Gina are just people, like everyone else."

"Yes, but they're different," she says. "And *different* means problems, no matter what. Everyone will be watching, no matter how sweet the girl is, no matter how intelligent or handsome her husband seems. You know how people are. They'll be watching the two of them, and they'll be watching you, too. You're the priest, Gregory. You'll set the tone. Mind what you say, no matter what you think."

"What I think shouldn't make one bit of difference."

"But it will. I'm not saying what they did was right or wrong. Although if it had been me, I never would have made the mistake she did and married outside the church. And while her husband seems like a nice enough man, I never would have married a man of… color."

I shoot her a fast look.

"But that's just me," she adds quickly. "I'm an old lady and the world is a different place now. What they choose to do is their own business. But no matter how much the world has changed, this isn't New York City or wherever he's from. James Bay is a small town. People here will need time to adjust."

Silence surrounds us as I round the corner and pull up in the rectory driveway. I cut the engine and sit behind the wheel, staring at the garage.

Mom watches me from the safety of her seatbelt. "Aren't you going to get out and open the door?"

"I don't know." I fold my hands across my lap. "Maybe I'll let the car sit out here all night. In fact, maybe I'll let it sit outside all winter."

"You're still mad, aren't you?" she says. "You always were a stubborn little boy."

My jaw clenches. "I am not a boy anymore, Mom. I'm a grown man."

"I know that, sweetheart." Her voice softens. "Gregory, I did not mean to upset you. I am only saying, as your mother, that you should be careful. Don't get people riled up. Don't upset anyone. Please, son, be careful."

But maybe I'm tired of being careful. Maybe I'm tired of doing what I'm supposed to do, of telling people what they want to hear, of doing what they think I should do.

Maybe I'm tired of following the rules.

Maybe it's because I'm getting older.

Or maybe it's something else.

Maybe it's time I started breaking a few rules myself.

CHAPTER THREE

"Like I already said, you're not in the book." A shrill voice fills the hallway as Lila and I push through the outside main door into the hallway leading toward the parish office. "Father Greg never sees people on Tuesday afternoons."

"Oops." Lila smothers a smile with a gloved hand as we exchange glances. "Sounds like someone is upset."

I glance at my watch. While Cynthia never needs an excuse, my three o'clock appointment has every reason to be upset. I'm running fifteen minutes late.

Mea culpa. My fault.

"Father Greg made the appointment for today. Three o'clock." The polite male voice with the European accent and firm self-assurance puts a grin on my face. It doesn't sound like Joe VanBrabant is taking any of Cynthia's guff.

"And I told you he's not available until next week."

"And tomorrow? He looks free then."

"You give me back that book right now! You have no right to barge in here and—"

Lila's eyes widen.

"Okay, I've heard enough." I push through the office

door, with Lila close behind me, before all hell breaks loose. "Joe, Gina, sorry I'm late."

Joe's jaw is clenched, his dark face taut, but Gina's relieved smile is like a ray of sunshine bursting through the clouds on this gloomy autumn day. "Father Greg, thank God. I was beginning to think you forgot about us."

"Never," I assure her.

Cynthia, behind the counter, grabs the calendar book from Joe and hugs it close to her chest. "They said they have an appointment," she tells me, with a mortified how-dare-they-invade-my-personal-space scowl.

"That's correct. Their appointment was for three." I manage to keep my sigh in check. Apparently, Cynthia and I need to have another chat. Scowls have no place on people's faces, especially people who work for the church.

Her beady brown eyes blink. "They are not in the book."

"That's because we set up the meeting last night. If you would remember to leave the calendar on your desk instead of locking it up when you leave at night, maybe we wouldn't have this problem."

I feel like kicking myself as a crimson flush climbs her neck and spreads across her cheeks. Chastising an employee in front of parishioners has got to qualify as some sort of sin. Still, Cynthia should know better. She's worked at the parish for years. Her job is to help people, not put up barriers.

I turn to Lila, hovering in the doorway, and motion her forward. "Come meet Joe and Gina VanBrabant, our newest parishioners."

"Welcome to Our Lady's." Lila offers her hand to both of them. Tiny laugh lines frame her brilliant blue eyes. "How long have you been in James Bay?"

"It is one month tomorrow," Joe says.

"Joe was brought in by VVA," Gina says with a proud smile. "He's their new Vice President of Operations."

News to me. And judging by Cynthia's raised eyebrows, news to her as well. VVA is an international company dealing with the aerospace industry and the leading employer in our area. Cynthia's husband, Leon, works in maintenance at the plant.

Sounds like Joe VanBrabant could be Leon's new boss.

"Sorry again about making you wait," I say. "I say Mass at the nursing home every Tuesday afternoon, and I thought I'd make it back in plenty of time. But today, unfortunately, Lila and I got trapped by some dirty laundry."

"I'm sorry?" Joe says with a puzzled smile.

Lost in translation, I realize with a smile of my own. "Nursing homes aren't allowed to restrain residents," I explain. "Some of them—with Alzheimer's or dementia— wear bracelets designed to set off alarms that lock down the outside doors if they try to leave."

"Someone escaped?" Gina gasps.

"Emma Smith's bracelet tried." I trade quick smiles with Lila. Less than thirty minutes ago, the two of us were virtual prisoners, caught between two steel doors. But somehow, with Lila laughing beside me, things hadn't seemed so bad.

"No one realized Emma's bracelet was snagged inside one of her sweaters when her daughter was taking some clothes home to wash. The alarm went off as soon as she got near the door."

Lila nods. "We made it through the first door, but then we were trapped."

"Total lockdown," I agree. "The alarm tripped every time they tried to reset the code. It took ten minutes before they figured out Emma's laundry was the culprit."

Lila laughs. "That poor nurse."

"Poor us, you mean," I say, chuckling. "It was damn cold in that doorway. Good thing we were both wearing warm coats." I eye Cynthia. "Have you registered the VanBrabants?"

"Not yet. I was just about to."

"Never mind. Hand me a registration form and I'll do it myself." I wave Lila toward us. "Those medallions you wanted for the meeting are in my office. Come walk with us and I'll give them to you."

She hesitates. "Are you sure? I hate to intrude."

And I hate to see her leave. Lila is an attractive woman, but the serenity radiating from inside makes her truly beautiful. "Come on, it will only take a minute."

Cynthia flags me as we head for the door. "Excuse me, Father, but I need you to sign a few checks."

"When I finish with the VanBrabants."

"They need to go out today," she warns.

"Later," I say curtly.

The four of us troop out of the office, leaving Cynthia alone with her scowl.

I slump back in my chair after Joe and Gina leave and ponder the options the three of us have discussed. If they were any other couple their issue of marriage outside the church would be easily resolved. They're wonderful young people, deeply in love, but my heart aches for them. An interracial marriage is vastly different than a marriage between people of different faiths. Guaranteed the road that faces them won't be easy to navigate.

"Father Greg?" The telephone intercom crackles. "Are you still in your office?"

I mutter a quick prayer, then hit the speaker. "Yes, Cynthia. What do you need?"

"I'm ready to leave and you still haven't signed those checks."

I'd like to ignore the disapproval in her voice, but instead I head down the hall to her office. Cynthia waits behind the counter, coat zipped. She hands me a pen and silently slides a pile of invoices and checks across the counter.

"What am I signing?"

"Telephone and gas bills plus the health insurance, too. I've held them as long as I can. Everything needs to be paid today."

I peer at the gas bill. "Good God. It cost nearly one thousand dollars to heat the church last month? It hasn't even snowed yet."

Cynthia shrugs. "Everything is going up."

"Except our collections." Our parish was pinching pennies before the economy went to hell, but not like this. With people losing jobs and moving out of town, Our Lady's is hurting. The lopsided figures on the past six months' of balance sheets is all the proof I need.

"Say some prayers," I say as I scrawl my signature on the checks. "We need to get our finances back on track."

"We never had these problems before," she says. "Father Mac used to contact the diocese and—"

"Forget it," I say curtly, shoving the checks back at her. "We are not taking out a loan."

"But if the parish needs money, wouldn't it make sense to—"

"No loan." I grab a lollipop from the container on the counter and jam it in my mouth before I say something I'll later regret. Cynthia and I have our differences, but she's been here forever and I can't afford to lose her. Not only does she keep the death registry, she knows exactly who has skeletons lurking in the closet—and where they're buried. "Am I free to go now?" I ask. "Or is there anything else?"

"Just one more thing." She flips open a folder and shoves it in front of me.

I scan the parish council meeting minutes. Everything seems in order. "I guess I don't understand. They look fine. What's the problem? Besides, we don't have a meeting until next month." I squint at the wall calendar hanging nearby. "Not until the week of Thanksgiving."

She taps a finger against the neatly typed notes. "I've brought it to your attention because I wanted to talk about the meetings."

"What about them?" I'm no good at basketball, but suddenly it's like we're lobbing a ball back and forth and I'm the one playing defense. Cynthia attends our monthly meetings as recording secretary, but until now, she's never said boo.

"Perhaps you are not aware of the history involved behind the council," she says. "Father Mac originally asked me to attend and take notes as a personal favor to him. Naturally, I said yes. And I've been doing it for years."

Suddenly I don't like the challenge in her eyes or the cool, condescending tone in her voice. What does she want from me? A compliment?

"You do a wonderful job," I assure her. "I know the parish and finance councils appreciate it."

Cynthia doesn't blink.

"And I do, too," I add stiffly.

"Until now, I've volunteered my time," she says in an I-couldn't-care-less-what-you-think voice. "It's two nights, every month, and everyone expects me to attend the meetings. But now Father Mac is gone, things are different. I'm not a member of either council. And I don't think it's fair. So from now on, I'd like to be paid." She eyes me steadily over the counter. "Nothing personal, Father."

Nothing personal? Of course it's personal. How stupid does she think I am? I blow out a long sigh. "Look, Cynthia, don't get me wrong. I appreciate what you're saying. But you've seen the books; you *do* the books. You know things are tight. We're fighting for every penny."

Her body stiffens. "As I said before, if you called the diocese and asked for a loan, I'm sure they'd be glad to see us through."

I don't bother to answer. Is the woman that dense? I already said *no*. How many times does she need to hear it?

Her chin tilts higher. "I believe I deserve some compensation for attending those meetings. I've done it for years. I've done it so long, everyone expects it. But it was never part of my job description. I think paying me is only fair."

Why me? Why today? Fighting with Cynthia is the last thing I need. But she does have a point. She deserves compensation for her time. The church needs to work harder when it comes to issues of justice, especially being fair with its employees.

"What about flex time?" I ask. "We could work something out. You attend the meetings, take notes, and then take two afternoons off every month."

"No, thank you, I prefer my regular hours." The look on her face implies I'm stupid for having suggested anything else. "Besides, even if I took the time off, the office needs to be open. Who would run things?" Cynthia shrugs. "If you want me to continue attending council meetings, I'll be glad to do so. But from now on, I want to be paid for my time."

My hands curl into tight balls and I force myself to count to three. I hate the challenging look in her eyes. I hate that what she says makes sense. I hate that I'm going to have to address the situation.

"I'll have to take it under advisement, but thank you for bringing it to my attention. And I apologize if you feel you've been taken advantage of. Quite frankly, I never thought about it. I just assumed..."

"And now you know," she says with a tight smile.

"The church owes its employees a just wage."

She nods. "Thank you, Father. I appreciate that."

I salute her with the raspberry sucker and try to shake off the note of triumph I hear in her voice. "I'll be at my desk figuring out a way to pay for this."

I escape down the hall, bypassing the spacious office of my predecessor, Father Mac. Shortly after my arrival, I turned it over to our Religious Education Department. They've put the space to good use as a parish library. My own tiny office doesn't have much of a view, but at least I'm not haunted by ghosts of pastors past. I slam the door, sink into my chair, and loosen my Roman collar. My private line rings as I prop my feet on the desk.

Caller ID shows it's Ray on the line. After last night, I'm not sure I'm ready to talk to him. But I've managed Cynthia; surely I can stand up to Ray.

I punch a button and put him on speaker. "What's up?"

"Just thought I'd give you a call and see how you're doing. I didn't like the way we left things last night."

As usual, Ray is right on target. "Neither did I."

"Don't get me wrong, Greg. Those two young kids seem like a nice couple. I just wonder if James Bay is ready for them."

"Looks like we'll find out soon enough," I say.

"Have you set up a meeting with them?"

"They left my office a few minutes ago."

A long silence sits between us. "I'm sure you'll handle things fine," Ray finally says. "They couldn't have picked a better parish, Greg, or a better priest. They're lucky to be working with you."

"Thanks." I'm slightly mollified by his words, but still cautious. If my old friend Ray, a priest, turns out to be a closet bigot, God only knows what I might expect from my parishioners.

"What are you and Mrs. K. up to tomorrow? The weatherman says it's supposed to be a beautiful day. I was thinking maybe I'd take a little drive up the shoreline. Care to join me?"

"Tomorrow?" I scratch my head. Getting away sounds great, but I've got work to do. "I don't know, Ray."

"Come on, you deserve to play hooky." His voice drops. "And I could use the company."

It's a tempting offer, especially when I eye the two thick financial ledgers looming on a corner of my desk. "Sorry. I'm sure Mom would enjoy it, but I've got work to do."

"Since when have you ever let that stop you?"

The same old Ray I've known since high school seminary. Always up for adventure, ready to make things happen. Let's shoot some hoops. Let's take in a movie. Let's go for a drink. And even though I've sworn off alcohol and he still indulges, he has never deserted me. Thank God for Ray.

"How can you afford the time off?" I ask. "Last I heard, you had a parish school to run."

"It's called the fine art of delegation, my friend, and I've honed it to perfection. The principal and staff manage just fine without me." He chuckles. "In fact, I'm beginning to believe they prefer things that way. Get the old man out of the way, and it works out just fine."

Delegation? I only have one person available to help me, and Cynthia already has a swelled head plus a bad attitude. Not to mention, she's looking to put more money in her paycheck.

"So, what do you say, Greg? Are we on for tomorrow?"

"Sorry, but I need to beg off. I've got a few fires to put out and some things around here that need TLC."

"Anything I can do to help?"

The concern in his voice lifts my spirits. "You could write the parish a check for one million dollars."

He laughs. "Don't tell me you're still screwing around with that stupid budget?"

"Even Jesus Himself couldn't avoid dealing with money," I remind him.

"Not quite the same," he says. "He lived in the desert, remember? I doubt He worried about utility bills. And as for you, my friend, isn't it a little early in the season to be strapped for cash?"

I sigh. "Try telling that to my parishioners."

"You plan on giving them a talk from the pulpit?"

"No," I say flatly. Far too many priests use the pulpit as a platform to pump parishioners for money. But no matter how bad things get, I have no intention to stooping to that tactic. To me, the pulpit is sacred, meant to be a place to speak God's word; not to balance His checkbook.

"Have you tried giving the diocese a call? If you're in a jam, they can make you a loan and you'll be able—"

"For God's sake, Ray, not you, too," I groan. "No loan. How many times do I have to say it? Between you and Cynthia, I'll never hear the end of it."

"If you don't mind, I'd prefer not to be lumped in the

same sentence as that woman," he says. "Why you choose to keep her around is a mystery to me."

"Some days it's a mystery to me, too," I admit. "Just a few minutes ago, she informed me that she now expects to be paid for attending council meetings and taking the minutes—something, I might add, she's been doing for years. For free."

A bark of laughter erupts on the other end. "Sounds like you've got yourself a little problem brewing at Our Lady's."

"Any suggestions?"

"Sure." Ray's voice booms over the speaker phone. "Do yourself a favor. Fire her."

I grab the phone off the hook and speak directly into the receiver. "I can't fire Cynthia. She knows more about what's going on in this parish than I do."

"Hey, you asked and I gave you an answer. If it were me, Greg, I'd fire her in a heartbeat. But it's your life. And your parish."

"Thanks." I sigh.

"Although you might consider this," he says. "Next month, why not have both councils appoint secretaries? Let them be responsible for taking notes."

"That's not a bad idea." I slouch back in my chair and contemplate the empty parking lot through the narrow window. "But who exactly tells Cynthia her services are no longer required?"

Ray chuckles. "You're the pastor, not me."

"You're a big help."

"Glad to oblige. Now, since I've solved some of your problems, what about tomorrow? Care to join me in playing hooky?"

For one brief moment, the promise of a golden afternoon beckons. Escape from this place? Escape from Cynthia's wrath?

I take a sideway glance at the finance ledgers. How long can I afford to let them sit? And what will Cynthia say when I tell her I've decided to take tomorrow off? I can already imagine the scowl on her face. "Sorry, Ray, but I can't."

"Another time, then. Don't work too hard, buddy."

Regret and resentment burn in my belly as we hang up. How many more beautiful days are left before I'm trapped by winter weather? And who is Cynthia to tell me what to do?

But even the thought of arguing with her leaves me tired. This isn't the life I envisioned when I signed up to be a priest. I was called to love God and serve Him all the days of my life; not serve the business needs of a parish. I'm fifty-four years old. Figure in the laws of probability and I've got another twenty to go.

Twenty more years of financial councils. Twenty more years of trying to figure out how to pay the bills, how to balance the budget.

Twenty more years of arguing with Cynthia.

I lean back and contemplate Ray's suggestion. Life without Cynthia. No more reminding her not to open my personal mail. No more hearing her fuss about how long it took to count the weekly collection. No more hearing her grouse about no longer being able to use a rubber signature stamp for checks like she did in the past.

No more hearing her mutter about "the way Father Mac and I used to do it."

Maybe Ray is right. Maybe I should fire her.

Then my common sense—or maybe the Holy Spirit?—gets the better of me. I'd have to be nuts to fire Cynthia. The woman is a genius when it comes to playing martyr. If I let her go, she'll have the entire parish convinced that, no matter what happened, it was my fault.

I can't fire Cynthia. I don't dare.

I swallow hard, grab the finance ledgers, and settle down to figure out how to afford a secretary I never wanted in the first place.

CHAPTER FOUR

Some alcoholics find holidays tough, but I never have. Especially not Halloween. No need for a mask around the AA table.

"My name is Greg and I am an alcoholic."

"Hi, Greg."

The chorus of voices washes over me like a refreshing wave of cool water and I think for a minute before I start to speak. The topic for tonight is gratitude, an issue I normally enjoy discussing. But this isn't my Sunday-night men's meeting or my regular Thursday-night group. It's a holiday meeting with twenty people, men and women of all ages, sitting around the table. I glance around with an equal smile for everyone.

Including Lila.

"Gratitude. Good topic." I let my thoughts briefly wander. "Personally, I'm grateful for tonight's trick-or-treaters that wiped me out of candy. At least there won't be any leftovers to tempt me when I get home. My mother was staying with me for a while, and she's a pretty good cook. I've gained a few pounds."

The twitters were expected and I wait for them to quiet. Meanwhile, I watch the glum young boy, probably still in his teens, slouched in a chair at the end of the table. He hasn't made eye contact with anyone since the meeting started. Court ordered, or here by his own choice?

"I'm also grateful for whoever got here early and made the coffee," I continue. "Our literature says doing service is important. I need to do more of it. Thinking of others and how I can serve them instead of being self-serving; it helps me keep my ego in check."

Pride. Arrogance. I struggle with my character defects on a daily basis, and probably always will. Much as I hate to admit it, there's a part of me that takes pleasure at being in charge, being in control, being *Father Greg.*

A part of me that likes to think the four hundred plus families at Our Lady's depend on *me.*

Talk about grandiosity.

I'm not the one they depend on. I need to remember that, because I'm dependent on Him, too. A Power far greater than myself.

Getting down on my knees helps.

Sitting around this table helps.

"There was a time in my life when I would have chosen to spend tonight alone with a bottle. Instead, I'm at this meeting, and I'm grateful to be here. I'm grateful to be sober. Thank God for that. And thank God for everyone here tonight." I send a smile circling around the table. "Thanks, everyone, for letting me share."

The meeting breaks up and I waste no time heading for the young man. "Good to see you tonight. How are you doing?"

"Fine," he mutters, head down, no eye contact.

"First meeting?"

"Yep."

Definitely court ordered, I decide as he bolts out the clubhouse door a few moments later. Kids that young, already alcoholic, still bewilder me. Then again, why should I be surprised? This disease has no respect for anyone or any age.

"You can't save everybody," a soft lilting voice says from behind me.

"Was I that obvious?"

"Perhaps," Lila says. "But if it's any consolation, I don't think he noticed."

I scratch my head and let out a long sigh. "Do you ever have moments when you wonder what's the point?"

"All the time," she says. "It's called being human."

I give her a wan smile. "Thanks, I guess."

"You're welcome, I guess." She throws me a curious look. "Is everything all right, Greg? You seem a little on edge tonight."

"Must be all that candy I ate." As usual, Lila looks and smells wonderful. I might be a priest, but I'm also a man.

I down the cold coffee in my cup in one quick gulp. "How's life with you?"

"Great, especially since I'm not the one who gorged myself on Halloween candy." The laugh lines around her blue eyes crinkle. "Some people never learn."

"Go ahead, I deserve it." I grin. "Hopefully now my mother has left, I'll lose some weight. I've been thinking about taking up jogging again. Lord knows I've got to do something, especially with the holidays coming. Thanksgiving, Christmas—"

Her eyes brighten. "That reminds me. I talked with Lucy yesterday. She and Max are staying in town for Thanksgiving, and I'll be hosting dinner at my house. We'd love it if you could join us. That is, if you don't have other plans," she adds.

"Will it just be Lucy and Max?" The thought of just the four of us sounds perfect, like a relaxed family gathering. But Lila isn't family; she's strictly a friend. And while friendship with a woman isn't forbidden, my vocation holds me to boundaries I do not dare cross.

"I've invited a few other people, but not too many. My house isn't that big." She smiles confidently. "Don't worry, I'm sure you'll know everyone."

Something swells inside my heart. I'll call it gratitude, for lack of a better name. "Thanks for the invitation. I didn't have any plans, but it looks like I do now."

"Wonderful." Her face lights up as if the sun had decided to make a miraculous appearance on this gloomy autumn evening. "And if your mother is in town, naturally she's welcome, too."

"Believe it or not, she'll be out of the country. One of her friends won a four-day Caribbean holiday cruise and invited Mom along."

"No doubt she'll have a much better time cruising the Caribbean than sitting at my dining room table," Lila predicts.

I merely smile. While I'm sure Mom will enjoy the holiday sunshine, I'm also positive that I've received the better invitation.

"Remember that young couple—Joe and Gina—you introduced me to a few weeks ago?" she says. "I invited them for Thanksgiving, too. I ran into Gina at the grocery store today. Bless her heart, she was wandering down the aisles and looked so lost and lonely. I couldn't help but ask her."

Regret rushes through me. I've been meaning to contact

Joe and Gina about their counseling sessions, but things keep popping up and their file is buried somewhere on my desk. "Do you think something's wrong?"

"Oh, I wouldn't worry about her. She'll be fine once she gets through the next month or so," Lila confides with a smile. "She told me about the baby."

It's a relief to hear Gina's problems are female oriented. And if she needs a maternal touch, I can't think of anyone more perfect than Lila.

"Lucy will be so pleased when I tell her you'll be joining us. Mind you, I'm not sure, but I'm thinking perhaps she and Max might be planning on making an announcement."

"Wedding plans?" Lucy and Max are a great couple, but they've been living together nearly a year, and the situation has been tough on Lila. She's a mother, she's concerned, and she's found it hard to remain quiet on the sidelines. She's come to see me a few times, and we've talked about it. She wants Lucy and Max to do things right, to make it official in the eyes of the state, but especially in the eyes of God.

But one thing I've learned in my years as a priest is that prayers aren't answered according to our wants. God knows what's in store for Lucy and Max. Things will work out.

God has perfect timing.

Meanwhile, I have another reason to look forward to Thanksgiving.

A middle-aged man, new to the AA tables but not new to me, edges up beside us.

"Hello, Dan," Lila says. "Good to see you tonight."

He nods absently at her, then zeroes in on me. "Sorry to interrupt, Father, but I..." Dan wets his lips and swallows. "Do I call you Father? I mean, I guess I don't know the protocol yet. They say it's an anonymous program, but I heard some people calling you Greg, and I didn't know..."

"Whichever you prefer," I reply in an easy voice.

"Have you got a minute, Father?" His pale face and hopeful eyes give him away.

Dan, a longtime member of Our Lady, is probably looking for a sponsor. Who better to turn to than the recovering parish priest? But I learned early in my sobriety it's better not to sponsor my own parishioners. They tend to take it personally when I practice tough love.

They can fall out of love with me, if they want. But I don't want them falling out of love with God.

Dan glances at Lila, then back to me. "I was wondering about this sponsor business, Father. Could you tell me how it works?"

"Have a good evening, gentlemen." Lila throws a small wave in my direction. "We'll talk later."

I watch her slip into the crowd, then force my attention back to Dan.

Later can't come soon enough.

"Greg, good to hear your voice. How's everything at Our Lady's?"

I yank my feet off the desk at the unexpected sound of the bishop's voice on the other end of the phone. "Fine."

Though if Holden has taken it upon himself to call, things are anything but.

"Things are fine," I repeat smoothly, trying to convince myself as I picture Holden in residence behind his mahogany desk at the diocese. Guaranteed his feet, in those shiny black leather, tasseled loafers he prefers, aren't propped on his desk, but planted firmly on the floor.

"I hope you've been enjoying this beautiful autumn weather we've been having."

"I'm trying to taking advantage of it as much as I can." I prop the phone under my chin and fumble fastening the collar hanging loose around my neck. "I suppose you're trying to get in a few more rounds of golf before the snow flies."

"Actually, I've got a two o'clock tee time," he says. "I'm making a few business calls before I hit the course."

"So I'm to assume this call isn't social?"

Holden's rich baritone laugh floods the line. "You've never been much for small talk, have you, Greg?"

I can schmooze with the best of them when the spirit moves me. But when it comes to Bishop Holden, my spirit gets stuck.

Papers rustle in the background. "I've been going over your financials. How have your collections been?"

"Steady." Something in his voice puts me on edge. "Why? Is there a problem?"

"I notice you made your annual diocesan tax target again this year," he says, ignoring my question. "You know how many priests I've got that can't hit their target?"

I don't bother to answer. It's not my place to figure that out. And it's not the priests' fault when parish donations come up short. Holden loves to play politics, but I'm not playing into his little game. Not today.

"I believe in paying compliments when they're deserved, Greg. Obviously you're doing something right at Our Lady's. Keep the people happy and their wallets stay open."

"I appreciate that." I stumble over the lie. God and money have no business lumped togethcr.

"Know why the people in your parish like you? You've got an easy style they can appreciate. God's given you a wonderful gift, Greg, for getting people to open up. They trust you. The communication flows. That's a good thing. I wish more of my priests could be like that."

Since when? Holden's never expressed an interest in holding frank and honest dialogue with his priests. In this diocese, things run one way. Holden's way.

Why doesn't he just get to it?

"That's one reason I called today. I heard there might be a little trouble in your parish, and I thought we should chat."

Trouble? I hunker down in my chair. With a parish count hovering at four hundred families, something's always simmering, but lately things have seemed quiet.

"What kind of trouble?"

"I had a call from one of your parishioners. What can you tell me about Charles Murray?"

That particular name comes as a surprise. "Chuck called you?"

"Don't go getting ahead of yourself," Holden says in an easy voice. "One of your parishioners called to talk about Mr. Murray."

Obviously to complain. A slow stirring of anger begins to simmer in my stomach. If someone has a problem with Chuck, why didn't they come to me?

"Who called you?"

"I don't believe that's relevant," he says. "People need to know they can speak freely to me. But I shouldn't have to tell you that. When it comes to anonymity, Greg, you, above all people, should understand."

Holding my alcoholism over my head is playing dirty, and Holden damn well knows it. And I'm no fool. He' not making this phone call merely because of some anonymous complaint. Whoever griped must have an open checkbook and plenty of money, enough for the bishop himself to pick up the phone.

"Tell me about this Charles Murray. I believe he's one of your parishioners?"

"He is," I say bluntly. "Chuck's a fine man: dedicated, faithful, devoted to God."

"I understand he's also divorced?" Holden's voice drops several degrees.

"Yes," I admit. The collapse of his marriage wasn't Chuck's fault. After twenty years of marriage, his wife had an affair, then demanded a divorce. Chuck was devastated. I counseled him for months.

"Did he serve as Eucharistic Minister during his marriage?"

I hesitate. Chuck was one of our regular Eucharistic Ministers and helped distribute communion on the altar until his second marriage a few months ago.

A marriage performed outside of the church.

My gut twists as I suddenly realize where this conversation is headed.

"I've been told Mr. Murray recently remarried. Is that true?"

"His wife is a lovely woman," I rush to confirm. "She's Catholic, and has never been married."

"A civil ceremony, from what I understand, not valid in the eyes of the church."

I snatch open my desk drawer and paw for the roll of antacid tablets I keep handy for times exactly like this. "There were extenuating circumstances. Chuck tried to get his ex-wife to cooperate with an annulment, but she refused."

"You know the rules as well as I do, Greg. He married outside the church."

"But he's been trying—"

"No excuses." Holden's voice is blunt. "He and his second wife are free to attend Mass, but neither of them are free to receive communion. And he certainly is not free to assist on the altar. Which, from what I've been told, is exactly what he did a few weeks ago. And you allowed it… knowing full well you had no right to do so."

The fire in my belly roars into full blaze as I recall that late-morning Mass when I found myself alone on the altar. Chuck, God bless him, saw my predicament. When it came time for communion, he made himself available by coming forward and offering to assist.

What was I supposed to do? Refuse his generosity? Order him off the altar in front of the entire parish?

Holden is bringing up a mere technicality. Why should Chuck's lack of an annulment matter? He was gracious enough to offer to help, and I accepted gratefully.

"It was an unusual situation." I do my best to keep my voice even. "One of the couples scheduled to serve didn't show up, and the third man was the father of one of our altar servers, who got sick during Mass. His dad took him out, leaving me alone on the altar."

"Doesn't matter," Holden says.

"The church was packed with visitors. No one else was available. And Chuck did not receive communion," I argue. "He was only there to help."

"Doesn't matter," he repeats. "You know the rules as well as I do. The man married outside of the church. He's not welcome to serve… on the altar, on church commissions, or teaching religious ed. He is not welcome."

"How can you say he's not welcome?" I sputter. "Didn't Jesus welcome everyone? Saints and sinners alike?"

"I would suggest you quit arguing semantics." Holden's voice doesn't budge. "The church laws are specific. Mr. Murray made his choice, and now he has to live with the consequences."

How can any of this be fair? How can the church be so

unjust? The pounding in my head vibrates like the hammering in my heart. My teeth ache from clenching my jaw so hard. "Chuck Murray is a good man."

"I never said he wasn't," Holden replies. "But I am also telling you he is not qualified to serve on the altar. And he will not do it again. Why? Because you are going to speak with him and make it clear that you will not allow it. He is not to volunteer again. Period.

"And one more thing." His voice hardens. "I don't want any more of your parishioners phoning me to complain that you've taken it upon yourself to allow Mr. Murray and his wife to sidestep church law about this marriage and annulment issue. Do I make myself clear? That's not the way things work in my diocese. If you've got any idea of acting on your own accord in pursuing a pastoral solution for the situation, I suggest you do yourself a favor and forget about it, right now."

Bile surges up the back of my throat. I've debated for weeks about raising the issue of a pastoral decision with Chuck. Save for his first wife's continuing refusal to cooperate, there's no impediment to his second marriage. A pastoral decision would allow Chuck and his new wife to receive communion. Their deep faith is obvious; I know they're both hurting spiritually. A pastoral solution is never a decision a priest makes lightly; it involves much discernment and discussion. Still, it's something I was willing to consider. Chuck knows his own heart; he only has to ask.

Correction. Chuck only *had* to ask… but he didn't. And now it's too late. I've been silenced by the bishop.

"I do not intend to have this conversation with you in the future, Greg. Do I make myself clear?"

"Perfectly." I pop three antacids in my mouth. The tang

of peppermint coats my tongue, but it can't touch the bitterness eating away at my heart. "I understand."

"Good. I knew you'd see things my way." Holden's voice softens. "Remember, Greg, people look to us for guidance. It's important we follow through. It can be a fine line, leading them down the right path while keeping them happy."

But exactly who are we keeping happy? The parishioner who complained? Meanwhile, what about Chuck? Who's watching out for his happiness? Certainly not the church. And certainly not his ex-wife, who for whatever perverted reason decided to exact her revenge by standing in the way of a good man who is only trying to make things right with God.

No, not with God. A man like Chuck, with an honorable loving heart, will always be right with God. Chuck only needs to make things right in accordance with the laws of the church.

But why is that so important?

I search for a reason. Any reason.

And come up lacking.

"Good chatting with you, Greg. Keep in touch."

There's a soft click as the line goes dead. I slam the phone in the cradle, but what I'd really like to do is slam my fist against the wall. Where do I stash the anger and resentment churning inside me? The church teaches us to be loving, tolerant, understanding. But where is the compassion? Where is the reason? I understand the need for laws. But why should they be set up to work against good people like Chuck?

How can all of this be fair, beheld through the eyes of God?

How can a loving God allow this to happen?

How can I allow this to happen?

I yank off my collar and shove it in the drawer.

Damn that parishioner for sticking his nose into other people's business.

Damn Chuck's ex-wife for deliberately allowing a good man to suffer.

Damn Bishop Holden and his precious church laws.

Damn, damn, damn.

CHAPTER FIVE

"Sorry I'm late." I stomp the slush from my shoes on the doormat on her porch.

"No apology necessary." A rush of cold air and blowing snow floods the hallway as I enter, but Lila doesn't seem concerned. She holds the door open, eyes filled with worry. "How's Marie?"

Truth? My new housekeeper is lucky to be alive. Her husband, Phil, is barely hanging on in his grief. And I'm feeling guilty for having wanted to be here at Lila's two hours ago.

"It was definitely a stroke. One side of her body is paralyzed. They'll be doing tests the next few days to determine the extent of the damage." I shrug out of my coat. "Phil was pretty shook when he called."

No way I could have left him sitting alone in the hospital, waiting to hear if his wife lived or died. No one deserves to be alone at a time like that.

"The poor man," she says. "I'm glad you were there to help him."

But I didn't do anything, except be with him. Like the

hospital staff, a priest is on call twenty-four seven, regardless of holidays. And while I'm comfortable counseling people, put me in a hospital setting and my spirit sinks into frustration and helplessness. Doctors save lives, but all I can do is sit with the family, hold their hands, help them through the waiting... and pray.

Those few hours Phil and I sat together this afternoon, we did a lot of praying.

I brush a hand through my hair, wet from melting snowflakes. I'm cold, tired, and happy to finally be here. "Sorry I spoiled your party."

I'm sorry about plenty of things. Sorry about what happened to Marie and Phil. Sorry that she's suffering. And though I know it's selfish, I can't help feeling sorry for myself, too. Just when things were going smoothly, I lost my new housekeeper. In the one month Marie has worked at the rectory, she's washed all the windows, spring-cleaned the kitchen, and banished the mice to regions unknown. Mom would be impressed.

But who knows when—or if—Marie will be able to work again? I need to find a replacement... before Mom and the mice reappear.

"I hope you didn't wait dinner," I say.

"We went ahead without you. Thanks again for phoning." Lila hangs up my coat and turns to me with a smile that nearly makes me forget my wet feet and empty stomach. "I saved you some turkey."

"Dessert, too, I hope?"

"I thought you gave up eating dessert," she teases.

"Not if pumpkin pie is involved," I say, sucking in my stomach. I'm in official uniform tonight, in my clerics and collar. But it's Thanksgiving, and my collar can be loosened. I intend to splurge.

I feel the tension start to lift and my shoulders relax as I follow her down the narrow hallway. Lila's house is small, but she has a flair for decorating. Her use of blues, yellows, and creamy whites has created an atmosphere of peace and home. If the church had the money, I'd hire her to redo the rectory. I could use some peaceful ambiance. Rambling around alone in that drafty old building, it's easy to allow problems to overwhelm me. Stepping into Lila's home is like being in another world where problems don't exist.

The dining room is small, dwarfed by a long table crowded with people. A sparkling chandelier gleams overhead. Lila has no dark corners in her house or her life.

"Hi, Father Greg." Lucy blows me a kiss from her seat next to Max. I glance around the table with a casual wave. Looks like everyone is here. Roberta and Bob Campbell, across the table, are cook and caretaker at the local boys' camp owned by Max. Bob and I are old friends. We often grab a cup of coffee together after our Sunday night AA men's group meeting.

"Happy Thanksgiving, Father." Gina beams at me from her chair next to Joe.

"And to the two of you as well." Working with them has been a joy. Just last week we finally set the date for the blessing of their marriage.

Only one face at the table surprises me. Jim Gillespie, the local district judge, sits on our Pastoral Council. I'm accustomed to seeing him at the monthly meetings as well as in the front pew at Sunday Mass. But I've never seen him at Lila's dinner table.

Not until tonight.

"Hello, Jim." I nod briefly at the man comfortably ensconced in the chair next to Lila. "Happy Thanksgiving."

Standing, he shakes my hand. "Same to you, Father."

Lucy pats the empty chair beside her. "I saved you the best seat in the house."

Max leans across her as I sit. "We missed you earlier, Father. I know it wasn't your fault, but it would have been nice if you'd been here sooner."

"Quit complaining. You did a wonderful job filling in, and you know it." Lucy pats his cheek affectionately, then turns to me with a knowing smile. "We made Max say grace, since you weren't here."

"Both of you hush and let the poor man eat." Lila serves me a plate with all the trimmings. I bow my head and offer up a hurried silent prayer. That Marie survived the stroke tops the gratitude list. That I am a welcome guest in Lila's home follows as a close second.

Roberta eyes me as I finish my blessing. "How's Marie?"

"It could be a long recovery." I fill them in on the details. "I keep thinking about that old two-story farmhouse where she and Phil live. She'll have a hard time managing those stairs."

"I'll give Phil a call tomorrow," Bob says. "Roberta and I don't leave for Florida until next week. I'll see if he'd like some help fixing up the downstairs before she comes home."

Lucy frowns. "Isn't Marie your new housekeeper?"

"Was," I correct her. "There's no telling when or if she'll be back."

"I'd be glad to help you out, Father, if Bob and I weren't leaving next week," Roberta says. "But we've got our space for the winter reserved, and the motor home is already packed."

"Would you like me to run a help wanted ad in the *Journal*?"

I can't help smiling. Lucy, owner and publisher of the *James Bay Journal*, is as generous as her mother.

"Let's hold off for now. Times are tight and the parish is having a few money problems." I sample some of Lila's delicious turkey and walnut stuffing, trying to shrug off my housekeeping problem. "Who knows? Maybe I'll clean the place myself."

Roberta hoots with laughter. "You mean you'd do all that cooking and cleaning yourself? Come on, Father, you've got to be kidding."

"You think I'm not capable of running a vacuum?" Once Pop died and Mom went back to teaching full time, I learned fast how to make my bed and do my own laundry. Those skills came in handy, especially when I entered seminary and was expected to do things for myself. It was only after ordination that I discovered how many priests consider housework and kitchen duties beneath them.

"Gina was just filling us in on the exciting news," Lila informs me as I slather butter on a flaky roll. "A Christmas Day wedding at Our Lady's should be beautiful."

The round of congratulations does my heart good. Celebrating weddings is one of the most joyful parts of being a priest.

"We are very grateful to Father Greg," Joe says. "He has been most kind in working with us."

"I still don't get it," Roberta says. "I thought the two of you were already married."

"They were married in a courtroom in a civil ceremony," I explain. It's difficult for non-Catholics such as Roberta to understand the subtle distinction mandated by the church, but to practicing Catholics such as Gina and Joe, it makes a world of difference. "Perfectly legal, but the church ceremony will validate their receiving the sacraments."

"And having our baby blessed," Gina adds.

Lila turns to the judge beside her. "Do you perform many marriages in your courtroom, Jim?"

"Never," he says curtly.

Lucy eyes him thoughtfully. "But isn't a judge qualified to perform civil ceremonies?"

"Am I qualified? Yes. Will I do so? No." His lips dissolve in a thin line. "As a practicing Catholic, I believe marriage is a sacrament received in church before the eyes of God. If some people choose to do things differently, that is their business. But I want no part of it."

Silence sits on the table like the picked-over turkey carcass no one wants to touch. Gina's face flushes a deep scarlet. Joe's eyes are wary. I stuff a huge forkful of mashed potatoes in my mouth before I say something I'll later regret. Who the hell does Jim think he is, passing judgment on Gina and Joe?

Jim may be a judge, but this isn't his courtroom.

"I'll be glad to help you with the housekeeping, Father, until you figure out what you want to do," Gina suddenly offers. "I've got time. The new college semester doesn't start until January."

Gina dusting, making beds, doing laundry, while carrying an unborn child? I'd rather mop my own floors than subject a pregnant woman to manual labor.

"Thank you, my dear, but I'll figure something out."

"If you're worried about the money, please don't be." She throws me a curious look. "I'm volunteering my time. I'm glad to help."

"No, it's not the money…" I jam another piece of roll in my mouth.

"Then what?" she presses.

I turn to Joe with a pleading look, but he merely shrugs and smiles.

"Wait, you can't be serious." Gina bursts out laughing as she catches the look that passes between us. "Just because I'm pregnant doesn't mean I'm helpless. If I can clean my own house, I can certainly clean yours."

"Sorry, Father," Joe says. "I have learned never to speak for Gina. My wife knows her own mind."

I don't want her overtired, overtaxed. Still, the idea of Gina rattling around the rectory in the dead of winter puts me in mind of springtime, of renewal, of new birth. Maybe a little dusting won't hurt her. I can handle the heavy work.

And having Gina around would definitely improve things.

Especially my attitude.

"I'll think about it," I promise.

"Don't think too long," she warns with a laugh. "I might change my mind."

"You shouldn't have to worry about cooking and cleaning, Father. You've got far too much to do as it is," Lucy says. "Just like today, spending your holiday at the hospital. It's as bad as being a doctor."

"I didn't mind," I say. Though it would have been nice to have been with Lila—and the others—sooner.

Max leans forward. "I read somewhere that doctors have a higher divorce rate than the rest of the population."

"Actually, that would be Protestant ministers," I mumble through a bite of turkey. "I know a Lutheran minister whose wife left him on Christmas Day, after ten years and four kids. They'd finally sat down, midafternoon, to have dinner and open presents when one of his parishioners phoned. Her husband was drunk, threatening suicide."

"The poor man," Lila murmurs.

"The woman begged the pastor to come. But his wife said he should tell her to phone nine one one, that his family had already made enough sacrifices for the church as it was, and that they deserved to have him home on Christmas Day. When he said he had to go, she told him she and the kids wouldn't be there when he got back."

My stomach still tumbles in free fall when I think of my divorced Lutheran colleague and the lonely path facing him in the years ahead. Was it his fault for doing his best to be a faithful minister to his people? Or was it his wife's fault, looking out for her children, her family?

Or perhaps it was no one's fault. Life happens, and often we're asked to make hard choices.

Living with the consequences can be the toughest thing of all.

Lila eyes me across the table. "Do you think priests should be allowed to marry?"

What do I think? I can't believe she brought up the subject. Of all the people sitting around this table, Lila should know better.

"Great question, Mom," Lucy says. "Yes, tell us what you think, Father Greg."

I mound my mashed potatoes in a pool of gravy, swirl my fork through the cranberry sauce. My appetite has disappeared, just like I wish this topic would. I'd rather not debate canon law around the dinner table. Especially not at Lila's dinner table.

But with eight pairs of eyes trained on me, it seems I have no choice.

"We're facing a serious crisis when it comes to vocations," I finally say, "and sooner or later, the Vatican will have to address the issue. Most priests today are past the age of sixty. Who are we going to get to replace them?

If celibacy was an option, many fine young men might consider the priesthood."

"Priests used to marry," Joe says thoughtfully. "Some of the oldest churches in Belgium date back to the tenth century or before. Priests passed church property and wealth to their sons."

"The Catholic Church has had its share of rascals," I agree. "A few of our earlier popes were married, too, with children of their own. Two of them actually successfully lobbied for their sons to succeed them. But once the money started leaving the church coffers, the Vatican clamped down. I believe it was around the eleventh century that celibacy became a mandate."

"A what?" Roberta says.

"No longer an option," I explain.

"You've given us the Vatican's position, but you still haven't told us what you think," Lucy says. "Should priests be allowed to marry?"

I concentrate on my plate, still half-filled with food, though my appetite is long gone. I don't dare look up. Is Lila watching?

"Honestly, it doesn't matter what I think," I finally say. "The Catholic Church has its rules."

"Well, I'm all for whatever makes people happy," Roberta says. She reaches over and squeezes her husband's hand. "Bob and I have been married for over twenty years. I can't imagine life without him."

"See what I mean?" Lucy huffs. "I think it's ridiculous that priests are forced to live by some antiquated rule mandated nearly a thousand years ago. The Vatican needs to get with the times. Don't they realize the world has changed? People have choices now. Including women." Her face tightens. "They're every bit as smart and spiritual as men. When are they going to start ordaining woman as priests?"

Despite the serious tone, I can't help chuckling. "I'll guarantee you that the Vatican will change its rule on celibacy long before they allow women on the altar as priests."

"They'd better do something soon," she mutters, "or we won't have any priests left to say Mass."

Lila lifts the crystal wine decanter. "Jim, would you like more wine?"

He smiles his thanks as she refills his glass, and the look that passes between them flips my stomach sideways. How did he get invited to this party tonight?

I lick my lips and glance away as the wine and conversation continue to flow. Jim's glass is constantly filled, his fingers dancing around the rim of the delicate goblet. He laughs at some joke Lila makes, looking completely relaxed. Why are some people able to drink and others, like me, not? Why are some people afflicted by this curse of alcoholism?

Since when have I begun thinking of my recovery as a curse?

For the first time in months, I find myself actually craving a drink.

Or is it something else I'm craving instead?

"Actually, if the Catholic Church allowed its priests to marry, I would be a priest today." Jim's voice rings with the quiet authority of a man accustomed to taking control and being in charge. "I spent two years in the seminary before I decided it wasn't for me."

Jim Gillespie, a priest? Though he's a devout Catholic, his words still catch me by surprise. It's not often someone admits they actively pursued a vocation, only to decide against it.

"Mind if I ask what changed your mind?" I say.

"My wife, Debra." He smiles briefly. "We met during summer vacation before my final year of seminary."

God or the girl. A few of my own friends in seminary made the same choice.

"We had some wonderful years together before she died," he says quietly. "But I made the right decision in marrying her. I have no regrets."

Despite what I think about Jim being one of Lila's guests tonight, I can't help feeling compassion for the man. Debra was in the final stage of terminal cancer when I arrived at Our Lady's. Her funeral was the first one I performed on that altar.

"What about you, Father?" Lucy eyes me thoughtfully. "Do you have any regrets?"

I swallow hard, acutely aware of Lila's eyes upon me. Regrets? I've had a few during my years as a priest. More than a few, in recent months.

"I consider myself blessed every morning I wake up," I finally say, answering her question with a mere thread of truth. Hopefully my light lie will go unnoticed. The people around this table are parishioners. What if I were to confess the truth?

That often I feel broken rather than blessed, helpless rather than helpful.

That I'm often sad and lonely and envy married couples such as Gina and Joe.

That I struggle every day, on my knees, to keep myself from battling depression, from heading for the liquor cabinet, from giving up entirely.

"Personally, I think priests should be allowed to marry," Gina says. "Maybe if they had families of their own, more of them would understand how hard it is to live in the real world. I realize the need for rules... but sometimes, when the rules don't make sense, they deserve to be broken."

I catch the look that flashes between her and Joe, and it puts me in mind of the prejudice they suffered at the hands of her father, plus the old parish priest. Gina has every right to be upset. She and Joe were treated unfairly, though it probably had more to do with race than religion.

"Rules—even church rules—exist for a purpose," Jim says. "Hopefully someday, the two of you will understand that."

I feel the anger pushing up inside me. Exactly who does he think he is? He's got no business passing judgment on the two of them. "Sorry, Jim, but I disagree. Some of the church laws are outmoded and ridiculous, and they deserve to be treated as such."

He blinks. "Excuse me?"

"Ridiculous." A vein throbs above my eye, and I rub my hand against it. "Heard the one about different countries deciding which holy days to observe? Nonsense. A holy day is a holy day. Who cares what nationality you are? Then there's the issue of standing versus kneeling during communion. At one time the U.S. bishops officially proclaimed that people are to stand. But what about those who feel it in their hearts they should kneel before the Lord? As long as they are devout in their worship, I'm sure God couldn't care less if they kneel. Yet I've heard of some priests taking wayward parishioners to task for that very thing, right from the altar. I'd call that sanctimonious, rather than holy."

Jim's face is redder than the cranberry sauce. "You've taken my words out of context—"

"And let's not forget the season of Lent," I add. "No eating meat on Friday, right? What about bishops—even our own bishop!—who lifts the obligatory ban when St.

Patrick's Day falls on a Friday? God forbid that our parishioners shouldn't be allowed to indulge in their traditional serving of corned beef. And so, Jim, I ask you... who do these laws serve, if they're so easily discarded?"

He squints at me. "Without rules or laws, there would be chaos. It is not our place to question."

"Even civil law is subject to interpretation," I argue. "Decisions made from the bench are reversed every day. Isn't that why we have the Court of Appeals and the Supreme Court? If you don't agree with the decision, you take it to a higher court."

His face stiffens like the collar around my neck. "I was not aware that the Catholic Church provided options for appeal. God's law is specific."

"God's law is not mandated through the church. Canon law was written by men. God's law is written in our hearts. It is infallible."

His eyes narrow, and I suddenly stop. Do I really want to argue theology over turkey and candied sweet potatoes?

And as for Jim Gillespie, why the hell is he sitting at Lila's dinner table?

"Would anyone care for dessert?" she asks.

"Hold on, Mom," Lucy insists. "I want to go back to that celibacy issue. It was just getting interesting."

"Lucy, I don't believe now is the time nor the place," she warns.

"Really? But what about the things you said the other night? Remember? You told me that you thought it wasn't fair, and that priests should have every right to make up their own minds—"

"That's enough, Lucy." Lila rises from her seat with a look for her daughter that would instantly freeze whipped crème on pumpkin pie.

"I still think it would make a great feature story for the *Journal*," Lucy mutters as her mother begins stacking plates. She shoots me a hopeful look. "Would you agree to be interviewed on the subject?"

"About what?" I'm finding it hard to concentrate. Does Lila truly believe that priests should be allowed to live regular lives as regular men?

"A feature article about celibacy and priests being allowed to marry," Lucy says. "We could cover the topic of ordaining women, too."

God forbid. The mere thought of what Holden would say when he found out I spouted off in print about celibacy and women priests leaves me aghast. The letter from Rome excommunicating me would arrive air express.

"Sorry, Lucy, but I'll have to beg off." I put down my fork. "Lila, as usual, everything was delicious. Thank you for the invitation and the wonderful meal."

Though her smile floods the room, it feels private, reserved just for me. "Would you care for dessert?"

"I'm stuffed." I pat my stomach.

"More coffee, anyone?" she offers. "I'll make a fresh pot."

I make my escape, trailing her into the kitchen where I place my dishes in the sink.

"Can I do anything to help?"

She shakes her head and smiles as she measures the coffee and starts it brewing. I lean against the counter, watching as she works. I'm loath to leave her company for the crowd back in the dining room. Plus, I'm still peeved at Jim.

"It's a nice mix of people you've got here tonight," I say after a moment. "Joe and Gina fit right in."

Lila smiles as she rinses silverware. "They make a sweet couple, don't they?"

"I wish everyone in town thought so." I noticed the stares

and raised eyebrows from the altar last weekend when Joe and Gina showed up at Sunday Mass holding hands.

She looks at me with eyes that hold a question. "Is there a problem?"

Prejudice. Ignorance. Bigotry. Where do I start? Joe has strong shoulders and I have no doubt he can handle himself, but Gina is different. This nagging sense dogging me, this feeling that I need to protect her, has me in a vise grip. Why can't I let go? Is it simply because she's pregnant? Because she's estranged from her family? Whatever it is, something about Gina brings out the paternal instinct in me, and not the Roman collar kind.

"I think she's having a hard time adjusting to life in a small town," I venture. "And I know she misses her mother."

"I'd be glad to keep an eye out for her, if you think that would help."

"That would be great." I lounge against the counter, feeling myself relax for the first time since I arrived. I should have known I could count on Lila coming to the rescue.

"I know exactly how Gina feels," she says. "It took me a long time to be comfortable in this town. The locals in James Bay definitely know how to make a stranger feel unwelcome."

I can think of someone in the next room who made two people feel unwelcome.

"What's with the judge?" I ask casually. "I didn't realize the two of you were friends."

"We're not, exactly." She begins to load the dishwasher in methodical fashion. "Jim sits on the board of directors at Max's camp. Inviting him tonight was Max and Lucy's idea. I think they decided to play matchmaker."

"You mean... you and the judge?" I'm momentarily rattled by the thought. "That's ridiculous."

A brief smile flits across her face. "Lucy and Max don't seem to think so."

Why do I find the thought of her dating so unsettling? Lila is an attractive woman. She's a widow. She's available.

And so is Jim Gillespie.

My stomach churns, but I don't think it's because of the turkey.

"Do you like the guy?" It's none of my business, but I can't stop myself.

"He seems nice enough. People in town like him." She rinses another plate, then suddenly halts and turns to me with a frown. "Why? Is there something about him you think I should know?"

My gut twists in a hard knot. I have no business meddling in Lila's love life. She's a grown woman and can make up her own mind about who she chooses to date. Still, this gnawing feeling in my stomach won't let go. Very few women bring out the protective urge in me: my mother, Gina... and Lila. But Mom is perfectly capable of taking care of herself. And as for Gina, she'd probably tell me the same thing. I know I'm overly solicitous, but she's vulnerable and pregnant. I don't want to see her get hurt.

But Lila is another matter completely. I didn't expect to feel like this. It's not that I'm suspicious of Jim. He's a good man, respected in the community, with the financial ability to provide for a woman's needs. Any woman would be flattered by the attention.

Would Lila?

He would treat her with respect. She deserves nothing less.

So why don't I feel happy and joyous for her? This

feeling inside me is anything but joyful. It's uncomfortable. It's ugly. It smacks of resentment.

I've got no business being resentful. I am a priest.

"Jim is a good man," I assure her. "I've never heard the slightest hint of scandal about him. He's got a good reputation in the community. He's active in the church."

We stare at each other a long moment.

"But...," she finally prompts.

I hesitate. Somehow, she's learned to read me well. Too well.

"It's nothing, really, just a feeling I have." I blow out a deep sigh. "He's a fine man. You've got nothing to worry about."

"But...," she eggs me on.

"Well, maybe he's a little..."

"Arrogant?" Her eyes twinkle, and a dimple plays peekaboo in her cheek. "A little too pompous for his own good?"

I grin. Just when I thought I'd lost her, we're back on the same wavelength.

"Actually, I was thinking more along the lines of stodgy," I say. "But now that you mention it, pompous works."

"He may be a judge, but he's no different than anyone else." Lila flashes me a sideways smile. "We all have our character defects."

She's talking recovery, and thank God for it. I need to keep my feet on the ground and my mind firmly rooted in the right neighborhood. I've got no business allowing my thoughts to wander down streets where they don't belong.

"I suppose if Jim were to ask, I would go out with him. Though it's not as if I'm waiting or hoping that he does," she adds. "Lucy and Max only invited him because they think I'm lonely."

Lila, lonely? The thought never occurred to me. I lean against the counter, watching as she moves easily around the kitchen. It's her comfort zone. "Is he someone you find interesting?"

"Don't tell me you're in on this, too?" She eyes me with a skeptical smile. "Has Lucy been consulting with you about my love life?"

Too bad she hasn't. At least then I could have set her straight. Lucy's capable and clever, but she has absolutely no clue about the type of men who belong in her mother's life.

"I'm sure she has your best interests at heart," I say. "Why shouldn't you be involved with someone? You're far too young to spend the rest of your life alone." I force a smile to my face. "Lucy and Max love you. They have every right to be worried about you. You live alone. You must get lonely."

"Not nearly as lonely as they think." She closes the dishwasher, then wags her finger at me. "And don't go giving me some quick little pep talk about how I shouldn't feel this way. You live alone, Greg, just like I do. You know what it's like. Don't you get lonely, too?"

Her question washes over me like a storm surge carrying the wreckage of broken branches and pent-up grief. How do I admit the truth? Do I dare?

I'm only human. Of course, I'm lonely. When am I not?

But never so lonely as I am this very moment, standing next to Lila in her kitchen.

We stare at each other a long moment. Does she have any clue how pretty she looks? How delicious she smells? How I wish things were different?

How, if the church didn't demand celibacy of its priests, I would be tempted to take her in my arms and...

I drag in a deep breath. There's no changing church law. It is what it is. And though I don't give a damn about myself, I refuse to subject Lila to the rumor mill.

"I'm sorry," she says abruptly. "I had no right to ask you that."

"Don't be sorry." I shrug off her question with a casual smile. If I dare admit the truth, I could bring everything crashing down upon our heads in a heartbeat. I doubt either of us is prepared for that. "Priests don't get lonely. We don't have time."

"Really?" She searches my face. "Funny, but I don't believe you."

God help me. I am only a man, and every instinct inside seems to whisper that she's leaving it up to me. And if she continues looking at me with those eyes, I am going to cave.

Mere inches separate us. One touch is all it would take and she would be in my arms. One word from me and she would give up everything. The slightest movement and my lips would be on hers, our breath mingling, her mouth warm and inviting. I would be kissing her, and I would want it to never end.

"You never did answer Lucy's question," she says softly. "What do you think? Should priests be allowed to marry?"

My hearts pauses, skips a beat, and restarts. Is she serious? I swallow, trying to find some spit. "If memory serves correct, you didn't answer, either."

"What I think doesn't matter," she whispers. "I'm not the one the church would come after."

Suddenly I realize how much I want it to happen. How close it is to happening. I've got no business being alone with her. I've taken sacred vows.

I need to move away, right now.

Because if I don't, there will be hell to pay.

For both of us.

"How about that piece of pie?" I back away from the counter, anything to distract myself from the sweet temptation of her perfume. "Pumpkin, with plenty of whipped crème?"

It crushes me, watching her face dissolve in an uncertain smile. She thinks she's read me wrong, that somehow it's her fault, that I don't want her.

But the longer I stay here, the more danger I put us both in. This is my fault. I never should have allowed it to happen. I have no business carrying on a friendship with Lila. To take things further would be insanity. The church would never allow it.

And my relationship with God means too much for me to dare allow it.

I head for the door and don't look back, escaping before she can say anything further or I do anything that puts either of us in jeopardy.

I know I've hurt her. I know she must be wondering what the hell just happened.

But how can I provide her with answers when I can barely grasp the truth myself?

Lucy stares as me as I slip back in my seat. "You look a little funny, Father Greg. Is everything okay?"

"I'm fine," I answer, though I feel anything but. If I were alone, I would sink to my knees and beg for help, for direction. Who knows what might have happened in that kitchen just now?

There but for the grace of God…

Lila silently serves my dessert. The pie looks delicious, but it might as well be mush. The whipped crème tastes like chalk in my mouth.

I finish my pie and coffee, say a hasty good-bye, and am the first one out the door. As soon as I get home, I'm giving Ray a call. Hopefully he's free tomorrow. Maybe we can take in a movie, go out to dinner. He's a man and a priest. Better that I stick to hanging around priests. At least they understand.

Because right now, when it comes to what's happening in my life, I sure as hell have no clue.

CHAPTER SIX

"I don't want you getting tired," I warn her. "Make sure you sit and rest. And I bought snacks, too. Help yourself to anything you find."

Gina smiles patiently and continues to fold towels fresh from the dryer. "Father Greg, you worry too much. Just because I'm having a baby doesn't mean I'm helpless."

I need to quit hovering. I don't want her getting tired and fed up and quitting on me. Pregnant or not, having Gina in the rectory on Monday mornings is a welcome distraction. She's a chatterbox and doesn't get much work done, save for the laundry and some light housekeeping. But she refuses to accept money, only lunch, and neither of us cares. Gina is a joy and a welcome diversion, especially after what happened on Thanksgiving at Lila's house last week. My mind hasn't stopped considering the possibilities of everything that might have happened if I hadn't walked away.

I could have risked everything.

I could have lost everything.

I could have been free.

Gina eyes me with a suspicious smile. "Don't you have work to do?"

"Plenty." My office desk is piled high, but the stack isn't as neat as her tower of folded towels in the laundry basket. Plus, since it's after ten, Cynthia will be in the office. I'm dreading what she'll say when I tell her about the decision made at last night's finance-council meeting. Since she no longer attends meetings, Cynthia has no clue we're going to begin using volunteer counters for the Sunday Mass collections.

Cynthia has been counting the collection for years.

Cynthia is not going to like being robbed of one of her regular jobs.

Cynthia does not like lots of things.

Including me.

"Did I mention there were snacks in the kitchen?"

"I swear, Father, you are as bad as Joe." Gina slams the dryer shut, folds her arms over the slight swell of her tummy and gives me a sweet, scolding frown. "Between the two of you, you'd think this baby was the first ever born."

"Well, and so it is, for both of us." I don't even bother trying to hold back the smile. "Try not to be too hard on him. Joe is a good man."

"Don't tell him that or it will go straight to his head." She brushes past me with the laundry basket. "He's stocked our refrigerator with so much food, it's bound to go bad. I told him it's impossible for one person to eat that much yogurt. I don't even like yogurt. But do you think he listens?"

I trail her into the kitchen, cringing as we pass the refrigerator. The top shelf is crammed with yogurt I bought yesterday just for her. "He loves you, Gina. He's concerned."

"I know. And he's so excited about the baby." A funny look flashes over her face. "He'll be such a good father."

She glances away abruptly, but not fast enough for me not to notice the sudden glistening of tears.

"Have I said something to upset you?"

"You, Father Greg? Of course not." Gina sets the laundry basket on the counter and quickly fingers away a few tears. "I was just thinking about Mama and how I miss her. Especially now, with the baby coming."

"Are the two of you able to talk much?"

"I call her every Wednesday. That's Mama's day off from the grocery store. We talk at lunch while my father is at work."

I lean against the refrigerator door, watching as she empties the basket. "What did she say when you told her about the baby?"

"She cried and said she wished she could be here with me." Her shoulders stiffen, but the tears are gone. "I told her you had agreed to bless our marriage. Mama said you sounded like a wonderful priest and a very good man. She asked me to thank you. And to tell you that she's praying for you."

God knows I can use all the prayers I can get. "I look forward to meeting her at the ceremony."

"I'm afraid you won't get the chance. She and Donny aren't coming." A wistful look flits across her face. "My father refused to allow it. Mama said she'd never seen him so furious as the night Donny accidentally let it slip that I'd married Joe."

How can one man be so stubborn, to deny his family the happiness and joy they deserve?

"Give him time, Gina. He'll come around." I'm not sure it will happen, but her face is so pinched and drained, I can't help but offer hope.

Sometimes hope is the only thing that keeps us going.

"No, he won't. You'd understand that, if you knew my father." Her voice drops. "He's not a nice man, Father Greg. Do you know the last thing he said to me before he threw me out of the house?"

I shake my head, certain I'll regret what I'm about to hear.

Her eyes narrow. "You're nothing but a black man's whore... and I'll kill you both before I'll let my daughter end up married to some nigger."

Hearing such evil knocks the breath out of me. What kind of hellhole did Gina grow up in? What kind of man lives and breathes hatred like that or treats his family that way?

If she was my daughter, I'd be on my knees, thanking God every day.

"I'm sorry you had to hear that, Father, but maybe now you understand how things are, and how my father is. But I have no regrets." She throws back her shoulders, flashes a brave smile, and heads for the laundry room. "No regrets about what I've done, except when it comes to Mama and Donny."

She loads the washer, slams the lid, and starts the machine. "I worry about them both. Mama isn't very old, but she looks like she's been through the wash cycle one too many times. And Donny has asthma. He's fifteen, and he gets sick a lot. Sometimes he ends up in the hospital. Mama worries about him. And my father is no help. I think she's been beaten down by him for so long, she doesn't expect anything else."

Beaten? "Does he..."

Curls fly in wild abandon as she shakes her head. "He's never touched her. I don't think he'd dare. My father is the worst kind of bully. He's a coward."

100

"Has she ever thought about leaving him?" I've made the suggestion to parishioners in similar situations. Sometimes, the only recourse people have is doing what they need to do in order to survive. And if that should mean walking away from a spouse, then so be it.

The Catholic Church might not agree, but a loving God will surely understand.

"Mama will never leave him," Gina predicts. "I think the spark got knocked out of her when Donny died."

I feel my face scrunch in a frown. "I thought you just said that he had asthma…"

"I had two brothers, both of them named Donny." A peculiar sadness draws over her face. "My older brother Donny died before my younger brother Donny was born. He fell out of a tree in our backyard when he was ten years old and broke his neck."

I sink against the doorway, sick and shaken by what I've heard. "Gina, dear, I am so sorry. I had no idea."

"It happened one summer a long time ago. I was just a little girl, about to start kindergarten." She leans against the washer, as if drawing comfort in the slow steady rumble of the machine. "Daddy was working, and I was outside playing in the sandbox. Mama was inside. I can still remember hearing her singing through the kitchen window.

"Then suddenly, there was a wild scream, and Donny came crashing down out of the tree."

The horror of her words settles between us like a heap of dirty clothes on the laundry-room floor.

"Mama ran out of the house and then she started screaming. Even today, I remember thinking how odd it was, her shrieking and circling him while Donny laid there on the grass. His eyes were open, and he looked so peaceful and quiet, except for the blood on his face. I suppose the branches must have scratched him when he fell. But I didn't know; I'd never seen a dead person before."

An odd look shadows her face. "There's a holy card from his funeral Mama keeps tucked inside our family Bible. It has a picture of Jesus on it. He has blood on His face, too. That holy card always scared me. For years, I thought everyone died with blood on their faces. I wanted to ask Mama, but I didn't dare. After Donny died, she wasn't the same. Nothing was the same. Daddy quit talking and Mama quit singing. She quit smiling. She quit doing much of anything except working and praying and worrying.

"And after my younger brother Donny was born, she had even more to worry about. Donny was always sick, ever since he was a baby. Daddy hates it; sometimes I think Daddy hates him. Maybe he's always hated him. He insisted they name him Donny, after my older brother, but it was wrong. Donny's not the same, and he never can be. It's not fair. Donny deserves more. We all deserve more."

Her face clouds with doubt. "Maybe Joe and I shouldn't have insisted on getting married on Christmas Day. Maybe then Mama and Donny might have found a way to come. I don't know. Maybe we should have—"

"Don't should on yourself," I say quietly, "or you'll drive yourself crazy. God has things under control."

Gina stares at me a long moment.

"He brought you and Joe together, didn't He?" I remind her. "Things will work out. They always do."

She still looks doubtful.

"I promise," I add.

Then suddenly she buries her head in her hands. I stand and watch helplessly as the washing machine roars in a spin cycle and Gina's tears drip down her cheeks. Every instinct urges me to wrap my arms around her, to comfort her as if she was my own child. But we're alone in the rectory, and I don't dare.

Gina is not my daughter. I am father to no one.

Damn that father of hers, for throwing her aside. She deserves so much more than that. She deserves all the love in the world. Thank God she has Joe.

"Please don't cry." I pat her shoulder awkwardly. "Would you like me to call Joe?"

"No." She swipes her eyes with the sleeve of her sweater. "He's seen enough of my tears."

"Are you sure?" Maybe she is, but I'm not. What if she collapses? How would I explain that to Joe? This overwhelming sense of worry, concern, of being responsible for another human being is foreign to me. No wonder parents who come to me for counseling are confused so much of the time. How can they possibly know the right thing to do?

Am I giving them the right advice? How do I know? What if I'm wrong?

"I think we should call Joe," I say uneasily.

"No, please don't do that. I'll be fine." Gina musters up a smile. "I'm sorry, Father. I didn't mean to scare you. I cry a lot lately. Joe's gotten used to it. Chalk it up to pregnant woman nerves."

"No apology necessary," I say, relieved to have some physical distance between us. "And never forget, no matter what, God is watching over the three of you. No matter what happens, things will work out for the best. I promise."

God help me if I'm wrong. I've got no business making promises I can't keep. None of us have any clue what the future holds. But her father has already yanked away her dreams. How can I let her walk through life without hope?

"What about Joe's sisters?" I ask. "Are they coming from Belgium for the wedding?"

"I don't think so. Annelies and Annelore both have families." Her face brightens slightly. "But they've promised to come in the spring, when the baby is born."

Slowly, surely, my prayers are being answered. When the time comes and she needs people most, Gina won't be alone.

"Lila Carter phoned me yesterday and invited me to lunch at her house. What a nice lady. Don't you absolutely love her?" Gina slowly heads back into the kitchen. "And guess what? She told me that she used to be a cashier in a grocery store, just like Mama. I never would have guessed. Lila doesn't look like she belongs behind a cash register. In fact, I'm surprised she doesn't have her own shop. Maybe something involving interior design. Her house is so pretty, just like she is. There's something about her I can't describe. Just being around her makes me feel calm and peaceful inside. Know what I mean?"

I nod slowly. If only Gina knew how well I understand. After what nearly happened between us in Lila's kitchen, I've tried my best to keep my thoughts from wandering anywhere in her direction. I can't afford the temptation.

I don't dare.

"I asked her to be my maid of honor," Gina prattles on. "Or, I suppose I should say my matron of honor. I understand she's a widow."

Lila never remarried after her husband drowned in a tragic boating accident on Loon Lake years ago. I've always been curious why she chose to remain single. No doubt she's had plenty of offers. She's an attractive woman. Perhaps she never found the right man.

Has Jim Gillespie invited her out to dinner yet?

Has Lila said yes?

None of my business, I remind myself bluntly. None of my damn business.

"Oh, Father Greg, look! It's starting to snow."

Together we watch as snowflakes float past the kitchen window and blanket the sidewalk between the rectory and parish center.

"Don't you love winter?" she whispers. "It's my favorite time of year. Things look so fresh and pretty, covered with snow."

Though I've been through enough winters to last me a lifetime, I'll gladly deal with a few snowflakes if they take away Gina's tears and put the smile back on her face. "There go my plans to start jogging. Guess I'll start walking laps inside church with my rosary."

"You should call Joe." She opens a drawer and puts away clean dish towels. "He jogs every day."

"Even in this weather?"

"Snow doesn't stop him. And neither does sun, rain, or fog. Every morning at six, Joe goes for a five-mile run. Once he gets back, he showers, eats, and he's off to work with his Blackberry and pager clipped to his belt. Joe is fanatic about keeping in touch."

"As long as he remembers to keep it turned off during Mass," I say, smiling.

Gina rolls her eyes. "Last weekend in church, a woman in the pew in front of us was texting during Mass. I couldn't believe she had the nerve. Honestly, Father, I felt like poking her and telling her God doesn't have a cell phone and that she'd be better off paying attention to you."

I can't help chuckling at the thought of Gina, indignant on behalf of God. But the issue of cell phones ringing in church has become commonplace. Usually I remind people to turn off their phones. Maybe I need to add *no texting*, too.

Gina turns to me with an expectant look. "Have you given any thought to Christmas decorations? Joe and I put up our tree last night."

"Vince has the tree stored in the garage. But we'll let it wait until my mother gets here. She'll take care of it."

"Why?"

I frown. "She always does."

"Because she wants to? Or because you haven't done it?"

The question throws me, as does the skeptical look on Gina's face. It's similar to one I've seen on Mom's face throughout the years when she's annoyed with something I've done or something I neglected to do.

"I'm not sure," I admit.

"I'll come back tomorrow and decorate for you," Gina says matter-of-factly as she grabs a dust rag. "I'll make sure it looks beautiful when your mother arrives."

"I don't know if that's such a good idea," I say uneasily. Just because Mom's retired from teaching doesn't mean she's given up control. "You don't know my mother."

"No offense, Father, but you don't know women." Gina smiles. "Trust me, everything will work out fine. And if she's upset," she adds, "you can just tell her it was my idea. Being pregnant is a great excuse. No one stays mad at me for very long."

She flashes me a sweet backward smile as I trail her into the hallway. "Why don't you go find Vince and tell him to bring in the tree. Meanwhile, I'm going upstairs and finish the dusting."

Gina heads up the stairs and I head for the kitchen door to do her bidding. If she's right, my life will be bright with twinkling lights by tomorrow.

But this morning, things still are gloomy.

Cynthia awaits.

"It was pointed out during our insurance inspection last month," I explain, "and the Finance Council agreed. This weekend, we start using volunteers to count the collection."

Cynthia sits rigid before me, hands clasped in her lap. I hold back a deep sigh. I'm not entirely unsympathetic. She's counted the collection for years. If it were me, I'd feel pushed aside, too. But this isn't a conversation we can put off having. Gossip runs rampant, especially in this parish. If I don't tell her, someone else will.

"The insurance rep was quite specific," I add. "The person responsible for handling the checking account and the money going out should never be the one counting or depositing the money coming in. He called it a check-and-balance system. It's an accounting practice that should have been established years ago. Or so I've been told," I add.

Cynthia looks like she swallowed a sour lemon ball that went down the wrong way. "Father Mac never complained."

That figures. From what I can determine, Father Mac didn't do a hell of a lot in his ten years at Our Lady's except say Mass, play golf, and let Cynthia run the parish. I'm not sure how deep her power base runs, but I know she still has his ear. And Father Mac is a crony of Bishop Holden. Who knows what the two of them discuss when they're out on the golf course?

If I take on Cynthia, it could mean bucking Holden and the diocese.

"The council's decision was based solely on the insurance recommendation," I assure her. "This isn't a matter of trust. You haven't done anything wrong."

Her eyes narrow.

"You do a wonderful job here at the parish. Your efforts are much appreciated," I add.

Her mouth tightens.

"By everyone." I swallow down the bile rising in my throat. "Including me."

I catch the gleam of satisfaction in her eye. Enough already. If she thinks I intend to continue spewing false compliments, she can forget it. I don't need the grief, plus I'm out of antacid tablets.

"I'll be in my office working on my Christmas homily this afternoon. I'd appreciate you not putting calls through," I say. "Speaking of Christmas, how are we doing on the flower collection? Have we brought in enough to cover the florist bill?"

The Christmas flower collection is another tradition started by Father Mac. I tried to do away with all special collections when I arrived two years ago, but the older parishioners love the flower collection. For a mere donation, they write down the names of their deceased loved ones to be remembered at Christmas. Like it or not, the Christmas flower collection is here to stay. I'm not about to start feuding with little old ladies over prayers versus poinsettias.

"We've taken in over two hundred dollars," Cynthia says.

"Seems like I remember the florist bill from Williams last year was double the money we took in from the flower collection."

She stares at me with flat eyes.

"Did you already place the order?" I ask.

"Williams has a standing order on file. It's the same every year. Fifty poinsettias, the larger variety, in reds, pinks, and whites."

If we can't afford it, we can't afford it. And while the Christmas season should be a joyful celebration of Our Lord's holy birth, the altars of Our Lady's have smacked of gaudiness rather than godliness for the past two years. I doubt Mary and Joseph had fifty poinsettias—the larger variety—surrounding the manger.

"Give them a call and tell them we're putting the order on hold."

Cynthia's eyes pop. "But we've been ordering from Williams for years. They're parishioners."

And according to my friend, the local funeral director, they're also the costliest florists in town.

"The fact that they're parishioners isn't helping us pay the bill. If they want to keep our business, they can cut us a break."

"You expect me to tell them that?"

A slow burn starts in my stomach. Why does she have to make everything so difficult? Why can't she simply do as I ask?

"If you'd rather that I phone them, I have no problem doing that," I say.

Her face tightens. "I'll make the call."

"Good. And while you've got them on the phone, be sure and mention we're shopping around," I add, trying to keep my voice light. I know she's fuming, but I'm done spending money on things we can't afford, including gilt-edged poinsettias. Baby Jesus didn't have anything so grand when he was born in that manger stall. "It might be a good idea if you call around and check with the other florists in town," I continue. "Let's see what kind of prices they can offer us."

I cut her off before she can protest. "And for what it's worth, I don't care what religion the florist is. A little friendly competition never hurt anyone."

She rises to her feet. "Fine."

I suspect she's itching to get back to her office and get on the phone. Not to call florists, but rather, Father Mac.

"One last thing," I say as she starts for the door. "I need a check. Make it out for one hundred dollars."

She halts in the doorway. "Payable to…?"

"Gina VanBrabant." She insists on doing the housekeeping without being paid, but I'm going to insist Gina take the money. She can buy herself something pretty. Gina deserves it.

"Thanks, Cynthia. And would you please close the door behind you as you leave?" I grab the yellow legal pad I use to scratch out my thoughts when preparing my sermons. I open my desk drawer, pawing for a pen.

Then I notice the bulky form still looming in the doorway, hand on the knob.

"Is there something else?" I ask.

A few seconds pass as a strange battle seems to rage across Cynthia's face. "I don't understand why we're writing her a check," she finally says. "If you're adding her as a member of the staff, she'll need to fill out paperwork."

"There's no need for that. She's not part of our staff."

"Then we're paying her as an independent contractor. We'll have to provide her with a ten ninety-nine at the end of the year. She needs to fill out the paperwork."

I hold back a long sigh. What is it with this woman? Does she not understand what she's told to do?

"Gina VanBrabant is here on a temporary basis. She's a volunteer."

Cynthia gives me a cool stare. "If she's a volunteer, then why did you ask me to write her a check?"

Because I'm a nice guy? Because having Gina around puts joy in my heart? Because I intend to cover the cost of the check by throwing some extra twenty-dollar bills in the Sunday collection on top of my weekly envelope?

Not that it's any of Cynthia's damn business. I'm the pastor at Our Lady's. I'm the one in charge.

Right?

"Just write the check," I tell her. "And close the door behind you."

She slams it behind her as she leaves, soft enough so I don't get up and follow her, hard enough to let me know she's furious about the way I've handled things.

For once, Cynthia and I are in complete agreement. Advent is meant as a time of joyful preparation spent awaiting Our Lord's birth. But at the moment, I feel anything but joyful.

More like smacking my fist against the wall.

CHAPTER SEVEN

Gotta keep up. Gotta keep up. The mantra pounds in my head as the pavement pounds under my feet. My knees ache, my feet are cold, the wind bites against my cheeks. James Bay must have had at least six inches of snow dumped on it overnight. I slow to a crawl and bend over double, grabbing my thighs, struggling for breath. For God's sake, who am I trying to kid? I'm fifty-four years old. No way in hell I can keep up with Joe.

He dances back to where I stand, clapping his gloved hands together for warmth. His jogging attire of Lycra suit with neon-glo stripes running down his legs and back stands out in the early morning light.

"You okay, Father Greg?" His breath blasts out in frosty puffs.

"Nothing thirty years off the clock wouldn't cure," I grunt, feeling every bit my age. My lungs ache like I'm locked in a deep freeze.

He jogs in place. "We will take a break and let you rest."

I need more than a break. I need coffee and dry clothes. Or maybe what I most need is to move somewhere warm and far away from this Godforsaken climate. I concentrate on the snowy road beneath my feet, counting on extra minutes to rest. "How's Gina?"

"Still in bed when I left," he says, jogging circles around me. "She is lazy, that wife of mine. I wonder, are all American women the same?"

What the hell is he talking about? Gina is anything but lazy. I peer up, ready to hit him with a reply… and spot the tender smile on his face.

"There's a comic in every crowd," I grumble.

Joe stops mid-stride, frowning. "Sorry, I do not understand? Where is the crowd?"

"Never mind." I stagger upright. "You do this run every day?"

"Alone, I would go farther," he admits. "But for you, I decided we would start off slow."

He's out of his mind, and I'm out of energy. "Look, Joe, I think I'm going to turn back. Go ahead without me. Finish your run."

"But we are almost halfway there." He keeps moving, still running circles around me on the icy road. "You can do it, Father."

"No, I can't." Joe is in superb shape from training every day, but I haven't jogged in months. This old body of mine is screaming *what the hell were you thinking*? We're just past the city limits. If I turn around now, I can probably make it back to the rectory in twenty minutes. Or five, depending on if I manage to snag a ride from some good Samaritan.

"Finish your run," I tell him. "I'll head back by myself."

Joe shakes his head. "No, I will go with you. Gina made me promise I would not let you run alone."

"Thought I might give up, did she?"

He returns my grin. "It was not your spirit she doubted, Father. It was your legs."

A car horn blares as it rushes past us, throwing slush.

"Good Lord, he could have hit us," I mutter.

Joe stretches his arms and legs, bouncing on his toes. "You get used to it."

"I think we should call this my first—and last—official run of the winter. From now on, I'll get my exercise strolling down the aisles in church. At least there's no ice to slip on. The only thing that might trip me up is the carpet."

"Maybe in a few days you will change your mind."

"Maybe," I say, though I doubt it. I wince as the pain shoots up my legs. The rectory is a good two miles away and I'm not looking forward to the hike or the shin splints I'm certain will develop by tonight.

We jog side by side down the road, then head back into town through the city streets. Thoughts of hot coffee and the rectory thermostat cranked on high keep me going. The traffic has picked up with the morning commute. Cars whiz past us as we hit the sidewalk and finish the last few blocks. A horn blares as one car slows, then passes us. Words shouted through the open window are lost to me, tossed in the wind.

I pick up my pace and catch up with Joe. "Someone you know?"

"Someone I do not want to know," he says curtly.

The car is already past us, but there's no mistaking the arm waving through the driver's-side window, third finger jammed high.

"The international sign of greeting," Joe says quietly.

My gut twists as I realize what I missed, the racial slur shouted. Hatred and bigotry are alive and thriving in James Bay.

"I'm sorry, Joe," I say as we reach the sidewalk of Our Lady's and slow to a walk. "There are lots of ignorant people out there."

"It is no concern to me," he says. "It is Gina that I worry about. She shouts at them and calls them idiots. I tell her she must ignore them."

He halts on the sidewalk beside me. His face is a quiet mingling of hope and sorrow. "Sometimes I wonder if Americans realize what a treasure you have in your country. Those of us who do not live here rejoice that there exists a country like yours. In our schools, we learn of Martin Luther King, of your American civil rights movement, that all men and women are created equal. And we think that in your country, it is wonderful that all people are free.

"But living here this past year, I wonder if that is the case." He slowly shakes his head. "Every day, I meet people caught up by their fears and prejudice. Either they are not friendly, or they try too hard, pretending that it does not matter. It is a disappointment to me. It is not what I believed America would be."

"Not all of us are like that," I say.

Joe shoots me a fast look. "No, my friend, you are much different, and for that, I thank you. You are like Gina. Both of you see the best in people. You are a wonderful man. And as for my Gina?" He smiles suddenly, his dark face radiating an inner light that brightens the dull morning. "My Gina, she is a free spirit. She is the love of my life."

God gives us what we can handle, and He's given Joe the grace to cope with people's prejudice better than me. There was a time when I was proud to wear my Roman collar everywhere I went, even while traveling, especially in airports. But once the priest sex-abuse scandal hit the news, I learned to travel in civilian clothes.

Joe has no choice. Thank God he's comfortable in his skin.

Nearly thirty years separate us, but I could learn a lesson or two from this young man.

A man Gina is proud to call her husband.

A man I am proud to call my friend.

"Got time for a cup of coffee?"

He shakes his head. "I must go home and get ready for work. Thank you for the run, Father."

"I'm the one who should be thanking you," I insist. "By the way, don't tell Gina I wimped out."

Joe hesitates, still jogging in place. "Excuse me?"

I've grown so comfortable around him, it's hard to remember he doesn't always understand American slang.

"Tell her I gave it my best," I explain with a grin.

He waves and heads down the street, never breaking his stride. While I'll never be able to keep up with him on the open road, I sense our hearts beating in the same rhythm.

The parish parking lot is already plowed, but the sidewalks leading into church are still plugged. A bulky figure in a faded snowmobile suit works fast and furious with a shovel, scooping snow.

I head toward the janitor instead of the rectory and a hot cup of coffee. "Got a problem, Vince?"

"Yep." Sweat drips from his face despite the frosty temperature. "Come on, Father, I'll show you."

He walks me to the rusty machine parked near one corner of the garage, kicks one tire. "The snow blower conked out again."

"Think it's the weather?" I ask hopefully.

"Nope," he says. "I think the engine's shot."

My spirits sink. "Any idea how much it might cost to fix?"

He shrugs. "I could call and ask around. But if you want the truth, it probably ain't worth it. Even if we get the engine fixed, we'll need to buy another chute control."

Together we mourn the worn-out machine, a relic from Father Mac's era. I'm reluctant to replace it, but if Vince says it's not worth fixing, I believe him. He's handy when it comes to tinkering with broken machinery. And while he's not book smart, he is dead-to-the-core honest and unfailingly polite. Two things that, in my book, beat brain power every time.

"Check around and get some prices on a new one," I decide, "but try and find something in stock. I don't want to mess around ordering something that could take a week to get here."

Vince's face brightens in the gloomy morning. "I'll get right on it, Father."

He drops his shovel and heads for his truck.

At least I've made someone happy today. I circle back toward the rectory, then notice the baby-blue Mercedes parked near the office entrance.

Suddenly, Vince isn't the only one smiling.

Though I am a bit curious as to what Lila is doing here so early this morning.

"Goodness, look at you." Her gaze sweeps over me as I enter the sacristy, coming to rest on my wet running shoes.

I halt in the doorway, making sure to keep a good ten feet between us. It's the first time we've been alone together since that night in her kitchen.

Lila halts her work folding altar cloths in front of the set of long, lined drawers. "Have you been out jogging?"

"Joe VanBrabant invited me to run with him," I say, leaning against the doorframe.

Her eyebrows rise slightly. "You managed to keep up with him? Gina says he's quite the athlete."

I knock back the swell of pride as I stomp the snow from my shoes. The nagging notion I should admit the truth isn't so easy to shake off.

She throws me a bright smile. "Are you and Joe going to start running together on a regular basis?"

My guilt is piling up faster than the snow outside the window.

"I doubt it, seeing how I conked out on him just past the city limits," I admit. "Poor guy. If we'd gone any further, he would have had to carry me back."

Lila laughs and so do I. Suddenly I don't feel so wet or cold or tired anymore. I venture a few steps inside. "That's a pretty coat you're wearing. Nice color."

"Thank you." A look of pure feminine pleasure spreads across her face as she glances down at the blue coat trimmed with a rich fur collar. "Lucy gave it to me for my birthday last week."

I missed her birthday?

"Sorry, I didn't know," I say, "or I would have sent a card."

A gift would have been inappropriate. Definitely inappropriate.

"I'll remember next year," I promise.

Tiny laugh lines crinkle around her eyes, making her prettier than she already is. Women like Lila don't need makeup. She's already wearing the natural, joyous kind provided by God.

"At my age, the only birthday I enjoy celebrating is the one which marks my sobriety," she says. "Twenty years, December thirteenth."

"The day after tomorrow." That's one birthday celebration I definitely remember. Anniversary dates are noted on the calendar down at the Club, and our regular

Thursday-night group has a small surprise celebration planned. When you work a strong program like Lila does, eventually the days add up. I've got fourteen years sobriety under my belt, but when it comes to recovery years, Lila is far older and wiser.

"Actually, my anniversary is the reason I'm here today. It's my morning to volunteer at the food pantry, and I thought I'd save myself a trip and drop these off first." She points at the neatly folded stack of altar linens lining the sacristy counter. "I took them home to wash last weekend and wanted to make sure I brought them back before I leave town."

"You're going away?" The words slip out of my mouth as the disappointment slides inside my heart.

"I'm driving downstate tomorrow to celebrate with my sponsor. She invited me and a few other friends from my original AA group."

How can I begrudge her taking time for herself? God knows she deserves it. And what business is it of mine what she does in her spare time? I push down the uneasiness growing inside and suddenly find myself wishing I was still out jogging those icy roads with Joe. Even with all the cars whizzing by, jogging seems safer than chatting with Lila.

"How long will you be gone?"

She throws me an amused look. "Worried I won't be back in time for Sunday Mass and you'll have to handle things alone?"

I know she's teasing and it shouldn't bother me. It wouldn't bother another man. But I am not a regular guy. I am a priest, and I gave my life to God nearly thirty years ago when I took my vows. And this woman before me, with her slim shoulders, small frame, and peaceful smile suddenly seems more dangerous than any patch of ice on a snow-covered sidewalk.

If I slip over Lila, I'm not sure I would recover from the fall.

I back up a few steps. "Have a good time with your friends. We'll miss you at the meeting on Thursday night."

She continues folding linens. "It's all right, Greg, you don't have to pretend. I already know about the surprise party."

Damn it, why can't people keep their mouths shut? "Who told you?" I demand.

"Don't be mad." Her laugh is as delicate as one of the icicles hanging from the window. "They told me last Thursday night at group after they found out I wouldn't be here." She blinks. "Oh, that's right, I forgot. You missed last week's meeting."

Not by choice. I was at the funeral home presiding over a rosary service.

"When they heard I was leaving town, they surprised me with a twenty-year medallion chip." She peers at me with a suspicious smile as she closes the linen drawer. "But I suppose you know about that, too."

Know about it? I'm the guy who ordered it; along with the newly published AA meditation book still on my desk. I planned to give it to her after Thursday night's meeting. A personal gift from one recovering alcoholic to another, in honor of twenty years' sobriety.

"How long will you be gone?"

"I'll be home on Saturday." She smiles suddenly. "Believe it or not, I have a date."

My heart thuds to a complete halt. "Oh?"

"With Jim Gillespie," she adds. A faint pink blush starts a slow crawl up her cheeks.

"He seems like a nice guy," I say, my brain racing furiously. Is it their first date? Second? How long have they been going out? And I suppose he remembered her birthday, too. Not that it's any of my business. Lila is a grown woman. She has every right to date who she pleases.

Suddenly I'm aware that I'm standing in a puddle of melting snow. My shoes are wet, my turtleneck clings damply against my skin.

"Jim's taking me out to dinner and then to hear the chamber orchestra. They're playing a program of Christmas carols at the Historical Society. Did you know that Jim sits on the board?"

"No, I did not." The judge is one busy man. He runs his courtroom, plus he's involved with the Hospital Foundation as well as Max's camp. And the Historical Society? Sounds like Jim Gillespie is involved with everything in town.

And now he's involved with Lila.

Maybe I shouldn't give her that AA meditation book. Maybe I should keep it for myself. God knows I could use the insight. The index of emotions listed in the back might lead me to some reflections and readings that could help me understand. And I need help.

Because I sure as hell don't know what I'm feeling right now.

Is it loneliness? Fear? Resentment?

Or jealousy?

That is one emotion that definitely has no place in a priest's life—or heart.

"Well, have a good time celebrating with your friends... and with Jim on Saturday night. I'm glad the two of you have hit it off." Every minute I stand here chatting with her, I'm growing colder. I've got to get out of these clothes, get away from her, hop in a warm shower.

A cold shower?

"I know a lot of people think he's stuffy, but he's quite

an interesting man," she says. "Especially once you get to know him."

Exactly how well has she gotten to know him? If memory serves correctly, just a few weeks ago Lila herself called him pompous and arrogant. Why the sudden change of heart?

Maybe because her heart is now involved?

"It's no wonder Jim is like he is, with all those people shuffling through his courtroom," she adds. "A few years of dealing with that would make anyone jaded."

Maybe. Or maybe not. Jim strikes me as the conservative type—a man who embraces traditional values in his courtroom, personal life, and his faith. I'm surprised he hasn't advocated our parish for the return of the Latin Mass.

I'm even more surprised Lila seems to like him.

"Sounds like the two of you have a lot to talk about."

"He talks, I listen." Her eyes soften. "He's lonely."

I lean against the door and hug my chest. Jim isn't the only one who's lonely.

"And he's quite the storyteller. Did you know he's traveled around the world? He's been to Australia and Africa, plus all over Europe. He and his wife, Debra, even had an audience with the pope when they visited Rome."

"I'm impressed." I knew he was devout; it figures Jim would be the type to pull a few strings and arrange for a papal audience.

"I believe one of his friends made the arrangements shortly after Debra got sick. Jim said he used to be the pastor here."

"Father Mac?" I guess, my stomach hitting my knees.

Lila frowns. "No, I don't think that was the name."

"MacAfferty," I correct myself.

She brightens. "That sounds right. From what I understand, he and Jim are quite friendly. They golf together almost every week."

Naturally Lila wouldn't know Father Mac. She hadn't moved to the parish yet when I took on my assignment at Our Lady's a few months before Debra Gillespie died. Father Mac was on vacation and I ended up officiating at her funeral. Jim was devastated. The church was jammed and I did my best, but it was apparent that as far as he was concerned, I was nothing but a second-rate stand-in for his friend and former pastor.

Poor Lila. The woman has no clue what she's getting herself into. The last thing she needs in her life is to get involved with someone who's involved with Father Mac. Although Jim seems like a nice enough guy, and Lila deserves some fun in her life.

And I've got no business being alone with her.

"Look, can you wait here a minute?" I say suddenly. "I've got something for you over in my office"

She hesitates and checks her watch. "I'm due at the food pantry soon."

"I'll be right back." I don't give her time to protest. I bolt out the side door and immediately hit a patch of snow-covered ice that takes me skidding across the sidewalk. My arms flail and my legs fly out from under me. Somehow I manage to grab the hood of a nearby car, miraculously ending up still on my feet. For once, I'm glad Cynthia is on the job. Her car saved me.

Someone's already unlocked my office door, but at least there's no need to spend time fiddling with a key. The AA mediation book sits on the corner of my desk, exactly where I left it. I ponder taking an extra moment to inscribe it, then nix the idea. There's no time and no need. Lila knows how I feel. When it comes to recovery, we're on the same page.

I hurry out of my office and back down the hall, past the office door. Lila is already outside. I spot her through the large double windows, huddled next to her car.

"Careful," she warns as I start through the door. "It's slippery. You don't want to fall."

"I'll make sure Vince sprinkles some salt." I hand her the book. "Sorry, I didn't have time to wrap it. I was going to give it to you on Thursday night."

"For me?" Her gloved hand brushes the embossed golden cover as she stares at the book, then back up at me. Her blue eyes are round and questioning. "From you?"

The words won't come. My tongue sticks like it's frozen to the roof of my mouth. My brain is cold and empty.

But not my heart.

"It's for your twentieth anniversary," I sputter. "I was going to inscribe it, but... well, I didn't have a chance. But congratulations anyway," I add lamely.

We're outside in the cold, snow swirling around our feet. But one look at her face and we might as well be in the furnace room smacked up against the boiler. What is wrong with me? Why the hell did I give her that book? I should have known better. She probably thinks I'm nuts.

Or maybe she thinks something else entirely.

Does she know? Can she guess?

What have I done?

"Thank you, Greg." She cups my face between her hands and kisses me.

One kiss, then another. A kiss for each cheek, European fashion.

"You are such a sweet, thoughtful man," she whispers in my ear. "I am so blessed."

Did I hear her correctly? Has the wind caught her words, tossed them senselessly about the parking lot, taunting me with what I want to hear?

But how can you mistake a kiss?

For one wild moment, I think about abandoning everything right there in the parking lot and pulling her into my arms. What difference does it make what God wants from me? How can this be wrong when He made man and woman to be together? What would it be like to have her lips melt against mine, rather than merely brush my cheeks? What would it feel like, our bodies pressed together? To feel the heat of her touch and the smoothness of her skin?

I catch her hand, squeeze it tight. Does she feel the same? Does she dream of me at night, the way I sometimes dream of her?

God help me. To carry on like this is madness. What am I going to do?

"Greg?" An uncertain look hovers in her eyes. "I need to go, or I'll be late."

"Sure. Sure." I let her hand go. My God, what have I done? I've embarrassed us both.

"Thank you again for the book," she says. "I'll think of you every time I read it."

"You're welcome," I sputter, rubbing the spot where her lips pressed against my skin. The warmth of her touch stays with me long after she drives away. I wander down the hall to my office and sink into my chair, acutely aware of the scent of her perfume hanging on my coat. Just a brief encounter between two people, but I came so close. I wanted to press her against me, to hang on, to never let go.

It is wrong. I know it is wrong. But something about this woman stirs something deep inside me. It is a longing, a sense that something is missing, something isn't right.

It is forbidden; they warned us in seminary. Never allow yourself to get too close to women.

I hug my coat closer, inhale the scent of lilac and roses that lingers.

Her scent.

This is why it is forbidden. This is what will bring down a decent man.

She is a woman, and I am a priest.

It is forbidden.

I bury my face in my hands. God, she smells good.

It is forbidden.

God help me.

CHAPTER EIGHT

"See that beautiful angel near the top of the tree? Gregory bought it for me last year when he visited Rome. And that clay angel with the funny halo is one of my favorites. I brought it back from Mexico."

Mom points out the glittering ornaments nestled in the Christmas tree. "Since Gregory was a little boy, we pretended our tree was filled with guardian angels." She turns to me with a fond smile. "Remember, son?"

How could I forget? We had the only celestial tree on the block. Instead of the usual candy canes, tinsel, and gingerbread, ours was adorned with heavenly creatures. The kids at school showed no mercy in teasing me.

"Guardian angels guarding the Christmas tree," Gina says. "What a beautiful tradition."

Mom looks pleased. "You and your husband could do the same, you know. And there's no better time to start a tradition than as you're starting a family." She ponders Gina with a little smile. "Who knows? Maybe there'll be a little angel tucked under our Christmas tree for that little one of yours."

Now Gina is the one who looks pleased.

A sigh of relief escapes my lips. Why was I so worried? The two of them seem to be getting along great, and Mom loves how Gina decorated the tree. It promises to be a good Christmas. With Mom settled in with me for the holidays, it will make it easy to get back on track, to keep my mind from straying where it shouldn't.

It is forbidden.

I'll focus on what I already have, rather than what can never be. I'll go to more meetings. I'll concentrate on keeping myself healthy and happy. I'll settle down and enjoy a happy, holy Christmas.

As soon as I finish preparing my Christmas homily, which for some odd reason, is giving me fits. Even the monthly homily guides arriving in the mail aren't proving much help. The suggested sermons seem stale. They're just the same old thing I see year after year.

This Christmas, I want my message to be something different. Unfortunately, I have writer's block. Perhaps it's because of some leftover guilt over what happened between Lila and me or some unspoken desire hidden deep in my heart. Thoughts of her surround me, everywhere I go, through everything I do. Is it any wonder I can't concentrate on my Christmas homily?

Maybe I should turn over my pen and paper to Gina and Mom. I'm sure between the two of them, they'd manage to come up with something far better than I.

"Gregory tells me there's going to be a special celebration on Christmas Day." Mom pats the couch cushion. "Sit down, dear, and tell me all about it."

Gina sinks down beside her. "Father Greg is blessing our marriage after the noon Mass. Joe bought a new suit. And I have a new dress." She throws a sudden doubtful glance at the swell of her belly. "I hope it still fits. I haven't tried it on in a few weeks."

"You'll look beautiful," Mom predicts. "All brides do on their wedding day."

"We're having a small reception at the Murray Hotel afterward." Gina smiles shyly. "Both of you are invited. We're looking forward to having you there."

"I wouldn't miss it," Mom assures her.

Nor would I. The handwritten invitation arrived in the mail last week, and I RSVPed for both of us, despite some misgivings about what Mom might say. But I have no intention of missing out on the chance to celebrate this happy occasion with Gina and Joe.

"We've only invited a few guests. Joe didn't think many people would come." She bites her lower lip. "I suppose he's right. After all, Christmas is a family holiday. Even if we had invited them, they probably wouldn't be able to make it."

Because it's Christmas? Or because they don't approve of an interracial couple? I can only offer an encouraging smile. Though I wish I could do more, there's no way to protect her from the ugliness and bigotry in the world.

"Being around that young lady breaks my heart," Mom announces later over a cup of tea once Gina leaves.

I look at her in surprise. "Why?"

"Because she's such a sweet thing. The life she's chosen won't be an easy one, especially once that baby arrives." Her face softens. "A black man and a white woman? People can be cruel. I hate the thought of her losing heart."

"That's not going to happen," I say firmly. Why should it? Gina is passionately in love with Joe and wildly protective of him. I can't imagine her losing spirit, no matter what people might say or what might happen. The world wouldn't stand a chance taking on Gina VanBrabant.

"What do people in your parish think, having them in the pews?"

I push down the nagging memory from last weekend, when Joe and Gina served as greeters before Mass. Some people seemed determined to make it their personal mission to be seen shaking hands with the new interracial couple in town. Others seemed just as determined to ignore them.

Prejudice is an ugly thing, with no limits, no barriers. Even uglier is the way it hides as it worms its way deep inside people's hearts.

"No one has complained. This is a church, remember? Everyone is welcome."

"I hope you're right, Gregory." Mom's tone doesn't hold much hope. "They seem like such a nice young couple. Perhaps it won't matter so much. After all, he is different than most of them."

I eye her carefully. "What do you mean, *different*?"

Mom blinks. "Why, you know very well what I mean. He's just different. For one thing, there's that beautiful accent of his. And… well, he's different."

"You mean he's not an American black man," I challenge.

"That's not what I said," she retorts.

I know I've offended her, but she's offended me. And though he's not around to hear it, she's offended Joe.

Even my own mother.

"Are you accusing me of being prejudiced?"

"You said it, Mom, not me." Of all the people I know, she should know better. Bigotry is born of ignorance. My mother was a teacher. Her job was to raise people above their ignorance.

But my job is to educate people, too, and to stand up in defense of others.

Especially when they're not able to do it for themselves.

"Answer me, Gregory. Do you think I'm prejudiced?"

"That's a question you'll have to answer for yourself."

"You should be more careful what you say and remember who you're talking to. I'm your mother and I love you, but people in this town won't be so quick to forgive if you question their moral judgment."

"Who said anything about moral judgment?"

"You did just a moment ago, when you accused me of being a bigot." She smoothes her skirt and rises, every inch of her five-foot-two frame in full regal stature. "I am going upstairs to lie down for a while."

"Come on, Mom, please don't be like this." She's been in town less than twenty-four hours. There's barely been time for us to bicker. "Are you mad at me?"

"Perhaps, Gregory, it would be best if I leave you alone so you have time to figure that out."

I watch as she disappears into the hallway.

"Ray will be here in an hour or so," I call from behind her. "Remember, the three of us have dinner plans."

The stairs creak and moments later I hear the sound of a door closing upstairs. She doesn't slam it. There's no need. She made her point. First and foremost, my mother is a lady, genteel and refined.

She is also a lady who is mad. Plenty mad.

I hang my head in my hands. Maybe I should phone Ray, beg off dinner. I'm not sure she'll join us. But I can't go off and leave her to fend for herself. Mom is nearly eighty. She needs looking after, despite what she thinks.

Why can't women be more like men? Say their piece and go with the flow. Why does she have to be like this now? I can't afford to have her mad at me. It's Christmas, the season of light and love. It's the time of year we are called to be patient and tolerant.

Patience and tolerance are worthy aspirations. But who's going to remind my mother?

Vince blesses himself with a hasty sign of the cross, then shambles over to where I stand in front of the altar.

"I'll be taking off now, Father, unless you've got anything else for me to do."

"I think we're good to go." I'm grateful for the interruption. Not that I'm anxious, but my Christmas sermon is still just a collection of rambling thoughts and I've only got two more days. "You're planning on coming in tomorrow, correct?"

"Yep." Vince scratches his beard. "Tomorrow, plus Christmas Eve, and Christmas Day."

"Good. Let's both keep an eye on the weather. Last I heard, they were predicting four to six inches of snow for tonight, plus another eight to ten inches tomorrow."

"Don't worry, Father, I'm on top of it."

"Are we all set on the parking lots? The snowplow guy isn't planning on leaving town for the holidays, is he?"

"I talked to him this morning," Vince assures me. "He'll be around."

"Great." Mom would never let me hear the end of it if we got snowed in on Christmas Day. "By the way, Vince, you're doing a great job keeping the sidewalks clean. Thanks again for convincing me to buy that new snow blower. It was money well spent."

Vince cracks a wide grin, rubbing a hand over his

shaggy chin that puts me in mind of a porcupine. He's been growing the beard since hunting season last month. He heads out the door, past one of the poinsettia plants delivered just this morning by the new florist we're working with this year.

I take a few steps backward, taking it all in. Twinkling lights peep from amidst branches of fragrant wreaths lining the aisles. The altar is draped in rich colors of scarlet and gold. The Christmas tree stands alone with an empty manger underneath, awaiting the newborn King.

All is calm, all is bright.

All is ready.

Except for my Christmas homily. I pat the notes shoved deep inside my shirt pocket.

"Father Greg?" A voice floats from above.

I whirl around and peer up into the choir loft.

"It's me, Carol. Hold on, I'm coming down." Footsteps clatter on the stairs. Seconds later, our choir director stands before me. Carol is a whirl of vivid colors with a shock of bright red hair and a dark frown on her face. "Was that Vince I just saw leaving?"

"It was." I confirm. "Did you need him?"

"When don't I need him?" She rolls her eyes. "Swear to God, that man has a radar that doesn't quit."

Carol is another leftover from Father Mac's era with a sharp attitude and even sharper tongue. Some of the choir members have complained, but I've been loath to interfere. She has formal training as a musician and works for a pittance. Hopefully after the holidays we can get things straightened out.

"He knew I wanted those music inserts in the pews before the Christmas Masses," she fumes. "I can't believe he ran out on me like that."

"He'll be in tomorrow," I assure her. "I'm sure he'll do it then."

"I've already told him twice, and they're still not out." She heaves a sigh of disgust. "I am tired of telling him what to do and him not listening."

Funny, I've never had that problem. Maybe it's the way she asks. Or maybe it's that she doesn't ask. Carol demands. No wonder the choir members are complaining. The choir loft has always been a hotbed of bickering, but why can't people cut others some slack?

"How about if I handle Vince?" I suggest. "Would that help?"

"Thank you, Father. Frankly, I'd rather not deal with him anymore." Her nose wrinkles slightly. "He smells."

My face hardens. She's right. Vince does smell... of gasoline, sweat and hard work.

"After the holidays, I think it would be a good idea if the two of us sat down and talked," she says. "With Helen leaving at the end of the year, I think it's a good time to make a fresh start. I don't know if you're aware of it, but things in the choir haven't exactly been... harmonious."

"I think that's a good idea."

Christmas is the season of forgiveness, and Carol seems to be offering an olive branch. Maybe she's finally beginning to understand that if you continually knock people down, it causes them to lose heart. And with our longtime organist Helen finally calling it quits, Carol is right. The timing couldn't be more perfect.

A new year, a fresh start. New songs. New attitude. New Carol.

"We need to get rid of some people, especially some of the older ones," she says. "They've been around for years. Too many years, if you ask me. They can't read the music, they mess up the instrumentals, they don't sing on key."

"Excuse me?" It feels like my ears are suddenly plugged with wax. Carol wants to cull the church choir? She wants to pick and choose who can belong?

"I didn't want to do it, not with Helen still around. They're all friends, and I couldn't afford to lose her. But now she's leaving, it's the perfect time to get rid of the dead wood. Once they're gone, we can figure out what we need to do to make Our Lady's choir the best in the diocese."

How do you fire a volunteer? How do you tell people who have been singing all their lives that the gift God gave them—no matter how much they sing off-key—is no longer desired?

What happened to living by the fruits of the spirits? Aren't we called to live by gentleness, patience, kindness, and love?

"Thanks for bringing it to my attention," I say. "I promise that once the New Year comes, the two of us will sit down and talk."

Thank God the altar flood lights are dim or she'd surely see me strangling on my tongue. I force myself to keep quiet before something utterly inappropriate slides out of my mouth within the walls of church.

Carol finally leaves and the church grows quiet, but not my spirit or my thoughts. I stride up and down the aisles with my feet moving faster than my fingers as they slide over the rosary beads. I pass the altar, the empty manger, and my thoughts turn to a young couple who trudged through a desert more than two thousand years ago.

A man and his pregnant wife, riding astride a donkey.

Was Mary a soprano? What kind of voice did Joseph have? Would Carol have dared tell either of them they weren't welcome because they sang off-key?

I march through the vestibule and start back up the aisle

of church. Would any of us recognize them if Mary and Joseph walked among us? What would we say if they knocked on our door? Were they turned away at the inn because it was full? Or perhaps the innkeeper didn't want to have them around. Mary's hair probably wasn't too clean. Perhaps she reeked like the donkey she rode. And I'll bet Joseph probably didn't smell much better than Vince.

I swing down another aisle, mulling things over. Why do so many of us think we are better than others? What gives any of us the right to judge?

I come before the altar and stare up at the cross.

A child is born to us. A son is given to us.

I think of Gina and the baby she carries.

I think of Joe, of how he protects her, of the good man he is.

I ponder everything that is in my mind, heart, and soul.

And suddenly there's no longer any need for me to keep thinking. Finally I know exactly what my Christmas homily will be about.

It takes only a few more steps to reach the vestibule. I scrounge in my pocket for the notes I've scribbled, crumple them in a ball, and toss them in the trash. Then I head out the door, down the hall to my office. My thoughts are coming fast and furious, and I want them on paper before they're lost completely in a swirl of sentiment.

Or before I lose my nerve.

This year for Christmas, I'm giving myself the gift I want: the sermon I want to preach.

CHAPTER NINE

Mom sifts the curtain aside and peers through the sacristy window. "I think the snow is finally letting up." She glances at me. "Were you able to reach Joe?"

I join her at the window. Together we watch the parking lot. It's definitely a white Christmas, especially with the heavy, wet snow James Bay received overnight. Power lines around town are down and traffic is barely moving. Midnight Mass was sparsely attended with only a few hardy souls managing to brave the weather. Even fewer were in attendance at this morning's Masses.

"Do you think they'll make it?" Worry wrinkles her face.

"I'm sure he and Gina are on their way."

Going to the chapel and we're gonna get married.

I'm still in my Christmas vestments, but there's no need to change. The rich, gold fabric of the chasuble and stole is appropriate for weddings.

"It will be a small wedding," Mom predicts. "*If* they get here. *If* there is a wedding."

"They'll get here. And there will be a wedding," I say, as

much to convince myself as her. It's times like this I could use a little space. The stress and busyness of Christmastime drains me. The cold weather drains me. Having Mom around twenty-four seven drains me.

I scan the empty parking lot. "There will be a wedding," I repeat. "All we need is Gina and Joe."

"Plus God," Mom adds firmly.

And Lila, who is scheduled as Gina's matron of honor. But it will take an act of God for Lila to make an appearance today. The Mercedes convertible Lucy bought her mother as a present on her fiftieth birthday is sleek and stylish, but not the greatest car for Northern Michigan winters. Maybe someone should volunteer to go get her. Do I have time? Will my coat fit over my vestments? But in heavy snow like this, my car isn't much better than hers.

"Here they are," Mom says with relief a few moments later as Joe blusters his way into the vestibule. He stomps the snow from his boots, then turns to hold the door for Gina, who is radiant despite the bulky navy blue ski jacket she wears.

"Merry Christmas!" She shares kisses all around, with an extra hug for me. "Merry Christmas, Father Greg."

Gina looks angelic on her wedding day. The cold weather has painted a rosy blush on her cheeks. Snowflakes sparkle and melt on her dark tangle of curls, a glorious diadem for a bride. Just the sight of her and this heavy tiredness filling my heart begins to lift.

"Merry Christmas to you, my dear."

Mom hovers between us. "You had us so worried. What with the weather being so bad, we thought maybe you wouldn't make it."

"God has quite a sense of humor, if He thought a little snow would stop Joe and me from getting here today." Gina steadies herself with one hand on Joe's shoulder as he crouches before her and removes her clunky black boots.

"Not what I intended to wear on my wedding day," she says with a cheerful smile, "but Joe insisted."

"We do not want you falling." He sets the boots aside and pulls a pair of pearl-white flats from his pocket.

Gina steps into the shoes and smoothes down her dress. The antique, ivory lace is iridescent with tiny pearl drops that shimmer as she moves, hugging the growing swell of her belly. Heavy with child, she looks more beautiful than any bride that has ever approached my altar.

Mom steps back with an admiring gaze. "My goodness, child, how pretty you look."

"How pregnant I look," Gina corrects her. "Not exactly the vision of a blushing bride."

"You are beautiful to me." Joe rises to a stand and grazes her cheek with a kiss. In his dark suit and elegant, ivory tie, he looks strikingly handsome, and my heart swells at the sight of the two of them.

"What about your witnesses? Have you heard from them?" I ask as they trail me into church and stand before the altar. Though Joe and Gina are married in the eyes of the state, the church still requires two people to serve as witnesses.

"My friend Henry has car problems." Joe scratches his face but can't remove the trail of concern. "Perhaps if you do not mind, we could wait? I do not know when he and his family will arrive. The snow has caused him to be stuck."

"In his driveway," Gina adds. "And I haven't been able to reach Lila. I tried calling her before we left, but the phone just rang and rang. What about her cell phone? Does anyone know the number?"

"I don't believe she has one," I say. Maybe I should

insist she start carrying one. What if something happened? She could be stranded on a road somewhere, cold and hurt. How would we know?

A small frown edges its way across Gina's forehead. "Will there be a problem, if neither of them shows up?"

"We need two witnesses," I say, but my thoughts are on Lila. God help her if she set out on foot. Her house is ten blocks from church, perfect for a summer stroll. But on a cold blustery day with half the roads clogged, she could be in danger.

"We'll wait a few more minutes." My stomach grumbles as I sneak a glance at my watch. No breakfast this morning and the day is wearing on. I try not to think about food. I try not to think about the wind picking up, howling around the corners of the church. I try not to think about Lila, whereabouts unknown.

Minutes later, the church doors open, and a rush of cold air blows Lila inside.

Jim Gillespie is close behind her.

"Sorry we're late." She stamps the snow from her boots with a grateful glance for Jim as he helps her with her coat. "My street isn't plowed yet. But Jim came to my rescue and volunteered to drive me in his nice, big four-wheel drive."

How did he know she was stranded? Did he call her? Did she call him?

The two of them were together at Midnight Mass.

Did they spend the night together, too?

My gut twists. It's none of my business, judging them. It's none of my business who Lila chooses as a houseguest. It's none of my business what the two of them choose to do in their spare time. They're both consenting adults.

Did they make love?

I can barely bring myself to look at her. The thought of

his hands on her body, his mouth covering her own, his arms wrapped around hers, makes my stomach heave. Lila allowing him to spend the night in her bed is a travesty of everything I thought she stood for. Goodness, pureness of heart, spirit, and body.

"Thank God I happened to tell Jim about the wedding today while we were in church last night," Lila rattles on. "I was so surprised when he showed up at my house this morning and offered me a ride. What an adventure we had getting here!"

He simply showed up? He didn't spend the night in her bed?

You are such a fool. The alleluia chiming in my head might as well be a heavenly chorus of angels singing in my ears.

"But that still leaves us minus Henry, Joe's best man." Gina watches me with wary eyes. "What do we do? We don't know when he'll be here."

"We still need two witnesses," I confirm.

Lila, standing before me, silently mouths a single name.

No. I won't do it. He's the last person I want to ask.

But Gina looks crestfallen, and Joe looks panicked. How can I deny them? They've waited so long for this day to come.

Jim Gillespie sits near my mother in the front pew. I take in the folded arms, the blank face, the tight set of his body.

What Lila sees in the guy is beyond me.

"Jim, it seems we're in need of another witness," I say. "If you wouldn't mind…"

He joins us at the altar before I get the rest of the words out of my mouth.

"I knew this would all work out," Lila beams.

"It's perfect," Gina agrees, shuffling to make room.

Perfect for the four of them, perhaps, but I have my doubts.

They stand quietly before me as I open the book that contains the familiar prayers.

Dearly beloved, we are gathered here today.

My voice echoes in the cold, empty church. Gina's eyes shimmer as she and Joe turn to face each other.

Father in heaven, hear our prayers for Joe and Gina today.

Lila couldn't look more beautiful in the rich red dress she's wearing.

And the Lord God said it is not good for the man to be alone.

I force my eyes away from her. It is madness, sacrilege to carry on like this. This is not about her. It can never be about her.

I will make a suitable partner for him... this one shall be called woman, for out of man, this one has been taken. That is why a man leaves his father and mother and clings to his wife, and the two of them become one body.

Joe reaches over and brushes away a few stray tears from Gina's cheeks. Are her thoughts on Mama and Donny, far away on this Christmas Day? Is Joe thinking of his sisters?

They clasp hands and gaze into each other's eyes. Are they thinking of the future, and the unborn child that will make them a family?

Love is patient, love is kind... Love rejoices in the truth. There is no limit to love's forbearance, to its trust, its hope, its power to endure. Love never fails.

Lila never fails.

Lord, bless these rings, which we bless in your name.

I sweep my hands across the two rings, make the sign of the cross.

Grant that those who wear them may always have a deep faith in each other. May they do your will and live together in peace, good will, and love.

"Do you, Johan Michiel VanBrabant, take Maria Regina King to be your wife? Do you promise to be true to her in good times and in bad, in sickness and in health, to love her and honor her all the days of your life?"

Joe's gaze never wavers from Gina. "I do."

"Do you, Maria Regina King, take Johan Michiel VanBrabant to be your husband—"

"Yes, yes, I do!" Her words rush out in a gasp of happiness that makes everyone laugh, including me.

"Let me clarify that," I say. "Gina, do you promise to be true to Joe in good times and in bad, in sickness and in health, to love him and honor him all the days of your life?"

"I do." This time her words are as soft and tender as a lover's whisper. When I finally pronounce them husband and wife, they share a long kiss that produces applause.

"Thank you, Father," Gina whispers in my ear as we share a hug. "Joe and I are so blessed to have you in our lives."

"My dear, it was a pleasure. There's no need to thank me." Joe and Gina are the ones who've done the hard work. They've chosen to take on the world and all its problems, allowing love to lead them through.

God, that I could be so brave.

The tight smile on my face feels like it's carved of wood straight from the cross.

I step back, faltering slightly. What is wrong with me?

Mom joins us on the altar as hugs and handshakes are exchanged. "And now, we celebrate."

The smile on Joe's face evaporates. "Unfortunately, I am afraid the snow has changed our plans. The Murray Hotel has no power. Their kitchen is closed, and we cannot host our party."

"Nonsense, of course we're going to celebrate." Mom doesn't even blink. "All of you will join us in the rectory. It's certainly not as fancy as the Murray Hotel, but we have some nice wine and plenty of food. I made a turkey yesterday, and there's cold shrimp leftover from last night. Not to mention the desserts and candies the RAS ladies have been dropping off the past few days."

I step forward. "Mom's right. Please, all of you, join us in the rectory. Let me change from my vestments and I'll be over shortly."

They gather their coats, a merry group, laughing and joking as they start for the door. I turn and head for the sacristy.

But not before I notice Jim Gillespie reach for Lila's hand and clasp it firmly in his own.

I crouch before the hearth, knowing without even turning that she's entered the room. The scent of Lila's perfume mingles with the snap of fresh, burning wood from the living room fireplace, but it only adds fuel to my resentment. I needed this time alone to pull myself together before rejoining the celebration around the dining room table. Why did she seek me out? Doesn't she realize that we shouldn't be alone?

I keep my head down and add another log to the fire.

Is there nowhere I can go to escape her presence?

Isn't it enough that she haunts my thoughts and dreams?

I poke the fire a few times, finally peer up at her. "Was there something you needed?"

She hesitates. "If this isn't a good time…"

"No, it's fine," I say brusquely. God, how can I send her away? She sounds confused, and I know I've hurt her feelings. But doesn't she understand that having her near is torture?

One kiss and she has obsessed me. One word, one look, one move on her part, and I could abandon everything. There would be no escape for either of us. It's like playing with fire. If I take her in my arms, there is no guarantee what will happen.

I stare at the flames, heat searing my cheeks. The hem of her velvet dress skims her knees, showing off a pair of shapely calves. I grab the tongs and thrust them through the burning logs, scattering the charred pieces. "Where's Jim?"

"Your mother talked him into another piece of pie."

I pile more wood on the fire. The insanity of *what if?* is torturing me. If only she would confirm what I already suspect, that the two of them are a couple, maybe I could finally let go of this obsession possessing me.

Maybe I could finally sleep at night.

"I don't think your mother likes me very much." Her voice falters. "I offered to help clean up, but she ordered me out of the kitchen."

"She likes you just fine," I lie, remembering Mom's admonition about Lila being pushy. The last thing I need is the two of them duking it out over the dishwasher. "She just likes to do things her way, especially as she gets older. But I'm sure she appreciated your offer."

"She didn't say no when Gina offered to help."

I shrug helplessly. What can I say? Gina is happily married to Joe. Gina is having a baby. Gina poses no threat.

"Try not to take it personally," I finally reply.

Lila looks doubtful for a moment. "Greg, is something wrong?" she finally asks.

Plenty. I've seen the hungry way Jim watches her when she doesn't know he's looking. I've seen the proprietary way his hand guides the small of her back, protecting her from God knows what, warning other men.

Back off, she's mine.

"What makes you think something's wrong?"

"You sound angry. And you've seemed upset all afternoon."

"Really? Well, you and the judge seem quite serious," I counter.

"You're crazy," she says, laughing in an uneasy way that tells me she thinks I might be right.

"He's crazy about you," I say quietly. "Come on, you can't deny it."

"Jim's a nice man," she agrees. "But we're not a couple, if that's what you mean."

Poor Lila. She's so clueless. I've met plenty of men like the judge; smart, driven, accustomed to getting what they want. And I've no doubt he wants Lila. Why would she say *no* to him? He's well respected in the community. He has a deep faith. He's devoted to the church. A woman would be crazy to turn him down.

But how could she be happy with a man like Jim?

Arrogant. Condescending. Judgmental.

Then again, Jim is a judge. It's his job to uphold the law.

Just as it's my job to uphold God's law.

My knees groan in protest as I struggle to a stand. "We should get back to the others."

She hesitates. "I wanted to thank you for the Christmas gift. The rosary is beautiful."

"You're welcome." I knew the rosary was meant for Lila the minute I spied it last spring in that little shop in Rome. The blue aurora beads immediately reminded me of the heavenly blue captured in her eyes.

Did Jim give her a Christmas present, too?

"I have something for you," she says. "I wanted to give it to you last night, but the weather was so bad, I decided to wait. I brought it with me today." She hands me a small box. "Merry Christmas, Greg."

I stare at the package done up with a gold bow. It's small but weighty in my hands. "What is it?"

"Open it and see," she suggests with a small smile.

I unwrap the box, aware of her gaze on me. My heart beats faster and the heat from the fire makes my face flush.

Or maybe it's not the fire making me sweat.

Why does she have to stand so close?

Why did she give me a Christmas present?

Why does she have to smell so good?

I tear away the last of the wrapping and toss it in the fire. The flames catch it and consume it in a death dance. My fingers fumble as I open the lid and draw out something hard and heavy, protected by tissue. I stare at the gleaming black stone with uneven edges. "It's a paperweight."

"I thought you could use it on your desk."

I trace one finger against the words etched deep in the veined marble. *As for me and my house, we will serve the Lord.*

Words that will last a lifetime. Words that serve as a weighty reminder of who I am, of vows I took nearly thirty years ago.

Vows that bind me to serve the Lord all the days of my life.

Somehow I muster up the strength to meet her gaze. My heart feels as cold and heavy as the stone in my hand. "Thank you."

Her forehead wrinkles, and she suddenly looks as if she wishes she'd chosen something else.

"It's great," I add. "Perfect."

Or would be.

If I had a house.

If I had a family.

Her eyes search mine. Logs snap on the hearth before us. The warmth of the fire heats the room. July Garland croons in the background, urging us to have a merry little Christmas.

"You don't like it, do you?" Her face falls. "You don't need to worry about hurting my feelings."

"No, it's not that," I say. "It's just…"

She hesitates. "Not what you wanted?"

What I wanted…

Who am I kidding? I know what I want.

Then Lila is in my arms and I am kissing her. Her lips are soft and sweet, open, welcoming, inviting. Her mouth is warm and moist against my own. A rush of primal instinct, of desire denied far too long, surges through me, threatening everything I am, everything I believe.

She murmurs something in my ear, whispers my name, and I realize she wants this as much as I do. I turn to her again, searching out her mouth, every instinct urging me on. Am I doing it right?

I haven't kissed a girl since I was in eighth grade.

God help me, this is sheer madness. It is all I can do to keep my hands from straying to her breasts, from pressing my body against her own, from taking her to my bed.

And damning us both for eternity.

But right now, I would willingly sacrifice everything for this woman who has brought meaning back into my life.

Lead us not into temptation.

I groan and bury my face in her hair, drinking in the delicate scent that surrounds her, crushing back the rush of desire.

148

Is this merely a physical desire, or have I fallen in love with her?

Am I willing to throw everything away? I was a boy when I entered the seminary, but thirty years later, I might as well still be that scared young boy.

Inadequate, helpless, frustrated, afraid; that young boy isn't sure what to do.

But the man in me—the priest in me—has no doubt.

It is forbidden.

Gently I try to push her away. "No, we can't. This is wrong."

"How can it be wrong?" she counters softly. "How could God have made this wrong?"

I want her. I want her more than anything I've ever wanted in my life. I want to take her to my bed, skin against skin, our bodies entwined together in the darkness. I want to enter her, to possess her completely, to know the fullness, the richness, the coming together of two people as one. As a man knows a woman. As a husband knows his wife.

But Lila is not my wife. She can never be my wife. The church mandates its priests remain celibate. No matter how we feel, no matter whom we love.

"No. We cannot do this. We must not do this." I force myself to pull away, though every inch of me strains to hold her closer. But if I allow her to remain in my arms, she will feel my desire, my overwhelming need for her. This is asking too much. I may be a priest, but I am also a man.

A man that has pushed away so much for so long.

And for what? Why?

"This is my fault. I never should have allowed this to happen. I am sorry."

"Sorry for what?" She searches my face with anxious eyes. "Sorry that you kissed me?"

"No." Never that. "Sorry that I let you down. Sorry that I'm the kind of man that allowed himself to give in to this. You deserve better."

"Better than what?" she demands. "Don't you realize who you are, Greg? The man I know is patient and kind, and filled with compassion for everyone he meets." Her gaze holds a challenge. "A passionate man, in everything you do. Why should you be sorry for that?"

Why indeed?

God help me. I draw her close and seek out her lips, allowing myself to succumb to the soft sweetness that is her. If this be madness, then surely I am lost forever, for I do not want this to end.

I do not want to let her go.

But being with Lila means forsaking everything I have been taught, and the sacred vows I made. I dare not go against them, no matter what she says.

Lila is innocent. I am the one to blame. I am the one responsible. It is my weakness, my sinfulness, that allowed this to happen. And while I don't care what happens to me, I dare not put her soul at risk. I have led her astray, and I have no choice but to let her go. Mine is by far the greater sin, for I knew it was wrong and did nothing to stop it.

I knew what I was doing and still I allowed it.

One last kiss, and I will say goodbye. I kiss her again, allowing my lips to linger on her own. Would she cling so close, if she realized this was goodbye? Allow me this one last kiss, and I will live on it for the rest of my life.

God forgive me.

But the muffled cry of horror does not come from God.

It springs from my mother, eyes wide with shock, frozen in the doorway.

CHAPTER TEN

"Lila Carter is on the phone again." Cynthia's voice squawks through the intercom. "It's the third time she's phoned this morning." Her tone hardens. "What exactly am I supposed to tell her this time?"

That I'm scared to pick up the phone? That thoughts of her have obsessed me these past five days? That she consumes my every waking moment, and my dreams at night?

That she has bewitched me, and I think—no, I fear—that I've fallen in love with her?

Guilt. How long can I continue to avoid her? It is not fair to either of us. But the memories of Christmas Day are as fresh as the fir boughs still draping the church pews. And the shame of being caught by my mother is as hot as the memory of Lila's lips on mine. My mother's fury is still evident. Five days later, with her safe at home some two hundred miles distant, she still refuses to speak with me.

Eventually Mom will get over it. She'll have no choice.

But Lila?

That's an entirely different matter.

"Tell her I'm busy. I'll have to call her back," I order Cynthia.

It's not exactly a lie. I didn't specify *when* I'd return the call. It could be an hour, it could be a day. Next week. Next month.

Or maybe *never*. Break it off completely. No more contact. That would be easier. The thought of talking to her, of seeing her again and facing that temptation, makes me break out in a cold sweat. It would be like uncorking the bottle and smelling the booze. Do I have the strength to resist?

"Fine," Cynthia spits into the intercom, cutting us off. She's still furious with me for messing up her routine. I've stuck around and buried us both in office work instead of taking a few days off like I normally do between Christmas and New Year's.

But I'd rather deal with Cynthia's wrath than stick around the rectory and face the hangover of my memories. The disappointment and disbelief in my mother's eyes, the pain on Lila's face, the fear in my heart over what I allowed to happen.

How long can I continue hiding out?

Hiding from Lila.

From God.

From myself.

I'm not even working an honest recovery program. The sober way to deal with fear is to admit it, talk it over with a sponsor or someone who understands. To face the fear, to embrace it.

But it is not the fear I want to embrace.

My private line rings.

"I've been phoning the rectory all morning," Ray complains. "What the hell are you doing at your desk?"

"I've got some things I need to work on."

"At Christmas?" He laughs. "Are you nuts? What's so important?"

"Some of us have things to do," I answer stiffly. "I'm busy."

Busy trying to forget.

"Greg, did I do something to piss you off? Because if I did, I'd rather you tell it to me straight."

"You didn't do anything."

It's not Ray's fault he has a friend who is a jerk.

A jerk with a guilty conscience.

"Okay, so if it's not me, then what gives? And exactly how long do you plan to keep up this solitary confinement act?"

"Until I get things straightened up around here." My eyes sweep over my desk. "I've made a dent in the office clutter, but I've got a ways to go."

He chuckles. "An early New Year Resolution?"

"Something like that," I agree.

"What about tonight? Everyone deserves some time off, and it's New Year's Eve. Got any plans?"

New Year's Eve. I'd nearly forgotten. A night meant for celebration. A night for making resolutions. A night to be with people you love.

What is Lila doing tonight?

Does she have plans with Jim? Dinner? Dancing?

Will tonight be the night he takes her home and doesn't leave till morning?

I push away the image that has tortured me these past few days. A man and a woman, the two of them together in the darkness of her bedroom. Twisted bed sheets, moans of pleasures, and two bodies coming together as one.

"Greg? You still there?"

It's none of my business what Lila chooses to do in the privacy of her bedroom. She is a grown woman. She answers to no one.

It is none of my business.

None of my damned business.

"I've got no plans," I tell him. "No plans at all."

"Great. Come on over, and we'll celebrate together."

But I don't feel like celebrating. Not when my life has fallen apart and my faith in everything shaken. Not my faith in God, but faith in myself. Faith in everything I thought my life was meant to be.

"Thanks, Ray, I appreciate the offer, but I think I'll stay put. The weather forecast is calling for more snow."

"For God's sake, man, we live in Northern Michigan. It snows. Deal with it. Shut the office, get in your car, and haul your ass over here. It's New Year's Eve."

"I know that, but…"

"Listen, Greg, you'd be doing me a favor." His voice drops a few notches. "I could use the company."

I hesitate. Ray doesn't sound right. What kind of a friend am I, to be so wrapped up in myself that I haven't given one thought to him? Then again, maybe he's worried about me. Ray's a good friend, and more than anyone understands what it means for me as a recovering alcoholic. It's been a long time since I've had a drink, but I was a professional drinker for years. And when it comes to alcohol, New Year's Eve is amateur night. Ray knows I've got a lot on my mind. He's probably worried about me.

Stay sober, no matter what. Drinking won't help; it only makes things worse. I know that. I haven't forgotten.

Just like I haven't forgotten that bottle of wine in the dining room cabinet leftover from Joe and Gina's wedding. I try to swallow despite my dry mouth, tasting the first swell of panic. There's no way Ray could have known that all morning long, I've been thinking about a drink.

Lila and a drink.

I've got to talk to someone.

Thank God for Ray. A man couldn't ask for a better friend.

"I'm on my way." I push away the half-eaten sandwich sitting on my desk, grab my coat, and ignore the flashing message light mocking me from the telephone. Another call from Lila. Maybe tomorrow. Maybe in a few more days. But not now, not yet. I can't handle hearing her voice.

I lock up the office, give Cynthia the rest of the day off, and head for my car. The skies, gray and flat, mirror my mood as I make the drive to Ray's. The roads are slushy and traffic is light. People are still working, or already home preparing for tonight's festivities.

Ray welcomes me in a warm bear hug and ushers me inside. He's been at his parish for over five years and has fashioned the rectory into a warm, relaxing retreat, courtesy of his family money. I shrug out of my coat, toss it over a chair, note the open bottle of whiskey on the table as I trail him into the dining room.

"Looks like you started celebrating early."

He eyes the bottle, then lifts a shoulder and smiles. "For you, I made coffee."

"I hope it's good and strong." I follow him into the kitchen. "I'm going to need it."

He pours me a mug. "Sounds interesting."

"Decide for yourself."

And with that, I confess.

"Did she lead you, Greg? Encourage you in any way?"

Ray eyes me across the table. "Some women get off on going after priests. It's the whole forbidden fruit thing, you know."

"Lila isn't like that," I shoot back. "I take full responsibility for what happened."

Ray gulps his whiskey, muses things over for a moment. "Okay, so you kissed her. But that doesn't mean you have to tear yourself apart."

I recognize the tone he's using on me. Patient, firm, and comfortingly familiar. God knows I've used it myself when dealing with parishioners bent on self-flagellation.

"I think you're being too hard on yourself. Just because we're priests doesn't mean we're not human. You can't beat yourself up over this."

I wrap my hands around my coffee mug. Exactly what Lila told me after we kissed. "Look, Ray, I know what you're trying to tell me, but—"

"No *buts* allowed," he presses. "Did the two of you end up in bed?"

"God, no!" Though I wanted it to happen. God knows, I wanted it more than anything.

And maybe if the rectory hadn't been filled with people, maybe if we'd been alone, maybe if Mom hadn't caught us...

Mom. The way she acted, she might as well have caught us in bed. I still feel sick, remembering the cold chill on her face as she turned her back on us without speaking a word. We returned to the dining room, and everyone at the celebration remained blissfully ignorant. But Lila's face, solemn and sober, continues to haunt me. She and Jim quickly took their leave. His hand lingered protectively against the small of her back as he escorted her through the door. Her eyes caught mine for the briefest of moments, and I read the wariness captured there.

Has she told him? Does he know?

"Take my advice, Greg, and let it go. You'll end up destroying yourself if you don't. For God's sake, man, it was only a kiss."

But it wasn't just a kiss. It was more than that, and I know in my gut that Lila felt the same. What happened between us was more than a kiss. So much more than a kiss.

Ray downs his drink in one long swallow. "That had to be quite the scene, Mrs. K. walking in on the two of you."

"She was furious," I admit. "She still isn't speaking to me. I phone every day. She hangs up as soon as she hears my voice."

"What kind of man are you, Gregory?" she'd hissed after everyone left. Her face was a mottled purple that scared the hell out of me. "You are a priest. You are my son. You have shamed our family. You should have known better. To think that you allowed yourself to be tempted by that... that woman."

"Can you blame her? You're a bad boy, Greg, breaking your mother's heart."

"Thanks a lot, Ray. I feel rotten enough as it is." I've spent countless hours on my knees praying for guidance.

With only silence for an answer.

I cup my hands around my coffee mug and stare at the dregs littering the bottom. They warned us about this very thing in seminary countless times, but I never believed it would happen to me. I think of the various priests I've heard about through the years. Priests caught *in flagrante delicto* with women. The whispers, the rumors as they were discovered, then confirmed, convicted, and banished by the church's swift retribution.

Is that what my future holds?

If God is for us, who can be against?

I am still for God. But what happens if I abandon His church?

Will He abandon me?

"What am I going to do?" My heart feels shattered in so many pieces, it might be impossible to put it back together.

As does my faith.

Faith in myself. Faith in the rules.

Faith that I can continue to follow those rules.

"What about Lila?" he asks. "What has she said about all this?"

"I don't know."

He throws me a hard stare. "What do you mean, you don't know?"

I swallow. It's one thing to know the truth, but it's something else to admit it to another human being. "She's phoned a few times. Cynthia's talked to her, but I haven't taken her calls."

He slams down his drink, causing golden whiskey to spill across the snowy tablecloth. "For the love of Christ, Greg, you mean you haven't talked to her?"

"No." The wrath in his voice makes me cringe.

"What the hell are you thinking? You can't avoid her. It's wrong," he accuses.

"I know, I know." I stare at him through bleary eyes. "I'm afraid."

Not afraid of what she might say, but afraid of what I might do. I'm afraid that I won't be able to resist her. Lila is like a drug to me, like my own personal brand of scotch.

I gave up drinking years ago.

"You son of a bitch." Ray's eyes narrow. "I never figured you for a coward."

The disgust on his face makes me want to crawl under the table.

"You're right. I know I need to move on this. But, if I do, this changes everything. I'm so messed up. I don't know… I think I need to talk to someone."

"Start with Lila," he says.

"I was thinking maybe the bishop."

Admit my fault, embrace the guilt, do my penance.

"Are you nuts? Take my advice and keep your mouth shut," he says bluntly. "One word to Holden and he'll yank you out of your parish so fast you won't have time to pack your bags. They'll whisk you off to some secret location and no one will hear from you for months. And when you return— *if* you return—any hope or ambition you had about getting ahead will be gone."

"I have no ambitions," I mumble. "Not anymore."

To love and serve God all the days of my life. That was my only ambition; that was the promise I made when I took my vows.

But why can't a priest be allowed to love and serve God while loving and serving a woman?

I slump back in my chair. "Remember when we entered seminary? We were just kids. How were we supposed to know what was right for us? What the hell is the church thinking? How can they expect fourteen-year-old kids to know what they want for the rest of their life?"

Even in grade school all I wanted, all I talked about, was being a priest. The other kids teased me, but I never questioned it. I spent twelve years of my life preparing for the priesthood, all of it in seminary. Four years of high school, four years of college, four years of theology.

Twelve years of my life.

Plus, nearly thirty years spent as a priest. Has it all been in vain? Has it all been for nothing?

I rake my fingers through my hair. "I feel like no matter what I do, it's already over. I've lost everything."

"Hang on, Greg." His voice softens. "You're just going down a rough path. Things will get better."

Easy for him to say. He's never had to deal with anything like this. Ray's got money, influence, no doubts, no anxieties. Life has always been easy for him. But my dad died when I was just a kid, and my mother struggled to put me through school. Scholarships helped, but there was never enough. She was so proud the day I was ordained. What will she think if I walk away now? How can I do that to her? Were her sacrifices, her dreams for me, all in vain?

"Maybe now would be a good time to take that vacation we've talked about," he suggests. "You could get away, relax."

"No, I can't." I think of Lila, how she accused me of living my life on the run. I can't leave now. That would be like running away. I have to stay and face it.

"Maybe I'm not meant to be a priest. Maybe I made the wrong choice. How do I know?" I swallow hard. "What if God wants something different from me?"

The words ring hollow, but the question haunts me. "All my life, I thought I knew what I wanted, what He wanted. But now, I'm not sure."

"What are you going to do?" he asks quietly.

"I don't know. But I can't keep living like this. It's not normal. No wonder people think priests are strange."

He fingers his empty glass. "Who's to say what's normal?"

"We don't even have a choice," I say sadly.

"Sure we do," he argues. "We made our choice when we took our vows the day we were ordained."

"What about Protestant ministers? They're being ordained in the Catholic Church, but they aren't called to make the same sacrifices. Lots of them are married. They bring their wives in through the back door. Is that what the church's future holds? Widowers with children, grandchildren in the rectory. And where does that leave guys like us?"

"Is that it, Greg? You're jealous of what other men have? Is that what you want?"

"I don't know." But Ray's question haunts me. Is that what I want? God *and* Lila? Under current church law, for ordained priests such as me, there is no way such a thing can be possible.

I would be forced to choose.

God *or* Lila.

What if I did leave the church? What if I took her for my wife? How would we survive? Would I be able to provide for her? After twenty-some years spent working for the church, what would I list on a resume? Counselor? Educator? Defrocked priest? And even if the economy was soaring, I would still be competing against eager young college graduates that I baptized as babies. I have to be realistic. I'm in my mid-fifties and probably unemployable.

I can't put Lila through it. It would be impossible, asking her to make those kinds of sacrifices. I can't do that to her. She deserves so much better than that out of life.

"What exactly is it that you want, Greg? Do you think you're missing out?"

Is that part of it? Do I think I'm missing out? How can I explain it to Ray, when I barely understand things myself?

"All my life, I've only had one thing in mind," I choke out. "A love for God... and a call to serve His church by sharing that love with others."

But can that be enough, now that Lila has come into my life? Will it be enough?

"Why must priests stand separate and above?" I wonder

aloud. "How can love for a woman be wrong? Celibacy isn't a discipline mandated by God. We're losing good men because of this insane rule. Things have got to change."

"I wouldn't hold my breath, Greg. You know how the church operates. The Vatican moves slowly."

"Maybe I'm sick of the Vatican." I shove my coffee mug aside. "I'm sick and tired of living by their rules. I'm sick and tired of trying."

"Are you sick of being a priest?"

His words stop me cold.

"Because that's what it will come down to." His eyes lock on mine. "Are you trying to take the easy way out? Forget it, my friend. There is no easier, softer way. Continue this way of thinking, and you'll have to make a choice. It's *God or the girl*."

As usual, Ray has nailed it, though he might as well have nailed me to the cross. No easier, softer way. I'll have to make a decision, and soon. I'm frustrated with the situation, furious with myself.

And worried about Lila. The past five days have been the worst of my life. She must be going through hell.

How could I have ignored her calls? How could I have been so stupid? How could I have put her through that?

"*Let go, let God.* Isn't that they what they tell you in that program of yours? Good advice, Greg, and I suggest you take it. We've all got things in our past we regret. Let it go, my friend. Give it a try. See how it works."

But Ray doesn't understand. I've been trying to let go, but it's not working.

Or perhaps it's not working because I am desperate to hold on to two things that I love.

God *and* Lila.

Did I enter seminary because of a true calling from God?

Was that what God wanted from me? Did I do it to satisfy myself, or to satisfy my mother? Did I join the priesthood to serve others, to serve God, or my own grandiosity? All my daily needs are met, courtesy of Mother Church. I don't live with the day-to-day burdens my parishioners face. The financial responsibilities, the daily toils and struggles of family life.

Did I follow my instincts? Did I follow God's call?

Or did I choose the easier, softer way?

You are a priest forever in the order of Melchizedek.

How can I turn away from this? It is what I am and what I thought I would always be.

Or is it?

You may be the only Christ some people will ever meet, Bishop Holden reminds his priests.

But does that mean I can't make a difference in people's lives unless I am a priest?

All this angst. My head hurts, but my heart hurts more.

"I should get going." I ease myself off my chair, though the thought of leaving scares the hell out of me. The last thing I want is to be alone in the rectory tonight with myself and my thoughts.

And that bottle of wine in the dining room cabinet whispering my name.

My mouth feels like cotton. Can I trust myself? Am I strong enough to say no?

Ray eyes me carefully. "Why not stay? I've got no plans, other than a date with a flat-screen TV and some college football games."

I grab my handkerchief and wipe the beads of sweat popping on my upper lip. "Thanks, Ray, I appreciate the offer, but..."

"We'll order a couple of pizzas, sit back, root for the home team."

"I've got an early Mass tomorrow."

Ray grabs my wrist. "Greg, listen to me. Don't go."

I stare down at his hand, firmly wrapped around my own. Does he know? Can he tell? God help me, I want a drink. I need a drink. I need a meeting, desperately need a meeting. I avoided my regular Thursday night since I figured Lila would be there.

"Don't go," he repeats. "I'll make another pot of coffee and we'll ring in the New Year. Together."

I rub my fingers against my chin, feel the rough stubble. I'm without a razor, toothbrush, and clean clothes.

But I'm not without a friend.

"Sure you want the company?"

He smiles and claps me on the back. "I wouldn't ask if I didn't mean it."

God bless Ray, I send a silent prayer winging toward heaven. He's always been there when I needed him, and once again, he hasn't let me down. I am so grateful to have him in my life.

"Thanks, Ray. I didn't plan... well, I appreciate it," I finish lamely.

He waves off the sentiment. "You'd do the same for me. Things will look better tomorrow."

I hold on to his promise. And though I've never been much for football, I settle down with Ray in front of the television, and we eat our way through an extra-large pizza. He flips the station after the second game ends, and we watch as the New Year's celebration unfolds around the world. In Rome, as doves are released from high atop the Vatican walls, the pope blesses the faithful gathered in St. Peter's Square. The Holy Father prays for a year and a world filled with peace.

I bow my head and whisper the same prayer, plus another.

Dear God, help me find the strength to phone her.

CHAPTER ELEVEN

I wait for the group hovering around her to disperse. Meeting nights are always crowded, and after meetings, Lila always attracts a crowd. I head in her direction when she's finally alone.

Before she can make a getaway.

Before I lose the opportunity.

Before I lose my nerve.

Will she even talk to me? Sweat pops on my forehead as I stroll up beside her. I feel just like a kid in middle school again, approaching the prettiest girl in seventh grade. The one who eyed me with that same what-do-you-want? look that's now on Lila's face.

She picks up her coat.

"Got a minute?" I ask.

She stares at me with eyes as cold and gray as the waters of Lake Michigan tossed in a November gale.

"I tried to phone you yesterday," I add.

"Really?" Her eyebrows arch as she slips into her coat.

The knot in my stomach tightens as I remember sweating through the call, only to be greeted with the endless ring-ring-ring at the other end. "I guess you weren't home," I add.

Her face is flat, and her eyes hold no smile.

Damn it, can't she see I'm trying? Even my mother finally thawed and started taking my calls, though she's still annoyed. Her twenty-minute harangue last night was proof of that.

But Lila isn't my mother. Far from it.

It's taken me awhile to come to grips with how I feel. The sexual attraction I feel for her is a natural desire. But there is no reason that it can't be quelled. Abstinence is difficult, but manageable.

You close your eyes.

You close your mind.

Closing your heart is the greater sin.

I still hunger for Lila's heart.

"I don't blame you for being angry. And I know you're upset—"

"You don't know anything." She cuts me off with a sharp look. "I don't hear from you for days. You won't talk to me. You don't return my calls. I haven't got time to play those kinds of games, Greg. You expect me to operate on your timetable? Forget that nonsense. Jim invited me out for dinner, and I accepted."

I push down the surge of disappointment. Where did he take her? What did they do? My New Year's holiday was spent taking an early afternoon jog through slushy streets with Joe, followed by dining on dried-out ham, courtesy of Gina. But even in the comfort of their home, chatting over dinner and dessert, admiring the nursery Gina has prepared, it was hard to stay focused.

God or the girl.

Ray's words from New Year's Eve keep churning in my

brain. I have to make a choice. I can't go on like this. The increasing isolation dragging me down; the growing discontent at the church hierarchy; the long, lonely nights and the doubts keeping me awake.

And Lila. Always, thoughts of Lila.

Thinking about her being with Jim is like picking at a wound that's barely scabbed over.

"I hope the two of you had a nice time," I say lamely.

Her blue eyes glitter. "Actually, we did not."

I'm no expert when it comes to women, but my guess is she's furious. At me? Or maybe it's him. The thought of Jim tipping a few too many on New Year's Eve doesn't equate, but I've seen straighter men do stranger things once they take the first drink.

"I suppose we both remember what it's like to do a little too much celebrating on New Year's Eve. Maybe you should cut him some slack."

"What in God's name are you talking about?"

I shift on my feet. What *are* we talking about? Obviously not the same thing that she seems to think we are. "I assumed the two of you had plans for New Year's Eve."

"You do a lot of assuming, you know that?" Her eyes narrow as she buttons her coat. "For your information, and not that it's any of your business, I spent New Year's Eve here at the Club. We hosted a twelve-hour AA marathon, remember? But since you didn't show up, I *assume* you forgot."

But I didn't forget. I stayed away because I couldn't risk the chance that she would be there. I was afraid to face her. I've missed a week's worth of meetings because I've been afraid to face her. And on New Year's Eve, that fear nearly cost me twelve years of sobriety. If it hadn't been for Ray's

167

intervention, I would have headed home and probably straight for that leftover bottle of wine, which quickly would have been followed by any liquor I could get my hands on.

Thank God that I've got a friend like Ray in my life. He sensed I was in trouble and on New Year's Eve, he saved me from a relapse.

And the only thing that will save me tonight is being honest. My addiction has brought me to my knees, and recovery has brought me to the truth. Over and over, I need to admit that I have no power over my life.

I have no power over alcohol.

I have no power over Lila.

The first truth I admitted to myself twelve years ago when I walked away from booze. The second truth I need to admit right now.

Am I ready to walk away from her?

She starts to turn away.

"Lila? Please?" I want to fold her in my arms, hug her close, and stop her from walking away from me forever, but instead, I keep my distance. It's better that way. Easier. Maybe I can get through this. "We need to talk."

She eyes me skeptically. "Really?"

"You know we do. And I'm ready and willing, whenever you like. Just name the time and place."

Her eyes narrow and she stares at me for a long moment. Then suddenly, she shrugs out of her coat and drapes it over a chair. "Fine. Start talking."

"Here?" I glance around the cavernous room, take in the usual few stragglers at the far end still hanging around the coffeepot. "Now?"

"I can't think of a better time." She slips into a seat.

My heartbeat quickens. Maybe she's right. The

clubhouse is as safe a place as any—safer, perhaps, than anywhere else. It's out in the open, but not in public. And with alcoholism the great leveler, both of us belong here.

"Let me grab some coffee," I say. "Can I bring you a cup?"

"No." She folds her hands together, still unsmiling.

Somehow I make it down the length of the room to the coffeepot. I pour myself a cup, mumbling the Serenity Prayer under my breath. To *accept the things I cannot change*, to find the *courage to change the things I can*. Somehow, these things have to be done.

But *the wisdom to know the difference*? The woman has me confounded. I've never felt so depressed or discouraged in my life.

A good three feet separates us as I take a seat across from her. I blow out a deep breath. I was wrong. There is no easy, softer way to do this.

"First off, I owe you an apology," I say. "I should have returned your calls."

"Yes, you should have," she answers icily.

Her face shows no sign of thawing. This is a side of Lila I've never seen. But I have to admit that I deserve it. I'm the one who avoided her for over a week. I gulp some coffee, wincing as the hot liquid scalds the back of my throat. The pain is welcome, but not nearly enough penance for the sin I've committed.

"I'm sorry, and I hope you'll forgive me. Not calling you back was wrong, and I never meant to hurt you. But maybe... well, at least now we've both had some space and time to think."

Her eyes narrow. "That's how you spent your week? Thinking?"

Something in her voice warns me to stop right now, that

I'd be better off doing some more thinking before I say the wrong thing. It feels like I'm in over my head, thrashing in the deep end of the pool.

Lila does not look inclined to throw me a life preserver.

"I think we both realize Christmas was a mistake," I finally say.

"A mistake," she repeats.

"Yes, and I take full responsibility." I steal a glance at her mouth. How could lips that taste so soft and sweet be set in such a firm, unyielding line?

"I should have been stronger," I add. "I should have known better. I never should have allowed it to happen. I never meant to hurt you, Lila. No matter what else you believe, you must believe that. And I hope you can forgive me… just as I hope we can go on from here. This doesn't need to change things. We can put this behind us. It can be the way it used to be."

"You mean we will pretend it never happened?" she challenges. "Is that what you're suggesting?"

"I don't know," I confess. "Maybe. I only know that, for both our sakes, we need to find a way through this." God, how can I lose her? "We can still be friends. And, if you're willing, I hope you'll agree to continue as sacristan—"

"Greg, are you really that dense? How do you expect me to still be your sacristan? How can I do that? For that matter, how can I even continue attending Mass at Our Lady's? Do you really think I can sit in a pew and watch you on the altar, after everything that happened between us?"

Her eyes narrow into tiny slits. "You are the most frustrating man I have ever met in my life."

I shrink in my chair. Lila suddenly is pure woman: feminine and furious.

"All week, I waited." Her low voice slices through the air. "Seven days I waited, dreaming up excuses for why you wouldn't return my calls. Every day that passed only made it worse... until I finally realized what was wrong."

Relief rushes through me. Thank God she's finally come to her senses. She understands what happened between us was a horrible mistake.

We can bandage the wound.

I will pray for both of us.

And I swear never to dream of her again.

"They tell us in program to concentrate on our own program, not to blame others," she says. "Fine, I won't take your inventory. But I have every right to tell you how I feel. And you are going to sit there and listen."

Color floods her cheeks. Passion chokes her voice. Lila has never looked more beautiful.

"Do you have any idea how I felt when I realized you were avoiding me? You didn't phone, you wouldn't return my calls. You abandoned me, Greg. How do you think that made me feel?"

Facing the reality of the hurt in her eyes, hearing the angry ache in her voice, makes me hate myself more than I already do. If I could take her pain and embrace it as my own, I would gladly do so.

"There's no excuse for what I did. I'm sorry. Truly sorry." I rake my fingers through my hair, but I won't allow myself the luxury of hiding from her anger. I've done too much hiding. It's time to stand up and face things like a man. Lila deserves that much from me. "I wasn't thinking straight. I let the fear get to me."

"What are you so afraid of?" she demands. "Me? Yourself? The idea of *us*?"

"There can never be an *us*." I shake my head. "It won't work. It's impossible."

"Why?" she presses.

"Because it is!" I pound my fist on the table.

Several people at the coffeepot turn and raise their eyebrows. I choke down my anger. Why is she making this so difficult? She has no idea what she's asking.

"For God's sake, don't you understand? It should be obvious. I am a priest."

I am nothing without God... yet I am nothing without Lila. How can I go on without her in my life?

Yet, to try and include her would be sheer madness.

She sits back in her chair. "I can see there's no use in arguing the point. You've already made your decision, haven't you? You're going to play the martyr and pretend this is the life you want, even though you're not quite sure. And what does that prove? How does that change anything?"

The fury on her face is gone, replaced by a quiet pity. "For a man of faith, you have quite an ego."

Sitting here in the clubhouse, it's easy to remember AA's definition of ego: *Edging God Out.*

My Lord, my God, is that what I have done?

"There's no reason this has to change things between us..."

"Of course it changes things. It changes everything. And quite honestly, Greg, I find it hard to believe that you don't think so, too."

She turns her head away. Are those her tears, or merely my imagination playing tricks on me? But she has every right to cry. It takes a tremendous amount of courage to confess how you feel. What kind of man am I, to sit here and do nothing?

But what kind of man would I be if I took her in my arms, brushed away the tears, and kissed away the pain and sorrow I have caused?

Then Lila lifts her face toward me and I see her eyes shimmer, but not with tears. The fierce determination makes my stomach crawl.

"Damn the Catholic Church," she says. "They've brainwashed you into thinking you should hold yourself to some unattainable level of perfection, that celibacy will raise you up and bring you closer to God. Well, they're wrong, Greg. None of us is perfect. Not you, not me, not even the pope. Don't you dare sit there whining about how hard it is to choose. Every one of us is called to make difficult choices, every day of our lives.

"You are not the only one involved in this relationship. Don't you dare forget that." Her voice shakes with fury. "I can't compete with God; I refuse to compete with God. I love Him, too, remember?"

Her words are a stinging reminder of exactly what I've done. I have committed a deep wrong, a grave sin. I followed my own selfish desires and put her soul in mortal danger. I have sinned in the worst possible way and led us both to the brink of temptation. Somehow, I must find a way to bring us back. Thank God we did not end up in bed together. If it had come to that, going on without her would be impossible.

Now will be hard enough. Damn hard. But it can be done.

It has to be done.

I want so much to reach across the table and touch her. Instead, I clench my hands together, like I'm praying. "We can put this behind us. No one needs to know."

"But you know," she says. "God knows."

And then I suddenly remember. Someone else knows, too. Someone who was at the rectory on Christmas Day. Someone who is friendly with Bishop Holden.

I eye her carefully. "What about Jim?"

Her breath catches. "This has nothing to do with him."

"Did you tell him?"

"That is none of your business."

I lean forward across the table. "Damn right it's my business. He's involved with you. Don't try and deny it. And don't say it doesn't matter, because it does."

"I'll only say it one more time," she warns. "Leave Jim out of this."

I slam back in my chair. Does she think I'm a fool? She won't confirm it, but I know that she's told him. But Lila is the fool if she thinks he won't talk. A few words from Jim in the right ear will make a difference. A huge difference.

Was Ray right about her after all?

"What's this all about?" I demand. "Why won't you talk about him? Are you keeping quiet because you figured that if things didn't work out with me, you'd have Jim to fall back on?"

Even as the words slide out of my mouth, even before the disbelief and horror slide across her face, I know I've made a huge mistake. How could I have thought it, much less said it aloud? I know in my heart that Lila is not that kind of woman. What kind of man have I become, to accuse her of something like that?

How low can I go? How long before I hit bottom?

It sickens me as I realize we are having our first fight. And very likely, our last.

She stands. "This conversation is finished."

"No." I lunge across the table and grab her wrist. "Don't go."

Her eyes blaze with fury. "Take your hands off me."

Instantly I release her, then shoot a fast glance at the group still hanging around the coffeepot. They seem oblivious.

She sinks back in her chair, rubs her wrist, glares at me. "Never, never touch me again."

My stomach rolls. What have I done? The last thing I ever want is to hurt her. The insanity that's invaded my heart has taken over to the point I no longer recognize myself.

"I'm sorry, Lila. And I'm sorry for what I said about Jim."

"Since you're so interested in talking about him, fine, let's do that. But just remember, you're the one who brought this on."

The cold look that settles over her face brings prickles of fear inching up the back of my neck. If hell hath no fury like a woman scorned, then Lila looks like she's ready to march straight into hell and do battle.

With me.

"Jim is a wonderful man who knows how to treat a woman. He's thoughtful and considerate. He knows what he wants out of life and who he wants to spend it with." She draws in a soft breath. "Last night during dinner, Jim confessed he was in love with me. He asked me to marry him."

I've lost her. I shut my eyes and fight the swirl of cold nausea filling my stomach. My heart has disappeared, and it feels like I'm teetering on the edge of a vast, dark hole. There's nothing left inside save for a deep, empty loneliness that scares the hell out of me.

What's waiting for me at the bottom of that hole?

Hell?

"Jim has so much love to give," she says. "He deserves someone who can love him in return. Any woman would be flattered if she knew he was interested."

And naturally Lila's interested. Why wouldn't she be? She loves him. I bury my head in my hands, when what I really want to do is clap my hands over my ears and stop her words from crowding my brain. How do normal men live through this kind of agony?

If this is what it is like to live as a normal man, then I want no part of it.

"Which is exactly what I told Jim last night," she says. "That while I was flattered, I wasn't interested."

Her words don't connect in my brain. I lift my head and stare at her through bleary eyes. "What did you say?"

"I told him that I couldn't marry him, because I didn't love him," she says, "that I could never love him. Stupid, I know. Stupid and foolish. But that's because I am a fool... a fool who fell in love with a priest."

"You're in love with me?" I whisper.

"I thought I was." She shakes her head slowly. "But after this week, I'm beginning to think maybe I fell in love with a dream. The man I thought I loved has disappeared. Or maybe he never existed.

"I don't know who you are anymore, Greg. I thought I loved you. For a time, I actually allowed myself to believe—to hope—that you felt the same about me. But that's not what I'm hearing you saying tonight. You're not telling me that I was wrong. You haven't said that you don't love me, or even admitted that while you love me, you love God even more. You haven't said any of those things. Instead, all I hear from you tonight is fear. And that's a horrible excuse not to go after what you want in your life."

Her voice lowers. "I thought you were the kind of man

who stood up for something. The kind of man who was ready to take on the world, to fight for others, including himself. But you're not like that at all. You're nothing but a coward." Her voice fills with sadness. "You know what you want, and you don't have the courage to act on it. You're afraid, Greg. Given a choice, you'll choose the easy, softer way, every time."

The easier, softer way. The same words Ray used on New Year's Eve. Is Lila right? Is that what I've done?

"You walk in fear and live in shadows," she says. "I lived like that for a good many years, but I refuse to live that way anymore. And if that's what you want, Greg, if that's your choice, then I want no part of it." Lila stands. "I want no part of you."

"But—"

"No more *buts*." She grabs her coat and slings it over her arm. "It's over. I'm finished. We're finished."

I sit there watching through empty eyes as she walks away.

CHAPTER TWELVE

I slump forward in the overstuffed leather chair, stare at the plush, patterned carpet beneath my feet. How long does Holden intend to keep me waiting? I've already examined every painting on the wall and glanced through all the slick coffee-table magazines.

"I'm sorry Bishop is running late." Denise offers me a warm smile from behind her desk guarding the inner sanctum. "I can't imagine what's keeping him."

Maybe she can't, but I can. A summons to the diocese is never good news. Forcing me to wait nearly an hour is merely the beginning of the punishment Holden has in mind. There's no question he knows about Lila and me.

Damn it, why didn't Jim Gillespie keep his mouth shut?

If only Lila hadn't felt the burning need to confess to Jim what happened. But there's been no chance to question her further or ask her why she did it. It's been two weeks since we last spoke and since I saw her.

She hasn't been at meetings. She hasn't been at Mass.

But every night, she shows up in my dreams.

"Would you like more coffee, Father?" Denise asks.

"No, thanks, I'm all set."

She throws me a pleasant smile. "I have to tell you, Father Greg, how much I love your parish. Sometimes my husband and I drive to James Bay just so we can attend Sunday Mass at Our Lady's. It's such a lovely church, and the people are so friendly."

A lovely parish? With Carol's mandate no members over sixty years old in the choir loft? With Joe and Gina snubbed by nearly half the congregation? With the Rosary Altar Society ladies bickering about the Finance Council's demand they hand over their checkbook? With Cynthia constantly harping about Vince and the lousy job he does cleaning her office? Cynthia, whose face stiffens every time I mention taking an afternoon jog with Joe?

Maybe Ray was right. Maybe I should take a vacation. Get away someplace warm. A place far away, where no one fights. Somewhere with blue skies and a sunny beach, with hot sand beneath my feet. Somewhere I can spend my evenings enjoying good food as the beat of calypso music drums on the night breeze, stirring my blood, urging me to…

No. I push the thought firmly from my mind. Lent hasn't officially started yet, but I've already made it my personal penance to refrain from thinking of Lila.

And forget the vacation, too. It's better I stay put, emotionally and spiritually, in Northern Michigan.

Even if my heart freezes forever.

It's exactly what I deserve.

"Hey, Greg, what brings you over to headquarters?"

I glance up and see Father Bob Koenig, Director of Finance for the diocese, planted in front of me.

"Command performance, I'm afraid," I say.

Bob folds his six-foot frame into the chair next to me. "Holden got you cooling your heels out here?"

"You might say that." I eye him casually. The bishop and Bob are friendly. How much does he know?

"Haven't seen you around lately. We missed you at the retirement dinner for Father Michael last week."

"I had a rosary service at the funeral home that night."

"Sorry you missed it. We had a great time."

While I'm sorry the man died, I was glad for the excuse to stay away. Hanging out with Ray is one thing, and Bob, plus a few other priests, aren't too bad. But the rest of the Diocesan crew does not fit in with my definition of relaxation.

The hot, steady beat of Calypso music continues to drum in my ears.

"You hear the news about Joe McCullough?"

"What about him?" In his mid-forties, Father Joe McCullough is Director of Vocations and one of the bishop's right-hand men. Not that I hold that against him.

"Joe has pancreatic cancer." A solemn look shadows Bob's face. "They diagnosed him last Thursday."

The news comes out of nowhere and lands like a swift punch to my gut. Father Joe is a great guy, one of the best our diocese has to offer. With an upbeat attitude and super personality, he's personally responsible for having recruited our current crop of five seminarians.

I swallow the sour bile rising in the back of my throat. "What's the prognosis? Can they operate?"

Bob shakes his head. "It doesn't look good."

My stomach heaves at the possibility we could lose him. Ten years younger than me, Joe has so much potential. Why him? Why now? What did he do to deserve such a death sentence?

Denise's phone rings. She listens, then turns to me with a bright smile. "Bishop will see you now."

Bob claps me on the shoulder as we stand. "Stop by my office when you're finished with Holden. I'd like your input on an idea I've been working on."

"What's it about?"

He smiles. "What else? Raising money."

Who cares about money? My mind's still trying to wrap around the thought of losing Father Joe. I grab my coat and follow Denise toward the inner sanctum.

"Greg, good to see you." Holden meets me at the door, a preemptive move that surprises me. Normally he greets visitors from the cushy leather throne behind his mahogany desk. He pumps my hand and ushers me into the room. The massive door swings shut behind us with a quiet oomph. "Have a seat. Would you like some coffee?"

"Thanks, I'm all set."

"I'd offer you something harder, but I don't want to offend you. Though if you don't mind…"

Holden doesn't wait for me to answer. He heads for a small, elaborate bar built into a wooden bookcase and pours himself a generous amount of top-shelf scotch. He sinks into his chair, folding his hands across a stomach displaying only a slight paunch. For a man in his late sixties, Holden is in good shape. Must be all that golf he plays with Father Mac.

And Jim Gillespie.

I steady myself for what's sure to come.

"We haven't seen much of you around here lately. I assumed you'd be at Father Michael's retirement party last week." He takes a slow sip of scotch. "You missed a great party."

I eye the crystal tumble in his hand. I don't miss the taste, and I don't miss the hangovers, but I do miss having something that takes away the edge. And there's definitely an edge to this conversation.

"I'm sorry I missed the party, too, but it couldn't be helped. We had a death in the parish."

"Nasty business, funerals," he agrees. "But parishioners come first. Still, don't forget that it's important to take time for yourself. How were your holidays? Did you get a chance to sneak away after Christmas?"

Sneak away or sneak around?

It's obvious Jim told him, so why doesn't he get on with it? Yet Holden's face is deadpan. I open my mouth, force the air in and out, and wait for the harangue sure to come.

Wait to hear my name linked aloud with Lila's.

"I see you and Bob Koenig were talking in the lobby."

"Yes." My stomach lurches again as I think of Father Joe. The survival rate for pancreatic cancer isn't great. In fact, it's damn poor.

"Did Bob tell you what he's got in the works?"

I frown slightly. Why is Holden stalling? "He mentioned something about money, if that's what you mean."

"Automatic deductions for Sunday collections and our annual diocesan tax." Holden gulps down more scotch. The crystal tumbler is already nearly half empty. "It's a simple method. Brilliant, and so simple, I'm surprised someone didn't think of it years ago. We use bulletin inserts to obtain people's credit and debit card numbers and then we provide the information to the bank. The money flows in on a regular basis, even if parishioners are sick or on vacation. We'll even be able to tap into our snowbirds who head for Florida every winter."

"Are you joking?" Isn't it enough that the church duns parishioners every weekend at Mass?

His eyebrows rise slightly. "I never joke about money, Greg. And the idea isn't new. More and more parishes are using it, with great success."

"Bully for them," I mutter. Exactly what the Catholic Church has allowed itself to become. A big bully.

Holden settles back in his chair. Ice cubes rattle in his empty glass. "Am I to assume that you don't agree?"

"Let's just say I question the method, especially given today's economy. Don't get me wrong. Everyone has bills to pay, including the church. But times are rough. People in my parish are hurting. Why strong-arm them into signing up for automatic deductions they can't afford? Maybe what the church should be doing instead is cutting back on expenses."

Starting with the diocese. It's harder to push aside the envy and resentment over how much they've got with every visit I make. State-of-the-art computer equipment, designer furniture, departments operating with full-time staff. The diocese is plenty good at spending other people's money. Some of my parishioners have lost their jobs and can barely afford groceries. How can I ask them to whip out their credit cards and make further sacrifice?

Who exactly are we trying to help? The church? Or its people?

I thought the church *was* its people.

"We can't operate without funds," Holden reminds me. "We've got bills to pay."

"Jesus didn't have funds," I argue. "He wandered through the desert and preached the Good News. Two thousand years later, His word still lives on. And not because somebody ran a credit card through a machine, posted a sermon on the internet, or ran a TV ad."

I feel my face growing hot. "Word of mouth has kept Him alive. Word of mouth brings people into the pews and keeps them there. It's in the way we live our lives. It's believing in something greater than ourselves. It's who we are, what we aspire to, what we…"

Holden applauds loudly. "Very good, Greg. Your points are well taken." He eyes me across the desk. "Perhaps I could interest you in taking over as Director of Finance?"

I chuckle. "No, thank you."

"Then perhaps you would be interested in the position of Director of Vocations?"

The question buries me like an avalanche of heavy snow. "What?"

"Father Joe won't be able to function much longer. I need someone to replace him. I've been thinking about assigning you to take over his position here at the diocese."

"Me?" I barely manage to croak out the word.

"Don't look so surprised. I've given this a lot of thought, Greg. I believe you're the best man for the job."

Me, Director of Vocations, working at the diocese alongside Holden and his cronies? Me, in charge of seminarians? Me, responsible for recruiting young men to serve a life of obedience and celibacy?

"I don't know," I mumble. "I'm not sure I have what it takes."

"Father Joe is still able to function. He'll work with you and answer any questions you may have."

"But I have nothing to offer." Nothing except my frustrations and insecurities... and the growing fear that perhaps I made the wrong choice thirty years ago.

I doubt that's the type of thing Holden wants me sharing with future seminarians.

"Don't let the title scare you. It's like anything else, Greg; you bring what you have to the table. These are young men interested in the priesthood. Surely you remember that time in your life. They're searching for answers. Basically, they need to be able to talk with someone they trust, someone they can look up to. A priest who is empathetic, who understands their concerns and can guide them through the discernment process. You would lead group discussion, put on workshops, sponsor weekend retreats. And naturally, you'd keep in touch with our current seminarians. But that shouldn't be too difficult. There are only five."

I shake my head. "I… I can't give you an answer today."

"We haven't got much time."

"I have to think it over." But it won't require much thinking. Just enough time to figure out a way how to tell Holden *no*. I can't accept the job. I'd be nothing but a fraud.

"Father Joe is dying," Holden states bluntly. "The doctors give him six months at most. I need someone to fill that spot now."

"I don't know," I murmur. "I just don't know."

"But God knows," he says. "I've prayed about this, Greg. And everything tells me you're the man for the job."

Director of Vocations. *Vocare*, a summons, a calling from God. Can I do it? Do I want to do it? Even more important, is it what God wants of me? How can I help young men searching for answers when my own spiritual life is in shambles? Priests commit themselves to a life of service. They give themselves to God by serving the church, serving the poor, serving His people. But it's damn hard work, and it takes a toll.

It's taken a toll on me.

"I don't know." I hang my head, close my eyes. What's wrong with me? Why am I so weak? Why can't I summon up the courage and admit the truth? Holden picked the wrong man.

"I don't know," I repeat.

Ice cubes rattle in his empty glass. "Let me tell you a story," he finally says. "Maybe if you hear about my journey to the priesthood, it will help you decide."

I stare at him through bleary eyes. Holden wants to help? It's got to be the scotch talking.

"I was in the seminary during the sixties. It was a tumultuous time in our country's history. There was so much turmoil and unrest. The civil rights movement, Kennedy's assassination, and the Vietnam War. People were angry and demanding change, including from the church. Then along came Vatican II and Pope John XXII with his remarks about opening the windows of the church and letting in fresh air. It brought about radical changes. Some were good. Others, not so good."

Holden slowly rubs his chin. "Sometimes I wonder if lifting the restrictions was a good idea. It produced so much infighting within the church. In a strange way, it seemed to mirror what was happening in our country. Suddenly, priests I'd looked up to for years walked away from the church. Some of my friends left the seminary, enough of them that I began to wonder if I'd made the wrong choice, too. And that maybe I should walk away while I still had the chance."

I stare at him in disbelief. Holden harbored his own doubts about being a priest once upon a time?

He eyes me with a smile. "You remind me of our Vocations Director when I was at seminary. He was a good man, and I had a lot of respect for him. He knew I was thinking about leaving the seminary. He spent a lot of time listening to my concerns, addressing my confusion. He told me to trust my vocation, to listen to the things God had put in my heart.

"But I was a stubborn kid, and his words couldn't stop me. I left the seminary before Thanksgiving. I told him I was going home to think things through. He warned me not to think too long. New Year's came and went, but I was still thinking, trying to decide if I should stay home or return to seminary. And then, the letter arrived."

I stumble, lost in the story. "A letter?"

"From the United States Government." Holden's smile is pensive. "It started out *Greetings*. I'd been drafted for the Vietnam War. I contacted the seminary and begged them to help, but there was nothing they could do. I'd left the seminary of my own accord, and my deferment had been lifted. They couldn't protect me from the draft."

He shakes his head. "The letter instructed me to report immediately to an induction center. I had no choice but to go. I spent the next two years of my life in the Army."

The story he's telling seems incomprehensible, given the man I see before me, comfortably ensconced in his leather chair. Bishop Holden, a man of impeccable taste, tasseled loafers, and crystal scotch glasses, crawling on his belly through steamy jungle terrain? Carrying a rifle? Pulling a trigger? Killing other men?

"It must have been hell."

"My own personal hell," he agrees, "though I never left the States. I had a college degree, plus I'd spent two years in seminary. They weren't about to put me in the Vietnam swamps. Instead, they stuck me behind a desk at Fort Polk, Louisiana, where I spent my days typing up reports and my nights sleeping in the barracks with twenty other guys. Talk about an education."

Holden laughs suddenly. "Don't get me wrong. Most of them were fine fellows. But it didn't take two years, or even two months, to figure out I wasn't meant to live like other men. Two weeks was plenty enough. Two weeks of constant talk about cars, beer, and women was all it took to convince me I was cut from a different cloth. When my tour of duty ended, I turned in my army uniform for something much better."

Smiling, he fingers the tabbed white collar around his neck. "I was ordained the following year. Two years of my life gone, but no regrets. I came out of that experience with a stronger vocation than I had going in. God gave me a gift, and I got the message, loud and clear. I was meant to serve as a priest. Who am I to question it?"

Holden's words rock my heart and spirit. There must be a reason he's shared this with me. I want to trust him. I want to believe.

God, help me find my way out of my own personal hell.

"What do you say, Greg? Will you take the job? Will you agree to be our new Vocations Director?"

I struggle to hold back sudden, hot tears that I never expected. "I don't know if I can do it. I have to be honest with you. Lately, I'm finding things... difficult. I'm struggling."

"We all struggle," he says softly. "If we didn't struggle, we wouldn't be human."

His words echo words I heard recently from someone else. Someone whose presence carries a scent of lavender and violets, mingled with a touch of rose. Softness, sweetness, serenity. God help me, somehow I have to let her go. I have got to get her out of my mind. I have got to forget the way I felt, the feeling that possessed me when I held her in my arms.

A feeling like no other.

Like I'd finally come home.

"What about my parishioners?" I mumble. "I've got responsibilities to them. How can I be a good priest to them and serve the seminarians, too?"

"You'll find a way. I have faith in you. I know we've had our differences in the past, but that doesn't mean I don't respect you. I like you, Greg. And I've always been able to count on you to get the job done.

"That's why this position is so important. We need to increase vocations. We need young men willing to serve our church. You know the statistics. Remember those three men we ordained last year? Two were widowers, one never married; but all of them were in their sixties. What kind of a career lifespan will they bring to the church? We need to revitalize our church and our youth. Somehow we need to bridge the gap. We've got to make ourselves available to the young men out there who are searching their hearts and trying to determine what God wants of them."

I try to shake off the scent of lilac still haunting me. "Maybe the church would attract more interest if it changed a few laws. Celibacy, for one. And the ordination of women."

His eyebrows lift slightly. "You may be right."

The ease with which Holden capitulates stuns me.

"But let's be reasonable, Greg. We both know neither of those things will be happening anytime soon. The church's laws exist for a reason."

"What if the reason is no longer valid? What if it no longer serves its purpose?"

Holden stares at me a long moment. "Is that what this is about?" he finally says. "You think you're going to be the one to change things?"

"I didn't say that."

"The Catholic Church has been around for over two thousand years. I don't think one man's opinion is going to make much difference."

"One man *can* make a difference," I say. "One man *did* make a difference." My gut tightens and I swallow down the quick surge of anger. "We both work for Him."

189

We stare at each other, and I realize that, for today, there will be no answers.

Or tomorrow, either.

"Take the position, Greg," he urges softly. "God has blessed you with a great gift, of attraction and ministry. You'd be doing a great service to the church."

To be of service. Isn't that what I vowed when I was ordained? What God asks of me? What I am reminded every week as we study the Big Book during our AA meetings?

How can I be of service to others?

I bow my head, remembering the next part.

Thy will be done.

But what is His will for me?

"Put your trust in God," Holden says. "He knows the secret longings and desires of our hearts. He is the one who put them there. And when we search for God, when we look to be of service to Him, that is when everything falls into place. Trust Him, Greg. He knows what is best."

"But how do I know?" I wipe away the tears streaming down my cheeks. "How do I know the right thing to do?"

"It's called faith," he says softly. "When we have faith, it doesn't matter what we want, for we already know He's given us exactly what we need. Faith leads us to trust, and allows us to believe that what we cannot see is truly there. Faith brings us to our knees. It leads us to prayer."

The same prayer has been in my heart for days, for weeks.

Please, dear God, take away this doubt, this fear. Never mind what I want. Give me what You know I need.

"We need you, Greg. I wouldn't have asked if I didn't think you were the right man for the job. The way I see it, it's best for everyone."

His voice drops, and his eyes lock in on mine. "And given everything that's happened, I think it would be the best thing for you."

He knows. Jim told him. My heart rockets against my chest. I search Holden's face, waiting for him to finally accuse me of breaking my vows.

Holden doesn't flinch.

Why doesn't he say it? Why doesn't he ream me out, give me what's coming? Why this awkward silence, why this pretending that nothing has happened?

Then suddenly Holden stands. I unfold myself from my chair and follow his lead. I eye him carefully as he strolls around the desk, moves toward me, grabs my arm. I shudder at the physical contact, bracing myself for what's sure to come.

But instead, he claps me on the back, then drapes a casual arm over my shoulder as he walks me to the door.

"God has given you a great gift, Greg," he says. "Help us find good men who have heard that calling in their hearts. Help us find good men who want to serve others. Help us bring them into the church."

Holden embraces me in a gentle hug, like a father would a wayward son. "Help me, Greg," he whispers in my ear. "Help God. Help yourself."

CHAPTER THIRTEEN

The season of Lent starts with Ash Wednesday, which is early this year. The outside temps continue to hover below freezing, and the piles of snow banked in the church parking lot tower above my head. The irony of Jesus wandering through a hot, dry desert for forty days isn't lost on me. But despite my pair of winter boots, I sink deeper with every step I take as I slog through my personal desert.

I lift the sacred book above my head and face the congregation. The church is less than half-filled on this midday Ash Wednesday service. I reach the pulpit, and my fingers tremble as I flip to today's reading, bow my head, and whisper the familiar prayer.

Almighty God, cleanse my heart and my lips that I may worthily proclaim your gospel.

But how can I be worthy? How can I stand here before them and proclaim God's words when I have sinned? How can I help them when I can't help myself?

I lift my hands and bring the people to a stand. "The Lord be with you."

"And also with you."

The returning chant is oddly comforting. I stare at the page, find the words, trace my finger across them. My hand still trembles.

When you give alms, do not let your left hand know what your right is doing, so that your almsgiving may be secret.

Dear Lord, you, more than anyone, know how little I have to give. Only my heart, dear Lord. Only my heart.

When you pray, go to your inner room, close the door, and pray to your Father in secret.

Yet, if this be your will for me, let me give what I can. Help me not to complain, so as to not deter others from finding their way to You.

When you fast, anoint your head and wash your face so that you may not appear to be fasting.

Help me to be of service to You. Send me where I am most needed.

And your Father, who sees what is hidden, will repay you.

"The season of Lent is a season of penance," I say. "Today's Gospel reading reminds us of that. We hear it every year. Lent is a time of self-denial, almsgiving, and works of personal charity. But let's be honest, shall we? I doubt there's anyone among us who enjoys making sacrifices. Personally, I love my candy bars, and I hate to think of life without them."

Polite laughter washes through the pews and I ease my grip on the podium. Maybe I can do this after all. I catch sight of some ushers at the back of church huddled in a group. It's one big social club for them every weekend as they chat together, ignoring me, ignoring the message. Mass ends and they hurry home, back to their ordinary lives.

Am I making a difference in their lives?

"I think the season of Lent has gotten a bad rap," I

continue. "Yes, it's a time of penitence. Yes, the church urges us to attend daily Mass if possible and to pray the Rosary. Now, don't get me wrong. Those things are well and good. But Lent is about more than saying a few Hail Mary's. It is a call into action. It reminds us there is plenty of work needing to be done. And therein, my friends, lies the crux of the matter. Someone needs to do the work. And if it's not you, if it's not me, then who are we going to get to do it?"

The church grows quiet, and the tremor in my hand kicks in again. Maybe I shouldn't have come on so strong. I don't want to lose them. The church has already lost enough people as it is. I fumble for my handkerchief and wipe the sweat from my upper lip. But what am I supposed to tell them?

There is no easier, softer way.

"The ashes we receive today remind us that we are mortal, that all of us will return to dust. We haven't got much time, folks. I suggest we all start thinking about that, rather than ourselves. Lent is a good time to break that cycle of selfishness.

"The Gospel today urges us to give alms, to fast, and to pray. As Catholics, we're good at praying together, especially in church. But what about at home?" I challenge. "Do you spend time in private prayer? Remember, it doesn't have to be on your knees. There are no rules when it comes to talking with God. You can pray while sitting in a chair, doing the dishes, taking a walk. God doesn't care. He listens to all prayers whispered from your heart."

One of the ushers turns his back on me and gestures wildly, causing the others to laugh.

Are they listening? Is anyone listening?

"Prayers knock down walls," I say louder. "No matter

what kind of wall you might be facing: a physical disability, a wall of doubt, of guilt, shame, or fear. Prayers are like pinpricks that poke holes in a wall. Enough pinpricks, and the walls come crashing down."

A man in the front pew glances at his watch. People cough. A baby starts to wail. My homily is a mess, and I'm losing them. One of the three altar servers slouches in his chair. His clunky athletic shoe beats a rhythmic tap-tap-tap on the wooden floor. He yawns, scratches his nose, and suddenly I start to drift, remembering when I was a kid, just like him.

Do parents steer their sons toward the priesthood anymore?

An usher whispers something to the others, probably another joke and they all break out in laughter loud enough to make several people turn and stare.

There's no use pretending anymore. No one is listening.

Four minutes. My heart sinks as I glance at my watch. How could four minutes spent listening to me change anyone's life?

I wind up my homily and start the distribution of ashes. I smudge my thumb against another forehead with ashes in the shape of a cross. *"Remember, man, that you are dust, and unto dust you shall return."*

Are they listening to me now?

An elderly parishioner waylays me after Mass. "Father, I'm confused."

Rita Moore, in her late eighties, is confused most of the time. She clutches my arm with a feeble hand. I see the panic in her faded blue eyes.

"I don't understand. Did you say we should—or shouldn't—say the rosary during Lent? When I was a girl, they told us we were supposed to say the rosary during

Lent. What did you mean? Did they make a new rule?" Her voice is nearly a whimper. "Am I supposed to say my Rosary or not? I don't want to do anything wrong."

I give Rita a gentle hug and tell her to keep her rosary close.

Dear God, even if they do listen, do they understand?

Head bowed, I walk back to the rectory. Marie, fully recovered and back at her housekeeping chores, serves me lunch.

"Would you like more macaroni and cheese, Father?" She hovers at my side.

"Thanks, but I'll pass." I push away from the table, head into the kitchen, and rinse my plate. Gina has me well trained.

"But you only ate a few bites." Marie's face dissolves into a worried frown. "Didn't you like it?"

"It was delicious," I assure her, patting my stomach, hoping it doesn't growl. I'm still hungry. But the church mandates fasting and abstinence on Ash Wednesday with one full meal and two smaller ones. "I'm trying to cut back. The older I get, the harder it is to lose weight."

"And here I thought it was my cooking." Relief washes across her face. "I should have known better. My husband Phil loves my macaroni and cheese. Still, Father, there's no need for you to be watching your weight, not with all that exercise you do. You need to keep up your strength. You need to eat."

What I don't need is to end up with a paunch like Phil. I'm glad Marie made a full recovery and is back at work, but I miss Gina. She was the bright spot in my week every Monday, and my frequent jogs with Joe remind me how much I miss his wife. Gina talked nonstop and her diatribes could be distracting. Sometimes the dishes didn't get done and the dusting went unfinished. But it didn't matter. Gina was, and still is, a delight in my life.

Like a gift from God.

Like the daughter I never had.

I head for my office, prop my feet on the desk, and pick up the phone.

"We haven't talked lately. Thought I'd check up on you and see how you're feeling."

"Tired of being pregnant," Gina says with a breathless laugh that whooshes through me like a rush of springtime. "But I'm not complaining. From everything I've seen and read, it's been an easy pregnancy."

Easy, save for her father's stubbornness that has ripped the pages of her family life to shreds.

"If you're calling for Joe, I'm afraid you've missed him. He's at work. And while I'd love to chat, Father, I'm headed out, too. I've got a psychology class at two o'clock."

"Then I'll let you go. I just wanted to see how you were feeling."

Hearing her voice is enough. I can make it through the day.

"While I've got you on the phone, Father, I've been meaning to invite you over for dinner. Do you like meatloaf?"

"Love it." Monday nights meant meatloaf when I was growing up. Our house smelled of onions, garlic, and roasted meat when I came home from school.

"It's Joe's favorite new dish," she says, laughing. "I guess they never heard of meatloaf in Belgium."

The thought of Gina bustling around her kitchen, apron barely covering her growing tummy, puts the smile back on my face. She's not much of a cook, but she loves Joe. She wants to make him happy.

"How does Sunday night sound?" she suggests.

"Great," I say, though the word is like mush in my mouth. Four months ago, I had a standing invitation for Lila's Sunday night get-togethers.

A lot can happen in four months.

I haven't seen Lila since she walked out on me.

"Anyone else coming?" I try to keep the hope from leaping in my voice.

"Just the three of us." Gina laughs. "Although maybe I should say *the four of us*. The way I've been eating lately, we should probably count the baby, too."

I grit my teeth. I've got no business asking. Gina might not even know. I should say good-bye, hang up, and let it go.

But I can't help myself.

"Have you talked to Lila lately?"

"No." She pauses. "Why? Is something wrong?"

"Just that I haven't seen her around for the past several weeks." I bluff my way through the conversation. "She's one of our sacristans, you know, and I was just wondering."

Wondering and worrying.

"She's usually so responsible," I say. "It just seems odd that she hasn't been around."

Odd to others, maybe, though not to me. Lila is making good on her threat.

"Maybe she's sick," I add. "Or maybe it's something else."

My mind has no problem conjuring up plenty of something else or someone else. I haven't seen much of Jim, either.

"Sorry, Father, but I don't know." Gina sounds rushed. "I hate to cut you off, but I'm going to be late for class."

We hang up and I sit there some minutes, mulling things

over. Lila hasn't been in church. She hasn't been at our Thursday-night meetings. I've made it a point not to ask about her around the AA table. Where she goes and what she does is none of my business. It never was. It never can be.

Not if I want to keep my sanity.

Not if I want to keep my sobriety.

Not if I intend to honor my vocation.

Bishop Holden gave me a one-week grace period to think about the Diocesan appointment, but it's clear what he expects my decision to be. Meanwhile, what about those five seminarians currently studying for their own vocations? I haven't made a single phone call. How would I feel if I were one of them? Would I be wondering why no one had bothered to call?

Would I think the new director is too busy?

That he'd forgotten?

Or that he simply didn't care?

But I do care. So much that I'm afraid to pick up the phone. Who am I to be offering advice to young men questioning their vocation?

What if I can't help them? What if I steer them wrong?

Why did I become a priest, anyway? Did I make the commitment too fast? Was I too young? Did I give myself enough time to think it through? My life is no longer my own. I gave it to God nearly thirty years ago because I believed I could make a difference in people's lives. Just like Uncle Jerry.

I close my eyes, remembering my mother's younger brother who came to live with us after my grandmother died. Uncle Jerry was a holy terror and put my mother through hell. He ran with a wild crowd and had a couple minor skirmishes with the law. Not his fault, he would complain when she hauled him to task. It was never Jerry's fault.

Until one night his senior year of high school when a cute girl, a fast car, and his own ego crashed in a wild burst of speed.

God wasn't responsible for putting Uncle Jerry behind bars in the county jail. A jury did that. But serving time for vehicular manslaughter was the best thing that could have happened to him. It offered Uncle Jerry a chance to turn his life around. Eighteen months later, he'd cleaned up his act, earned his GED, and planned to spend his life counseling troubled teens. But being diagnosed with leukemia shortly before his release from jail changed those plans and he died six months later.

I never forgot the lesson Uncle Jerry taught me. His resolve to turn his life around and make a difference in people's lives convinced me I was meant to be a priest.

I clasp my hands together, prop them under my chin, and mull things through. Maybe Holden was right. Maybe I am the man for the job. I can offer my experience, strength, and hope. If these five young men studying for the priesthood truly have vocations, God will see them through.

The seminarian list is buried somewhere on my desk. I paw through stacks of papers littered with sticky notes from Cynthia, toss aside the latest financial reports, sift through back issues of the *James Bay Journal* I haven't gotten around to reading. Yesterday's front page snags my attention. There, beneath a bold headline announcing the beginning of Lent, I spot a familiar grainy black and white image.

I study the two-year-old photo of myself in chasuble and stole praying at the altar. Back then, I was the new priest at Our Lady's. My hair was darker, but the circles under my eyes have deepened. I skim the article covering standard Lenten practices and follow up with its conclusion inside on page five. The editorial page is on the left, and I scan the headline. Typical *Journal* outrage, but the byline, featuring Kris Henderson's name, comes as a surprise. Kris is the managing editor of the *Journal*, but Lucy Carter is the owner and publisher and the one normally responsible for the daily rant.

I grab a thick stack of *Journals* littering the floor and thumb through some of them. Every editorial in the past ten days carries a byline from Kris.

What happened to Lucy?

I snatch up the phone and put in a call to the one person guaranteed to know the answer to that question. Maybe to all my questions.

"Hi, Father." Papers rustle in the background, followed by a loud thud. "What the hell?" Another clunk, then more swearing. "Sorry, Father; pretend you didn't hear that."

"Everything okay, Max?"

"Life in general? Yep, I suppose. But here at camp, it's chaos." He sighs. "I'm trying to get things organized for next season, and it's been a bear. Hopefully once I get our new staff in place, things will settle down and I can relax."

Max sounds distracted, but it doesn't appear anything is wrong. Lucy isn't sick.

Obviously no one else is, either.

"What can I do for you, Father?"

Fill me in on the details. Tell me how she is. Tell me that she's happy, that she's alive and doing well.

Without me.

Perhaps if I hear that, my heart will finally be at peace. Maybe then I can find a way to pick up the pieces and start living again.

"Remember the PreCana test you and Lucy took last month?" I grab some pages and scan them briefly. "I finally have the results of your paperwork back from the diocese. The three of us should talk."

Max chuckles. "What's up? You sound worried. Did they find out we're living together and decide to excommunicate us?"

"Nothing like that," I assure him and flip the papers upside down. There's no need for Max to know about the blistering note the diocese attached. I've been directed to counsel Max and Lucy on the evil of living together in sin and to instruct them that they are to live apart until their marriage.

"We need to set up an appointment. When could the three of us meet?"

"It will have to wait until Lucy gets back."

"She went somewhere?"

Empty air sits between us for a moment.

"Sorry, Father, I thought you knew," he finally says. "Lucy rented a villa in Saint Martin. She and Lila flew down there last week."

My forehead wrinkles. "Saint Martin?"

"In the Caribbean."

My heart drops. No wonder I haven't seen her in church or at meetings. Not only did Lila make good on her promise to walk out of my life, she flew out of my life. Now she's thousands of miles away.

"Well, good for them." I try to keep my voice light and easy. "How long will they be gone?"

"Two months. I don't remember the date offhand. I think Lucy said they'll be back before Easter. I'm flying down there once I get things squared away here at camp. I'm looking forward to it. Lucy hasn't been gone that long, but I miss her." Max chuckles. "Guess that's why they call it love."

Sandy beaches, blue skies, warm trade winds kissing the breeze. Once upon a time, I thought about running away to the Caribbean. Now Lila has done the same thing.

Correction. She didn't run away. She walked away. She flew away.

From me.

"Look, Father, I don't know what happened between you and Lila. She's never said, and Lucy and I didn't what to ask. God knows it's none of our business. But Lucy is only looking out for her mother's interests. She loves Lila. She wants what's best for her."

"We all do, Max." Is this my punishment? It feels like my soul has been yanked from my body and tossed to the wind. It hurts like hell, knowing Lila didn't bother to tell me she was leaving.

But maybe she couldn't.

Maybe because she was hurting, too?

Why do we end up hurting those we love most?

Those we love most. The words smart. At least Lila had the guts to admit she loved me. And what did I say? What did I do?

Nothing.

"Lucy calls every night." Max hesitates. "I could ask Lucy to give her mom a message, if you want me to do that."

A message for Lila. Max's offer widens the sick yawning in my stomach. What would I tell her? What would I say?

That I've been offered a position as Director of Vocations?

That by accepting the job, I'd be assisting young men in

their journey toward the priesthood?

That I've never felt so broken, empty, or so lonely in my life since the night she walked away?

Come to me, all you who are weary... and your souls will find rest.

"I'm sure Lucy would be glad to pass along a message," he says.

My heart and spirit cry out in silent longing. If only I could take Max up on the offer. If only I could tell Lila how I feel. That I'm sorry for the way I hurt her. That I'm sorry for what I've done. That I'm sorry for allowing my selfish desires to lead her down the wrong path.

It was wrong. It was sinful.

It was my fault. *Mea culpa.*

I made a dreadful mistake, and I must never allow myself to make it again.

"Father Greg?"

"Thanks anyway, Max," I say quietly. "No message."

And I hang up.

CHAPTER FOURTEEN

Gina's eyes are tearstained and swollen. "Donny had an accident this morning. He's been learning to drive. Mama said the car jumped the curb and hit a tree. They took him to the hospital."

I slide the Kleenex box across my desk. "Is there any word on his condition?"

"Mama said he'll be okay. They're only keeping him in the hospital overnight for observation. But that still doesn't make me feel any better." She wipes away a few more tears. "I'm sorry, Father, I didn't mean to bother you. But Joe's out of town at a conference, and after Mama called, I had to talk to someone."

"I'm glad you chose me," I say, meaning every word. She looks like a waif, sitting there with a sodden Kleenex in her hand, wearing a bulky red coat that no longer buttons across her belly.

Gina sniffs. "I should have been there. I can't help thinking about what might have happened."

"Let's be grateful it didn't."

"But what if it had?" She wads the tissue up in a little ball and rolls it around in her hand. "When I saw it was Mama calling on the cell phone I gave her, I knew it had to be something horrible. She never uses that phone, except for our weekly calls. Then she told me that she was in the ladies' room in the ER, and she started crying. That's when I started crying, too, even before she told me about Donny. I hate myself for not being there with them. And I never can be. He makes it impossible."

"Was your father there?"

Gina grimaces. "Oh, he was there all right. Mama said he made a terrible scene. He swore at Donny for crashing the car and cursed the nurses for moving so slow."

Her father sounds like every bully I've met in my life.

"What if Donny had died?" She shudders and fresh tears shimmer in her eyes. "What would have happened then? Mama would have been all alone. I don't think I could live with myself, knowing I hadn't been there for—"

A sharp rap from outside interrupts us, and the door swings open.

"Greg, my man, got a minute?"

Gina and the balled-up tissue in her hand halts Ray in the doorway.

"My apologies," he says quickly, backing up. "Cynthia said you weren't busy."

"No, that's all right. I should be going anyway." Gina blots her eyes, grabs her purse, and struggles to rise from her chair. "I have a class starting soon."

"Give us a minute, will you, Ray?" We exchange quick glances, priest-to-priest. "It won't take long."

"Sure thing." He heads out the door and closes it quietly behind him.

I eye Gina carefully. Her face is still the same chalky white it was when she appeared in my office doorway ten minutes ago. While she might think she's ready to leave, I'm not certain I'm ready to let her go.

"Are you sure you'll be okay? I'm worried about you."

She sighs. "I'll be fine. Sometimes my mind runs away with me, especially when I think about Mama and Donny. I know we all make our choices, and Mama made hers a long time ago. But honestly, Father Greg, I think she must be crazy, staying married to a man like him."

Her shoulders sag. "I get so scared for her and Donny. It feels like I've abandoned them. Sometimes I think maybe I should go back. Maybe if I did, I could make her see things differently, that life doesn't have to be this way. Maybe I could help them… "

"Do you really think that would make any difference?" I ask quietly.

"I don't know." Her eyes take on a faraway look. "How do any of us know what's the right thing to do? Everyone has their place in life. Maybe mine was meant to be with Mama and Donny." She shakes her head slowly. "I never should have left. I should have stayed and helped them fight.

She breaks off and sits in silence for a moment. "Sometimes at night when Joe is sleeping and the house is quiet, I lie in bed and think about the way things used to be. Before I left home. Before I left Mama and Donny to fend for themselves. And I play *what if*. What if my father was a different kind of man? What if Mama had never married him? What if I had never married Joe? What if I made the wrong choice, like Mama did?"

"*What if* is a dangerous game," I caution. "You don't want to go there. It's not good for you or Joe, or the baby—"

"I know." Her voice is barely above a whisper. "I try not to think like that. And most of the time, things are fine. It's only on those nights when I can't sleep and I'm lying in the dark, listening to Joe breathe, that I get to wishing things were different. I wish I hadn't been forced to choose between the people I love."

God or the girl.

"I love Joe so much, and being married to him is like a dream come true. But honestly, Father, sometimes I think I'm in the wrong place. Sometimes it feels like I've been plopped down in the wrong kind of soil, just like those Belgian tulip bulbs his sister Annelies sent us last fall. We planted them in our front yard, and Joe said come this spring, they'll bloom for sure. He's got faith, but I'm not so sure. What if he's wrong? What if they don't take root? What if the soil isn't right for them? What if being with Joe isn't right for me?"

"I know things seem rough now, but it will pass." My voice is ragged, even to my own ears. "Try to focus on the positive. Think how much Joe loves you. Think about the baby."

She smiles suddenly. "That's exactly what Joe says. He tells me I need to be easier on myself, that I ramble like a pregnant woman. I don't know, maybe he's right. Sometimes my mind gets going so fast, it feels like I'm having a mental derailment." She gives a short laugh. "Crazy, isn't it?"

"Crazy," I agree, relieved to see her finally laughing again.

Gina blots away the last of her tears and labors to a stand. "Thank you, Father. I don't mean to be such a bother, always running to you about something. But you have no idea how good it is to know you're here. I know I can count on you."

"Don't ever be afraid to give me a call. I'm here when you need me," I assure her. "And for today, no more worries, understand?" I grasp her by the shoulders and look deep in her eyes, try to see past the shadows of panic. "Things will be fine."

I say it as much for myself as for her. If only I could be certain. If only I could make all her problems—and my own—go away.

Ray strolls in a few minutes later and flops in the chair still warm from Gina. "How's the little lady?"

"She'll be okay," I say, hoping to God it's true.

"Isn't she the one married to the black guy?"

For some reason Ray's comment irks the hell out of me. "His name is Joe."

His eyebrows rise. "They have a fight?"

"Her brother was in a car accident this morning." It's a struggle to keep my voice even.

He frowns. "Sorry to hear that."

"It's a difficult situation. Her mother and brother live downstate with the dad, but Gina and her father are estranged."

Ray shakes his head. "What is it with families? You grow up thinking they'll surely stand by you, no matter what, only to find out that they're the ones who always let you down." He scratches his head. "Go figure. My two brothers don't even talk to me."

"I can relate. My mother barely takes my calls." I regret the words even as I say them. Ray knows the situation with my mother and Lila, but I've no wish to revisit that nightmare.

"What brings you over here today?" I eye him across my desk. "Everything okay?"

He shrugs. "Just the usual crap. I got antsy and felt like taking a drive."

I glance out the window, where sunshine and blue skies greet me. Except for the snow banks, it could be June. I don't blame Ray for sneaking away on a gorgeous day like this. We all need a break, and he's got more pressure than me, running a parish school.

"How about buying me dinner?" he asks.

I feel my face relax in an easy grin. "You're the one with family money, remember? I'm just a poor priest."

The massive gold ring on his left hand gleams as he pulls at his collar. "Okay, fine, I'll spring for dinner."

It's not often Ray concedes so easily. Too bad I can't take him up on the offer.

"Sorry, but tonight's out. I've got the Annual Rosary Altar Society awards dinner."

"And you're going?" He chuckles, but I catch the glimpse of disappointment wash across his face. "What sin did you commit to deserve that kind of penance?"

"A command performance, I'm afraid."

"Better watch yourself, Greg," he warns. "Those RAS ladies will have you signed up as a card-carrying member before you know it."

"They're not so bad. Besides, they only invite me so I'll bless the food."

"And what's got you so interested in having dinner with them? Wait a minute, let me guess." He cocks a smile. "You're got your eye on their checkbook. Am I right?"

I give an easy laugh and ease back in my chair. Being with Ray always puts me in a good mood.

"Come on, spill it. You figure they had a bang-up year selling pies and you're going to hit them up for a check, right? What are you planning to buy this time?"

"Why do you assume everything always has to about money?"

He grins. "Because it is?"

Truth be told, I don't mind spending time with the RAS. Those elderly ladies with white hair and rosary beads are living relics of the church's glory days. And besides my mother and Ray, those ladies are the closest thing I have to family.

"Everybody's got an angle, Greg. You, me, and the RAS ladies. Even Bishop Holden." He eyes me thoughtfully. "And speaking of Holden, why didn't you tell me that you'd changed your mind?"

I frown. "About what?"

"From what I hear, you're fully on board with Holden and the Diocesan staff."

I stare at him. "What the hell are you talking about?"

"The automated giving program they're trying to implement. I thought you wanted nothing to do with it."

"That's right," I say bluntly. "I don't."

"Well, you might mention that to Cynthia." Ray jerks his head toward the door. "I was in her office just a few minutes ago and heard her on the phone with the diocese. It sounded like she setting things up."

My heart rate skyrockets. After everything Cynthia and I have discussed in the past about her going over my head, Cynthia has gone ahead without my direct authorization and proceeded to set up automated giving payments? My ears buzz, and I feel the anger harden on my face.

"Oooh, baby, you mean you didn't know?" Ray croons. "Let me tell you, *you've got trouble, my friend, right here in River City.*" He hums a few bars from the old song. "*Trouble with a capital T and that don't stand for pool.* When are you going to wise up and fire her?"

"Believe me, I'd like nothing better than to do just that." If I had the balls, I'd charge straight down the hall to her office and order Cynthia off the premises. Wouldn't she be surprised?

And then what? Cynthia has friends in high places. There'd be hell to pay and bigger trouble ahead if I don't keep in mind who—and what—she knows.

"Firing her isn't an option."

"Really?" Ray's eyebrows arch. "Let me ask you a question, Greg. Who's running this parish? Cynthia? Or you?"

Half an hour later, his question walks us down the hall and keeps me company as I wave him out the door, then head into the parish office. I mumble the Serenity Prayer and swallow over the sourness filling my stomach. I hate confrontation.

"I was only trying to get things organized so we wouldn't be caught last minute." Cynthia's voice rises in self-defense. "Denise at the diocese told me the automated giving program starts soon, and I thought…"

"You thought wrong," I state bluntly. "I'm the one who makes the decisions around here."

I fold my arms against my chest, try to keep a check on my temper as that old song Ray crooned keeps plinking through my head. *Trouble in River City* is right. Maybe she thinks she can get away with playing the innocent victim, but I'm not buying. Cynthia is many things, but innocent is not one of them.

"But Denise told me—"

"You don't take orders from the diocese or Denise. You take orders from me."

Two bright red spots flame on her cheeks. I can almost see the gears working in her brain as she stares at me from being her desk. Cynthia isn't used to being challenged.

"All the parishes are supposed to be online with the

company by Memorial Day," she finally says. "Denise said it's a diocesan mandate."

"And I just told you that I am the one who decides what we do. What part of that do you not understand?"

Her eyes narrow, and she stares at me a long moment. "I understand perfectly."

"Good." I force a deep breath, try to unclench my jaw. "I'm glad we got that straight."

"I'm sorry, Father." Her voice is tight.

And we both know she's not the least bit sorry. For one brief moment, I think about Ray's advice and contemplate the utter pleasure that firing her would give me. But who would finish the bulletin? I don't know how to do it. Hell, I don't even know the password to access the program.

Come to think of it, nobody knows how many passwords she's set up on the computer. There's financial data, the census database, not to mention all the spreadsheets. Cynthia has created her own little kingdom in the parish office.

And I was stupid enough to let her do it.

How could I have let her grab control? How could I have let things get away from me?

"I need to finish the bulletin." She turns her back on me, but I catch the smirk.

"After you finish the bulletin, I want you to draw up a list of all the passwords for our computer programs."

She whirls around in her chair. "What?"

"A list for the passwords."

She blinks. "Why?"

"Just in case."

"Just in case," she repeats slowly.

"That's right. Just in case." I match her stare with one of my own, daring her to ask me. I'll be happy to share the plenty of just-in-case scenarios I've got.

Cynthia sits back in her chair and contemplates me. The quiet tick of the wall clock counts off the seconds between us.

"It won't work," she says. "You can't get rid of me that easy."

"Excuse me?"

"Maybe you think you can con everybody else, but I'm not stupid. I've seen things."

"I don't know what you're talking about." I lick my lips and rack my brain. What has she seen? What has she heard?

"I've seen the way you look at her. I've watched you sneaking around for months. You thought no one knew, that no one noticed. But I did."

A triumphant smile lights her face. "I saw you kiss her in the parking lot."

My heart hits my stomach as I remember that frosty December morning when I came back from jogging and found Lila in the sacristy. That moment we kissed in the parking lot is etched in my heart like a snowflake pattern on delicate crystal.

"You're wrong," I choke out. "Nothing happened."

"I know what I saw." Cynthia shrugs. "And let's not forget Mrs. VanBrabant."

My gut twists. "What about her?"

"She puts on a nice act, playing the pregnancy card for all it's worth. You told me that she's not on staff, she doesn't work for the church. Yet, she works for you." Her mouth twists in a nasty smile. "Exactly what kind of work does she do, Father, while she's supposedly dusting up there in your bedroom?"

I open my mouth, but no words come.

"No wonder she runs to you, crying on your shoulder whenever something happens. My Leon works at the plant with that black man she's married to. Leon says no one likes him, that he's cocky and arrogant, a real uppity sort."

"My God, woman, you have no idea what you're talking about." I shake my head, dazed. "You've committed a terrible wrong against some fine people."

"Me? I'm not the one who's been sneaking around."

The evil before me makes my stomach heave. If the devil exists in human form, he has found a home in Cynthia.

"You have no right to make these kinds of accusations. You are wrong—"

"Am I?" Cynthia's eyes glitter. "Well, we'll see about that. Denise told me Bishop Holden is plenty interested in hearing your side of the story."

The truth burns like a hot slow poison invading my body. All this time, I never noticed we had a viper in the rectory office, coiled up, waiting to strike.

"You were the one who contacted the bishop," I guess. "You were the one who told him."

Poor Jim Gillespie. All this time I thought he was guilty, yet he wasn't to blame. I've done the man a terrible injustice, even if it was only in my thoughts.

"How could you have done this?" I ask. If it was simply about me, I would gladly take the heat. But Cynthia has dragged both Lila and Gina into this sordid mess. Things have been set in motion that could be irreversible. "If you thought there was a problem, you should have come to me. We could have talked."

"Talk about what?" she scoffs. "Why would I want to talk with you? Do you think I'm crazy?" She eyes me with a bold stare. "You have no right to tell me who I can or can't talk to. I am a parishioner, and I have every right to voice my opinion… and I also have a duty to tell the diocese if something is wrong. This is my parish, and I love it. I've lived here a lot longer than you, and I'll be here long after you've left."

"Get out." The words taste delicious coming out of my mouth.

"You can't fire me."

"I think I just did." The rush of adrenalin surging through me nearly lifts me off the floor. If I'd known firing Cynthia would feel this good, I would have done it months ago.

She stares at me for another moment, then grabs her purse and slams it on the desk. "Fine." She struggles into her coat. "I'll leave, if that's the way you want it. But you're going to regret this."

Regret firing Cynthia? I don't think so.

She marches toward the door, then suddenly whirls to face me.

"I'm glad you fired me. At least now I can sit home and collect unemployment instead of sitting behind that desk and watching you trash our parish." Her eyes narrow. "You're nothing but a pathetic little man. You make me sick. It's men like you that give the priesthood a bad name."

The door bangs behind her.

She's finally gone.

And so is my elation. I wander around the counter and stand near her desk. A lipstick-stained coffee cup sits beside the computer. The monitor still glows. I scan the program she left open, then groan. The weekly bulletin is due today. Who's going to finish it?

I sink onto the secretarial chair, and stare around the office. Who will I find to sit here now? Who's going to type the bulletin? Who's going to pay the bills? Who's going to manage all the tasks Cynthia did?

Then I remember her parting words, the accusations, the threats.

No bulletin on Sunday isn't the worst thing that can happen.

I slump forward and bury my head in my hands.

God help me, what have I done?

CHAPTER FIFTEEN

"Would you care to join me in an afternoon jog?"

"What's with the break in routine? It's a little late in the day, don't you think?" I glance at the clock. It's already past three, but Joe's phone invitation is a welcome diversion from the stack of paperwork piled on Cynthia's desk. I've been fighting my inner demons for the past twenty minutes, trying not to succumb to the impulse of heading to the rectory for a nap. "Didn't you run this morning?"

His deep laugh floods the line. "I came in early to finish a project. Now I need to stretch my legs and clear my thoughts. I could use the company."

And I could use a break from this desk. I've been inundated with phone calls for the past two days as people learn the news about Cynthia.

What's going on at Our Lady's? Why did you fire her? What did she do wrong?

But no one is asking the real question. What did *you* do wrong? Cynthia thinks she knows the answer. She's not right, but she knows too much, even if most of what she believes to be true is distorted.

I can't risk it. I don't know where to turn or who to ask. Even Ray, someone I've always been able to count on, is unavailable. I've tried phoning him repeatedly, but he isn't returning my calls. Has he heard about Cynthia? Has he heard the scuttlebutt from the diocesan pipeline? Does he think I'm a coward?

God help me if I've alienated Ray, too.

"Give me ten minutes to grab my gear," I tell Joe.

Half an hour later, we're on the open road. The skies are semi-overcast with clouds, but tomorrow's forecast is promising. I take care to keep my eyes on the street as we jog along in comfortable silence. A spring thaw two days ago started things melting, but a dusting of snow from earlier this morning still covers the road and some icy puddles.

"How's Gina?"

He flashes me a quick grin. "Very good. Getting bigger."

I grin right back. "That baby will be here before you know it."

"Hopefully not before she finishes her classes," he says. "She studies very hard. She is most concerned to keep up her schoolwork."

We keep jogging. "How are things going at the plant?" I ask after another few blocks.

"Very good. Very busy."

"I suppose your friends at work are excited about the baby, too."

He merely smiles.

We turn a corner and I think of Cynthia's rant about her husband Leon. How many others like him are out there? How can people be so bigoted and narrow-minded?

We take another corner. I try to keep up and match his pace. "Is everything okay, Joe? I mean, out at the plant? If you need to talk, I'm always available."

Joe fires me a fast smile without breaking his stride. "Perhaps you know something I do not?"

The tug of a smile starts across my own face. Am I that transparent?

"There are people there who would like to cause me trouble," he finally admits, "but there will always be people like that. I cannot allow them to hold me back."

His breath comes in long puffs. "Sometimes I do not understand the people here in James Bay. Many of them are unfriendly. Perhaps it is because it is a little town. But things are much different in my own country. We do not have your history of slavery. Still, my parents experienced difficulties themselves. My father was white, my mother was black. Hatred has no international borders. They were greatly inspired by the words of Ghandi. *Be the change you wish to see in the world*, they told my sisters and me. When things are difficult, I think of what they taught us, and I do my best to try and rise above it."

I keep running. Joe is a good man—so much a better man than any of us, including me.

"Gina worries about this," he continues. "I have never met her father, but perhaps it is best that, for now, he is not a part of her life." He floods a sigh. "Maybe, or maybe not. It is not my decision to make. Things will work out as they are meant to be. In the end, each of us must decide the right thing to do."

I ponder Joe's words as my feet pound against the hard, wet pavement. Is that the way I live my life? What is the change I wish to see in the world? Evil is an ancient concept, but it is still alive and flourishing today, even among the clergy. I think of the parishioner last Sunday who mentioned a friend had asked her parish priest for a travel blessing, but he responded that he didn't have time.

What kind of priest refuses to give a blessing? What happened to spreading the gifts of the spirit? Of espousing patience, tolerance, kindness, acceptance, and love to all?

How can we expect parishioners to follow if we do not set an example ourselves?

Do I have the courage and strength to tackle the prejudice and ignorance that surround me?

In my parish? From my fellow priests? With Ray? My own mother?

"You're a smart man, Joe," I say, huffing out short breaths. "You should have been a priest."

"No, Father, that is impossible. I love God with all my heart, but I could not be a priest."

"You would have made a good one," I say, puffing out a short laugh.

"No. Being a priest would mean living without Gina, and that I could not do. She is a gift from God. She sustains me. She is my breath, my life." He shrugs with a simple smile. "She helps me be a better man."

There is no need for me to answer. His words stand in firm testament to the beauty of a love between two people. And no matter what challenges face them in the years ahead, I know Joe can take care of himself, plus Gina, too. He is a quiet man of deep, gentle faith.

We reach the county road which is our usual halfway point and make a long, looping turn back toward town. I struggle to keep up the pace, but it's a losing effort. Joe, with his long legs, has his own rhythm, and I slow down, as I always do. The road in this section is lined with evergreens and filled with shadows and icy patches. I fall behind and soon I'm one, two, three, then five strides behind him.

And then from behind me, I hear the whine of a motor.

Turning, I spot a car in the dim dusk of late afternoon, coming low and fast in our direction.

Much too fast.

I watch in horror as the car hits an icy patch and spins out in our direction. I go numb, frozen where I stand in the road, watching as the car slams past. It misses me by mere inches. But Joe, some yards ahead of me, is a direct target.

"Joe!"

My scream comes too late.

Metal screeches, followed by a hard whomp and a high-pitched scream.

"No!" My stomach lurches and for one agonizing second, I shut my eyes against the horror of Joe's body pinned against the tree.

Dear God, not Joe.

Not Joe!

"It was the ice. I couldn't stop." The driver staggers to the front of the car, then collapses in a moaning heap. "Is he dead? Oh, God, I couldn't stop."

I reach Joe's side. The car, lurched away from the tree, has finally freed him. His body is on the ground. The sight of gray tree bark, dirty white snow, and bright red blood mingled together makes me want to vomit. Joe moans. I sink to my knees and grab his hand. He's alive. Thank God, he's alive.

"Hang on, Joe," I whisper. "Hang on."

A woman appears at my side. "I phoned nine one one." One look at Joe and her eyes go wild with horror. "Oh my God," she whispers.

"Get back," I order brusquely. "Go watch for the ambulance."

It's growing dark. The last thing we need is another casualty.

She staggers away and I turn my attention back to Joe. Blood streams from his mouth. It runs down his cheek and neck, staining his jacket, seeping into the snow. I crouch low beside him and shield his body with my own. It would be a sacrilege to allow anyone to see him like this.

He clenches my hand and tries to speak. "Sorry," he gasps. "Sorry for…"

I swipe away my tears and grasp his hand tighter. "You have nothing to be sorry for." I'm the one who should be sorry. I didn't warn him in time.

Blood bubbles from his lips and he continues struggling.

"Joe, listen to me. Don't talk. You need to save your strength."

He shakes his head and will not listen. He is determined to speak. I crouch lower, putting my ear near to his mouth.

"S… sorry for my sins," he whispers.

And then the truth hits me. Joe is making his last confession.

It is hideous, horrendous, and one of the holiest moments of my life. I would fall to the ground if I wasn't already on my knees.

"Bless me, Father, for I have sinned…" His words release in tiny gasps of spit mingled with blood.

"May God Almighty have mercy upon thee." My own tears anoint him as I trace the sign of the cross on his forehead.

The wail of an ambulance draws near. Dear God, how could this be happening? Less than ten minutes ago, Joe and I were chatting about nothing, and now he is on the ground, covered in blood, wounded beyond…

I swallow down the nasty taste of vomit surging up the back of my throat.

Within minutes we are surrounded by the emergency

crew tromping through the snow. They cluster around us, crowding the ground with medical equipment and a long tubular stretcher. I start to move back and let them do their work, but Joe struggles to keep my hand.

"Don't go," he begs.

The rational part of me whispers I should step aside. The emergency crew is working feverishly. I should let them do their jobs. But something in his voice urges me to stay. His eyes are lit with a fevered passion. I grip his fingers tighter, praying I am not a hindrance to the medical team. "You got it, Joe. I won't leave you."

"Promise," he says.

I squeeze tighter. "I'll be right here with you, all the way."

The minutes seem to crawl as they take his vitals and manage to get an IV flowing. Finally they lift Joe and strap him in the stretcher. Can't they work faster? I struggle to a stand, then gag as I finally glimpse the extent of his wounds. Though I have been at other accident scenes, nothing has prepared me for the sight of Joe's injuries. I want to run from the horror of what is sure to come.

But I can't. I made Joe a promise.

I stumble behind the ambulance crew as they haul the stretcher back to the road. An eerie pattern of red-white-blue zigzag lights flashes against the asphalt pavement. Cars line the shoulder and icy patches cover the ground. My feet slip out from under me and I nearly fall.

"Careful there, Father." One of the ambulance crew says as he catches me by the elbow.

"Thanks." I know the man, though not his name. I've seen him in church before at Sunday Mass. I grab his arm as two other techs load Joe's stretcher in the back. "Let me ride with him," I urge.

He shakes his head. "Sorry, Father, it's against regulations."

"Good God, what does it matter? Can't you see he's dying?" I choke out the words. "He's Catholic, just like you. Let me be with him in his last moments. Let me give him the last rites."

A nearby tech averts his gaze.

"Please?" I will beg, if that's what it takes.

"All right," he finally relents. "Go ahead."

I clamber into the back of the ambulance and crouch beside the gurney. Joe's hand is cold, but his eyes open briefly and he manages a small smile. "Father Greg. I thought you left me."

"Never." I clench his hand with so much force I'm afraid I might break his fingers. I ease up on my grip. "You can't get rid of me that easy."

"Tell Gina... *do not be afraid.*" He squeezes my hand, barely. "Tell her *I am with you always.*"

My heart clutches as I hear him repeat the familiar words taken from the Gospel.

"Promise you will tell her. Promise me," he whispers.

"I'm not promising anything." It cannot end like this. It cannot. I will not allow it.

Blood no longer gushes from his mouth. Joe's lips curl in a slight grimace as his hand slips through mine. His eyes have lost focus, but his words are steady and sure—just like his heart.

"Tell... tell Gina I love her."

"Damn it, Joe, tell her yourself." I push my face near his, growl the words. "Don't you dare give up. You're going to make it."

He answers with a faint smile. "You must tell her for me," he says. "Tell her *I am with you always.*"

The ambulance lights swirl in the snow. Damn driver, can't he go faster? Joe's face is a blur, for I can no longer see through my tears. But to swipe them away, I'd have to let go of his hand, something I refuse to do. I made Joe a promise. I am not letting go.

I sink against the cold metal wall of the ambulance. Dear God, this cannot be happening. He is so young. Why him? Why now? This is so unfair. Joe has so much left to do with his life, so much left to accomplish.

And what about Gina? Twenty-two years old and she will be a widow.

"Father, excuse me, but we need to take his vitals." The med tech gently pushes me out of the way.

The rocking cradles me as we rush along the icy streets. I am without holy water, sacred oils, and my breviary, but not without my faith. Never have I been more certain that God is with us now. I trace a cross upon Joe's forehead. "May God Almighty have mercy upon thee, forgive thee thy sins, and bring thee to everlasting life."

I whisper the words of the last rites of the church as the techs continue to work on Joe. "May the Lord Jesus protect you and lead you to eternal life."

Finally we reach the hospital. I slump back in the ambulance as Joe's hand slips from my own. I offer no resistance as the medics take him. I have done what I can. The rest is up to God.

But in my heart, I know it is finished.

Gina stalks the small private room off the ER like an animal caught in the wild who suddenly finds herself trapped in a cage. She shadows the walls, then turns back and repeats her track. It's a common reaction, one seen frequently when people are in shock.

"I should make a list of people to call," she says in a low voice. "Annelies and Annelore should be first." She stares at the cell phone in her hand, then back at me. Her eyes are huge black holes. "But it's the middle of the night in Belgium. How can I phone and... wake them with such news?"

"Wait until morning," I advise softly. "That's perfectly acceptable."

Gina pushes her hair away from her face, thinks for a moment, then tosses the cell phone on a nearby chair. "You're right. Let them sleep. It doesn't matter when I call them. It won't change what happened."

She resumes her pacing, and I resume my watch on her.

If only she would cry. I'm used to Gina's wild exuberance, but these past few hours in the hospital have left me unnerved, for there have been no tears.

No tears as she flew through the doors of the ER, eyes wild with terror.

No tears as the nurses sneaked sad glances in her direction.

No tears at the solemn timber of the doctor's voice as he gave her the news. *Internal injuries... beyond help... nothing we could do.*

No tears as she cradled Joe's hands in her own and I murmured a final prayer.

No tears as she faced the stark reality of the long, dark body laid out on the bed before us, shrouded in a crisp, white sheet.

If only she would cry. If only she would break down. But Gina has disappeared, slipped away to some faraway place where no one, no pain, can touch her.

A place where no one is invited, including me.

And she's refused any medical help for herself, rejecting the pills and sedatives they've offered, all because of the baby. But I am not nearly so brave. I want a drink. I need a drink. My hands tremble. I knot them together, fold them in my lap, surprised to find myself still in my jogging clothes. As soon as I get back to the rectory, I intend to strip and bury them in the trash. Better yet, I'll burn them. I never want to see these clothes again.

I will never jog again.

"Why are we still here?" She turns suddenly to face me. "I want to go home."

Once again, Gina has changed her mind. Her grief has left her inconsolable and inconsistent. Just minutes ago when I suggested leaving, she insisted on remaining with Joe's body until the funeral director arrived.

I stumble to a stand. "If you want to go home, then that's what we'll do. Whatever you like."

"No, wait. Maybe we should stay." She halts. Deep smudges darken the skin beneath her eyes. "What do you think?"

Me? I think it would be best if she spent the night.

"Would you like me to speak to the doctor again? Let's see what he says."

"She'll be fine," he'd told me privately an hour earlier. But what does he know? The doctor is new to the hospital, new to me. But he is the one in charge, and he has determined it will be safe for Gina to leave. "Just make sure to keep an eye on your daughter tonight."

"She's not my daughter," I'd told him, wishing fiercely that she was. At least then I'd be free to take her in my arms, hush away the hurt and horror, brush away the tears sure to come. "She's not my daughter," I repeated.

"No kidding." His eyebrows shot up. "And all along, I thought... well, I suppose it doesn't matter. Just make sure she has someone with her. Maybe it would be a good idea if you called your wife."

There was no use explaining things. The doctor is a new guy in town. He'll discover soon enough who I am and what I am.

But I'm willing to face him again, if that's what it takes for Gina to stay the night.

Morning and its new set of fresh horrors will dawn soon enough.

"Are you sure there's not someone you would like me to call?" I offer for the fourth or fifth time. If the doctor doesn't relent and I take Gina home, she'll need a woman with her. I can't spend the night, and she shouldn't be alone. "A friend, perhaps?"

"No."

I stare at her, wishing beyond all hope there was something I could do. "Maybe someone from school?"

"I don't need anyone. I'll be fine."

But it's obvious she is anything but. Her eyes are large dark pools, and a look of disbelief hangs on her face. She strokes her belly in soft, random movements, and I catch a glimpse of something shift beneath her clothing. The baby is moving. Has it instinctively sensed the distress of its mother?

Gina is not the only one grieving. This poor child lost its father tonight.

"You should eat something," I say. The cafeteria closed hours ago, but the nurses have offered sandwiches.

Wild curls swing in every direction. "I'm not hungry."

"You need to eat," I urge. "Remember the baby."

An odd look flits across her face. "Tomorrow night was

going to be our first prenatal class," she says softly. "But we won't be going now."

A dull ache settles in my heart. I'd like nothing more than to escape this horrible place. I want to go home, shed the clothes covered in Joe's blood, burn them. But I refuse to abandon her. I'm willing to do anything if it will help. But there's only one thing I can think to do. Something that helps in my own pain.

"Would you like it if we said more prayers?"

Gina hesitates.

I pat the couch beside me. "Come sit for a moment and rest."

Finally she eases herself down onto the cushions next to me. I have no rosary, no prayer book to steady the trembling of my hands or in my heart and soul. I reach for her hand, close my eyes, and begin the familiar prayers.

"I'm glad you were there with him, Father," she murmurs when I finally finish. "I'm glad Joe wasn't alone at the end."

Then her face contorts, and from somewhere deep inside her comes a sound like no other, like a mortally wounded animal. I squeeze her hand, giving her something to hold onto, and wait for her to cry.

But no tears come.

Gina stares into empty space. "What do I do now? How can I go on without him?"

Her question takes my breath away. She still is not crying, but I am. Perhaps this is the right time to tell her. "He talked of you at the end. And he asked me to give you a message."

Quietly I convey Joe's final words, that she be not afraid and his promise to be with her always.

"You're a strong woman, my dear," I say after a

moment. "God will see you through. And remember Joe's promise. He will be there, also."

She nods numbly, then pulls her hand from my own, labors to her feet, and resumes her pacing. I lean forward, close my eyes, rake my fingers through my hair. I've consoled countless widows and grieving husbands in my years as a priest, but I might as well be fresh out of the seminary for all the good it does me tonight. If I could, I would take all her pain and grief and bear it as my own. That would be easier than what I have been called to do this evening... to sit and do nothing. What Gina needs most is another woman beside her. I am nothing but a poor substitute.

Perhaps if I called, Marie would be willing to come. She has grown children and would know what to do.

If Lila was in town...

Lila loves Gina. If it wasn't for me, she would be in town. She would be here in a heartbeat. All of us are suffering tonight because of poor choices I made.

But no matter how much I wish things were different, I can't take it back. There's no use wishing for what can never be.

As Joe told Gina, *be not afraid.*

I have to go on. I have no choice.

Somehow I find myself on my feet. My legs ache, and my body feels weighted down by a weariness that drags on my spirit and seeps against the very edges of my soul. Gina stands at the window. Her eyes are closed, her face drawn in deep shadows. I touch her hand, and her eyelids flutter open.

"I'm going to find the doctor. Can I get you anything?"

She shakes her head.

"You're sure?"

Gina closes her eyes and turns away, shutting out the world.

And me.

I stand there another moment, then start for the door. I only want to help, but I've never felt more powerless in my life.

My rumpled windbreaker lies in a heap on the floor. I bend and throw it on the chair next to Gina's. Her cell phone lies where she tossed it earlier. I stare at it a long moment. Though I've never seen her texting, Gina is of a different generation than me. Cell phones are a lifeline.

Right now, I need a lifeline.

Gina needs a lifeline.

I snatch up the cell phone and slip out the door. I fumble with the keypad, wait for service as I stroll down the hallway, scroll through the directory, searching for the number. I've got no business making this call, but someone has to do it.

Will she talk to me?

Or will she hang up when she hears my voice, before I can give her the news?

I hit connect and make the call to the one person guaranteed I know can help.

Her voice is soft and hesitant. I talk fast, not allowing her a chance to speak as I share the tragic new. She gasps, and my heart sinks as I hear her plaintive cry.

"I know you can't be here, but I thought you should know."

A few moments later, I slip back into the waiting room and offer Gina the phone.

She shakes her head. "I don't want to talk to anyone."

I urge the phone on her. "But she wants to talk with you."

"Who is it?"

I hold the phone out, and she has no choice but to take it.

"Hello?" she says in a hesitant voice, then listens. Immediately her face crumbles. "Oh, Mama."

And finally, Gina's tears start.

CHAPTER SIXTEEN

"I still don't understand why you waited two days to call," Mom says. "You know I would have been here in a heartbeat. But I suppose it's no surprise; you always were a stubborn child."

I shove the last few knives in the dishwasher, bunching them together in a crooked row. They probably won't rinse right, but egg-stained knives are the least of my problems. If I had the guts, I'd tell her to go home. I never asked her to come. She took it upon herself to show up on my doorstep yesterday afternoon, and now she's making it sound like I've stuck her with a sink full of dirty dishes. I don't need the stress or the grief. I've grieved enough the past forty-eight hours.

The police investigation into Joe's death remains ongoing. I've been questioned twice, including yesterday when they took me for a ride in the police cruiser to revisit the scene. Seeing the tree skinned naked of its bark brought the horror of that afternoon screaming back to mind. The screech of tires, the snow mixed with blood. I barely made it back home through the rectory door and to the toilet before I lost my breakfast.

I punch the start button on the wash cycle.

"Gregory, for heaven's sake, pay attention to what you're doing." Mom yanks the door open and straightens the knives. "If you're going to do something, at least take the time to do it right. And why are you running the dishwasher, anyway? It's only half full. You're wasting energy."

Who cares? I jam my thumb against the start button once again and bring the machine rattling back to noisy life. I don't give a damn about a few kilowatts. What does it matter?

Given what's happened, nothing matters.

Joe is dead. How could this have happened?

More important, how is Gina?

"I keep thinking about that poor girl." Mom wipes down the kitchen counter. "What will she do now?"

"Get through the funeral service tomorrow," I say woodenly. "Joe's sisters were scheduled to arrive last night. They're taking his body back to Belgium for burial. Gina is flying back with them."

"In her condition?" Mom clucks her tongue. "In my day, pregnant women weren't allowed to fly."

If only that were true today. The thought of losing Gina to another continent, even for a brief time, widens the hole in my heart.

"I wonder if she plans on staying over there with them?" Mom presses. "That's what I would do, if something like this had happened to me. At least then she won't be alone. Poor little thing. Whatever she decides, she'll have a difficult life ahead of her, no matter where she chooses to live."

I cannot envision a life without Gina. I force away the thought. "It's too early for her to make a decision."

235

But is it? Maybe she's already decided. But there is no way I would know. Gina has shut me out.

There's been no contact between us since that night in the hospital. Everything has been handled by others. Her doctor, friends from school, the funeral director. I've phoned her daily, only to be rebuffed by unfamiliar voices on the other end.

Gina is resting. Gina will return your call.

And so I wait, hearing nothing.

Her emotions are completely understandable. I was the one with Joe at the end. I was the one with her in the hospital. It's only natural she wants to forget. Her grief is still fresh. I'm a living, breathing reminder of what happened.

But I am human, too. I lost a good friend the day Joe died. The thought that I might be losing Gina, too, puts me beyond sadness.

"And no wake service tonight?" Mom shakes her head. "What an odd thing to do. Was that her decision?"

"Gina wanted it combined with the funeral," I say, remembering the funeral director's instructions to me.

"You would think she would have wanted to give people a chance to pay their respects at the funeral home. People can be funny about things like that, especially those who aren't Catholic. Many of them don't feel comfortable being in our church. You should have pointed that out to her, Gregory. She probably never thought about it. She's so young, and you know her family background isn't the best. That poor girl has no idea the way things should be done."

But Gina is no stranger to tragedy. She was only a child when her older brother Donny fell from a tree and broke his neck. Even after all those years, the memories of his death she shared with me that afternoon months ago were vivid. I'm sure that's one reason behind her decision on how she's chosen to handle things for Joe. And she has every right to do so. Joe was her husband and the father of her unborn child. Gina needs to do whatever she has to do to take care of herself. And if that means no wake service at the funeral home merely to accommodate non-Catholics uncomfortable in church, then so be it. Gina has never been one for following the rules.

That makes two of us. Damn what people say. I'm sick of the rules, too.

Mom slips off her apron. "I wonder if her family will come for the funeral."

"I doubt it."

"You never know. She's such a sweet girl. I'm sure they'll forgive her, now that he's gone. Everyone makes mistakes."

"Their marriage was no mistake." I grind out the words through clenched teeth. "It was other people who made the mistake: bigoted, narrow-minded people."

Mom's eyes widen. "I understand you're upset, but there is no need to snap at me."

I pull out my handkerchief and wipe the sweat beading on my upper lip. Good God, what is wrong with me? I need to get a grip before the funeral service.

"Are you all right?" As usual, Mom's eyes don't miss a thing.

"I'm tired."

"You should rest more."

"I should do a lot of things." It's a struggle to keep my temper in check. I am fifty-four years old and I don't need my mother telling me what to do.

"I'm worried about you, Gregory. You've got circles under your eyes. Have you been getting enough sleep? You're not getting any younger, you know."

I don't even bother to answer. I head out the kitchen door, teeth on edge. If I don't get out now, I'll say something I'll later regret. Why did she come? When is she going home?

"You're working too hard." She trails me into the living room. "When was the last time you had a vacation? Maybe you should think about taking some time off after Easter."

"I can't afford it," I mutter. Salary-wise, or conscience-wise.

"If you're worried about money, don't be." She catches my arm and stares at me in earnest. "I've got some savings. You're welcome to it, son."

My heart instantly softens as I catch sight of the worry in her faded blue eyes. "I don't want your money, Mom," I say. "But thank you."

"I'm serious, Gregory. We could go together," she offers. "Remember when you were a little boy and we went to Disney World?"

Despite the anxiousness, I feel the tug of a smile starting on my face. "I'm a little old for Disney World, Mom."

"A cruise, perhaps." Her face brightens. "That one I took with Helen at Thanksgiving was so much fun. I could check the Internet when I get home. I'm sure they'll be offering good deals once the spring-break season ends. The Caribbean is supposed to be lovely that time of year—"

"Not the Caribbean." There was a time when the thought of long, lazy days lounging on a beach under blue skies and hot sand was the only thing that kept me going, but that dream ended weeks ago.

Leave Lila to enjoy the island life.

Gloomy gray skies and dirty snowbanks are my penance and exactly what I deserve.

"Or maybe we should go to Hawaii," Mom muses. "I've

never been there. And Raymond loves to travel. Maybe we should invite him, too. Why don't you call him, Gregory, and see what he thinks. I haven't been anywhere with you boys lately."

The hole in my heart yawns into a deepening chasm. "I'll pass the idea along," I promise halfheartedly.

"Why not call him now," she urges. "Hopefully he'll say yes, and that will give us all something to look forward to."

I throw up my hands. Anything to get her off my back.

I head for my office and make the call, but Ray's private number rings through to his voicemail. I hang up. There's no point in leaving another message. I've tried both his cell and private line repeatedly in the past couple days, but he hasn't picked up or returned my voicemails. Ray must be off on some vacation of his own, though if that's the case, it's unusual that he didn't call and gloat before he left.

Ray still has no clue that Joe has died or that I fired Cynthia.

Meanwhile, my own answering machine has been flooded with messages from parishioners and other priests, but I've ignored returning the calls. I'm in no mood to discuss why I fired Cynthia.

But I need to talk to someone. Only a friend will do.

I yank open the bottom desk drawer and paw through catalogues. I finally come up with the glossy diocesan directory and search for St. Rita's parish listing. A few seconds later, I've got Ray's secretary on the phone.

Linda's sobs starts as soon as I say hello.

"Oh, Father Greg, thank God it's you. It's been horrible; it all happened so fast, I didn't know what to do."

"Whoa, slow down." Linda's words mingled with her tears come so fast, I can barely make out what she's saying. "Take a deep breath, then tell me what happened."

She gasps. "You mean you don't know?"

My heart thuds to a resounding stop. Know what?

"Oh, Father, I wanted to phone you right away. Father Ray would have wanted me to. But there was no time. The diocese got here so fast…"

Her voice drops into a frantic whisper. "I would have called you, but they ordered me not to say anything. I didn't know if that meant I wasn't allowed to talk about it to anyone, or if I could confide in another priest…"

I swallow down the terror clawing at the back of my throat. Ray's eating-and-boozing, laissez-faire lifestyle put him front and center for a heart attack years ago. Has it finally happened?

Is Ray dead?

I bite my lip hard, welcoming the rush of pain. At least it blocks the fear rattling my heart.

First Joe, and now Ray.

"The diocese showed up right away. They're here now, going over the books." Linda's voice is barely above a whisper, as if she's shielding herself from being overheard. Idly I find myself wondering if there's someone in the room with her right now. "They're treating me like I've done something wrong. Father Ray would hate it, if he knew what they were doing. And the way they're talking about him?" Her breath catches. "It's horrible, Father. It makes me sick."

Linda gulps, and breaks into noisy sobs.

I pinch the bridge of my nose and squeeze my eyes shut. There's no use trying to get more information out of her. It's standard practice for the diocese to swoop in and freeze the accounts when a parish priest dies.

"Linda, listen to me," I urge. "The first thing I want you to do is—"

Suddenly the line crackles.

"Hello, Greg." A smooth voice floods the line. "I figured we'd be talking sooner or later."

My mind goes numb as I recognize the voice of Father Bob Koenig, Director of Finances for the diocese. If Bob has taken charge of the phone, then he's also in control of St. Rita's finances, and my worst fears about Ray have come true.

I close my eyes and fling a silent prayer at heaven. Dear God, have mercy on his soul and bless your faithful servant, my dear friend Ray Davis.

"Damn it, Bob, someone should have told me."

"Sorry, but you know how these things work. It's confidential."

I stare at the phone. How can someone's death be confidential? "What the hell is that supposed to mean?"

"Look, Greg, do us both a favor, and calm down." His voice is not unkind. "I know you're upset, but this isn't easy for any of us. And how do you think I feel, being sent over here to deal with all of this?"

Ray is dead, and I'm supposed to worry about how Bob feels? I always thought Bob Koenig a decent enough guy, but the thought of him rifling through Ray's desk and personal effects leaves my skin crawling. I grind my hand against my temple. My head feels like it's been hot-wired with explosives, and if Bob isn't careful, he'll ignite the fuse. "Why don't you just get on with it, and tell me what happened," I mutter.

"I'm not at liberty to discuss the details."

"Ray Davis was my friend," I say through clenched teeth. "The least you can do is have the decency to tell me how he died."

"What the hell are you talking about? Ray's not dead."

My heart hammers to a stop. "What?"

"He's not dead. I don't know who told you that, but they're wrong."

I don't know whether to sob or shout for joy, but it doesn't matter. The whole situation doesn't make sense. "Well, if he's not dead, then where is he? What the hell is going on?"

Seconds pass, and I swallow over the sudden panic snaking its way up the back of my throat. *He's not dead... It's confidential.*

Remembering Rita's sobs leaves me cold. *You should hear the way they're talking about him.*

What exactly is Bob Koenig doing at Ray's parish, rifling through his files?

"I want some answers, Bob."

There is a long pause, enough to make me wonder if the connection is broken. Then I hear a long sigh.

"Just so we understand each other, you didn't hear this from me," he says. "But when Holden found out about the lawsuit, he had no choice but to remove Ray from St. Rita's."

"Lawsuit?" My stomach drops. "What the hell are you talking about?"

"A civil suit filed by a classmate of Ray's," he says, "alleging unwelcome homosexual advances and sexual abuse. The diocese was named as one of the defendants. Given the potential liability, Holden had no choice but to act."

I clutch at the Roman collar choking my neck. Ray, a homosexual? No way in hell. The thought of him and another man together is vile and revolting—and flat-out wrong. For someone to accuse him of what the lawsuit alleges is insanity and pure evil. Ray never would have been involved in something like that. He's a good man and the best friend a man could ask for.

It's not true. It can't be true. We've known each other for years. I would have suspected something. I would have sensed something.

Wouldn't I?

"Look, Bob, I don't know who's behind this, but whoever it is, they're wrong. Dead wrong. There's no way in hell Ray could be guilty of any of those charges." I growl through the phone. "Do you hear me?"

"I'm sorry, Greg. I know the two of you are friends. It's got to be tough, hearing the news like this." His voice is low, filled with compassion. "I'm just passing along what I know."

"He's innocent," I insist. "They've got it all wrong."

"No, Greg, you're the one who has it wrong." Bob's soft voice swells with pity. "According to Holden, Ray has already confessed."

"I'm sure Bishop would be glad to speak with you, but unfortunately he's scheduled in meetings all afternoon."

"And I suggest you look again," I say firmly.

Denise ducks her head and consults her calendar. I'm sure she'd probably like to duck under her desk. The sight of a priest with no appointment and a definite attitude planted in front of her has got to be unnerving.

But I'll be damned if I'm giving up.

"I need to see him," I repeat. "Today."

Denise flips through the pages. "He has some time later this week. Perhaps Thursday afternoon?" she asks hopefully. "Would that work?"

"Why don't you pick up the phone and tell Holden I want to see him now," I coolly suggest, cursing myself as I watch her apprehension turn to fear. My God, what kind of man am I turning into? This isn't who I am or what I want to be. If I'm not careful, I'll turn into a monster.

Then I remember my purpose here today and force down a fresh surge of rage. The diocese has already labeled Ray a monster.

Holden himself ushers me into the inner sanctum a few moments later. He shuts the door behind us. "I don't appreciate you harassing my secretary."

And I didn't appreciate finding out about Ray the way I did. I fling myself into one of the chairs facing his massive desk. Just thinking about my friend, silenced by the church, current whereabouts unknown, makes me want to spit.

"I assume this visit of yours today concerns Ray Davis?" Holden levels me with a cold stare as he takes his own seat.

"Damn right it does." The knot in my gut hardens. None of them know the first thing about Ray. Not Holden, not any of the diocesan crew. "Where is he?"

"Quite frankly, that's none of your business." He settles back in his chair with hard eyes. "Although I'll admit I'm surprised to see you here today. I expected you over here sooner than this, huffing and puffing about his honor and dignity."

"Ray Davis is a fine man and a fine priest. You have no right to treat him like this."

"I have every right. It's my job to protect the diocese from further slander or potential litigation. And as for you, just exactly who do you think you are, barging in here like this, demanding I talk to you?" Holden's eyes narrow. "I would caution you to tread carefully, Greg. Don't say something you will later regret."

I match his cool stare with one of my own. I refuse to be intimidated by this man. He may be a church leader, but he is not my boss.

I have only one boss, and his name starts with G.

"You're wrong about Ray," I say. "He didn't do this."

"Funny, but that's not what he told me two days ago. In fact, Davis was sitting in the exact same chair where you're sitting now when he admitted the allegations were true."

Ray, a homosexual? Ray, forcing himself on another man? Committing lewd acts against another's will? I fight the nausea swirling inside. Could I have been wrong about him all these years? I think of Ray, of the boy I met in high school, of the man I've come to know and respect throughout the years...

No! Ray may have his faults, but he is not a predator. He doesn't have it in him. There's got to be some other explanation.

"Davis has done tremendous damage to himself, and the diocese," Holden says. "From what I understand, he was contacted by the man in question some months ago, who demanded money for his silence. I'm sure, had the funds been available, Davis would have paid him off and no one would have been the wiser—including me or the church. But it seems Davis' money is tied up in a family trust, and his brothers refused to sign off on the payment. Hence, the lawsuit."

My brain scrambles in a wild free-for-all. The thought that all of this could possibly be true is beyond belief.

Holden's eyes soften. "Don't get me wrong, Greg. It's a tragic situation for all involved. Davis is a fine priest, and it's a shame things had to unfold the way it did... especially given that all of this happened so long ago. But with the current public attitude about the clergy sex-abuse scandal, I simply cannot afford to put the diocese in a position where people think we're sheltering a priest who is guilty. My job is to protect the innocent."

I rake my fingers through my hair and stare at the thick, purple carpet beneath my feet. It is plush and obscene, just like the subject matter we're discussing. All this time, despite what Ray was going through, he never said a word. Not once did he give me any hint there was anything wrong happening in his parish or his personal life.

"I've known him since seminary. He's a decent man. He's a good friend."

Unwelcome homosexual advances. Sexual abuse.

"It can't be true. He would never…"

But supposedly Ray has already pled guilty to Holden. I fumble for my handkerchief and wipe away the tears streaming down my cheeks.

All these years, and I had no clue.

"If it's any consolation, Davis did deny most of the allegations. It's my understanding the relationship between the two of them was brief. A few encounters at most during the course of one summer when he was fourteen."

"Fourteen?" My stomach swims as the nausea takes hold. "But… but we were just kids.

"Yet you never saw or heard—"

"No." I shake my head fiercely. "Nothing. Never."

"I assumed that was the case. He must have tried to shield you from the truth."

"You said he was fourteen. We would have just started high school seminary."

Holden shrugs.

"We were only boys," I push the truth at him.

"Boys grow into men," he says bluntly. "Davis may be a priest now, but he's also a man. A man with a past… a homosexual past."

"All of us have pasts." My thoughts turn to Christmas and the rectory living room, the scent of her perfume, the warmth of her kiss. "How can you judge him based on something that happened over thirty years ago? Ray hadn't been ordained. He wasn't a priest yet, he was only a kid. A fourteen-year-old kid, struggling to figure out who he was."

I grip the wooden arms of my chair. "Regardless of what happened that summer, no vows were broken. He wasn't a priest. And I refuse to believe the other charges against him are true, or that he broke any vows after he was ordained. Celibacy is celibacy. Who cares whether a priest is gay or straight? Last I knew, ten percent of the population is gay.

"And who are we to judge? As long as a priest abstains from sex and remains true to the vow of celibacy, who gives a damn what his sexual orientation is? It shouldn't matter."

"It shouldn't matter, but we both know that it does," Holden says, "especially given everything the church has been through in the past several years." He eyes me with a bold stare. "The news will break soon, probably in the next couple of days. What do you think people will say when they find out? There'll be a lot of flak over this. And I guarantee you, it will not be pleasant."

"I don't give a damn about what people will say." My voice shakes with fury. "What about Ray?"

"You think I should have left him where he was? That I should have allowed an admitted homosexual priest to remain in charge of a parish school?"

"But he's done nothing wrong. He's the victim here. We should be comforting him, not punishing him, not taking away everything he's worked so hard for all these years. It's wrong." I bang my fist against my knee. "It's wrong."

"No, Davis is the one who was wrong," Holden counters. "He dragged the diocese into this mess. I have no choice but to listen to counsel. Our attorneys and the insurance company tell me that—"

"You're condemning an innocent man."

"I didn't condemn him. He did that all by himself." Holden's voice softens. "Greg, listen to me. Surely you realize that the world, as well as the church, demands we live by certain rules. Davis has to face the consequences of his actions. He has come to understand that. From what they tell me, he is contrite and apologetic. He is ready and willing to make amends—"

"Amends to whom?" I demand. "For what? He's got nothing to apologize for."

"He most certainly does," Holden says. "He needs to make amends to all of us—to you, to me, to every one of us who wears a Roman collar. He has tainted our calling. He's made every priest in this diocese look bad, including you. That fact alone makes him guilty." His face contorts in a vile scowl. "For God's sake, do I have to spell it out for you? Think of what he's done."

What *he* has done? What *has* Ray done? Isn't the more tragic question, what have *we* done? I think of Ray and the last time I saw him—blustery, opinionated, filled with laughter, life, and love. One could never wish for a more compassionate, empathetic friend.

What the hell does it matter if he is gay? Who the hell cares?

And a stronger truth burns in my heart. If the situation were reversed and I were the one who'd been accused and Ray were the one sitting here in this chair before Holden, he would fight for me with every breath inside him. He would never accept this.

So how can I?

"Damn the rules," I say quietly, "and damn what people

think. Ray Davis is my friend, and he is one of your priests. How can we turn our backs on him now? He needs our help and support. What did Saint John tell us? *Whoever loves God must also love his brother.* It shouldn't matter what people think. Jesus did not concern Himself with what people thought."

Holden levels me with a cool stare. "Jesus is not in charge of this diocese."

Our eyes lock, and I read the truth chiseled on his face. The church, in her ultimate wisdom and authority, has decided to cut her losses and cut Ray adrift.

My poor dear friend. Regardless of what happens in court, Ray will not be coming back.

My God, my God, why have You abandoned me?

"Hopefully someday you'll understand that I am not the villain you'd like to make me out to be," Holden says. "I did what had to be done. I could not afford to expose the diocese to further risk. It's my job to protect our people and our assets."

What's done is done. I stare at him through bleary eyes. "What happens to Ray now?"

"He's in a safe place where he's undergoing counseling. He will use this time to reflect on what has happened and what he wishes to do with the rest of his life."

I come to my feet with an unspoken question lying heavy on my heart. Finally I summon up the courage to ask.

"Is he done as a priest?"

"As a parish priest? Yes." Holden's voice is brusque as he joins me around the desk. "The rest will be determined once the lawsuit is resolved."

But we both know what he means. Without a parish to call his own, Ray's career is over. There will be no future for him in the church. Holden and others will see to that.

And regardless of what the courts decide, the verdict is already in. From now on, whenever people think of Ray, they won't remember the good works he has done or the lives he touched.

They will only remember the scandal.

CHAPTER SEVENTEEN

The church lies in semi-darkness, save for the glow of the sanctuary lamp. In the choir loft, our new organist rehearses for her first funeral liturgy. Soft strains of Bach follow me as I move around the altar making final preparations. Sometime during the morning, my mother has slipped into one of the front pews. She sits there now, rosary in hand.

A rustle at the church doors makes me turn. There, emerging from the shadows, I see Gina. The sight of her in her wedding dress nearly brings me to my knees.

Somehow I make it off the altar and down the steps to where she stands. The tiny pearl drops on Gina's dress shimmer, looking like they're about to pop against the round swell of her belly. "I thought Joe would like it," she offers simply.

"I'm sure he would," I whisper, brushing her cheek with a kiss. The two of us are of the same mind. No mourning garb, no black for Joe. My own liturgical garments for the funeral Mass today will also be white. It is the color the church uses to celebrate Jesus's resurrection, and His triumph over sin and death.

*I am the resurrection and the life… whoever believes in
Me will never die.*

"I have someone I'd like you to meet," Gina says. A
woman stands behind her, and she pulls her forward. "This
is my mother, Anita King. Mama, this is Father Greg."

An older woman with washed-out, strawberry-blond hair
and faded blue eyes takes my hand and grips it with more
strength than I would have thought possible.

"Bless you, Father." Anita King's voice is hushed and
reverent in the quiet of the sanctuary. "Thank you for taking
care of my daughter."

"I'm afraid I wasn't much help."

She shakes her head. "You were there when I couldn't
be. If that's not helping, I don't know what is."

A teenage boy with a shock of black curls hangs in the
background. With olive skin and dark, watchful eyes, he is a
younger, painfully thin, masculine version of Gina.

She drags him forward. "And this is Donny."

"He drove us here today," Anita says.

"Glad to meet you, Donny." A swell of emotion floods
through me. God answers every prayer, and today He has
answered mine. Gina needs all the love and support she can
get, and she has that now, surrounded by her family.

But someone is missing.

Tragedy often brings out the best in people. If only that is
the case today. I search Gina's face, hoping for the miracle.

She shakes her head. "My father refused to come."

"Everyone makes their own choices," Anita says quietly,
"and my husband will have to learn to live with his. But
from now on, he'll no longer be making decisions for
Donny or me."

Has Gina's mother finally found the courage to walk
away?

Gina glances toward the gathering space where Joe's casket stands. The funeral director stands discreetly to one side. Two women stand before the open coffin, one with her arm cradling the other.

"Joe's sisters," Gina whispers. "They asked for a moment alone with him." Her voice drops. "I haven't seen him since that night in the hospital. Have you?"

I nod.

A hint of dread slides across her face. Her eyes are deep, empty pools and her face is pale with exhaustion. "How does he... I mean, is it still Joe? Does he look...?"

Her fear is understandable. I had a hard time myself earlier today when the funeral director brought Joe's casket into church. I anointed it with holy water and my own tears as we opened the coffin. But Joe, in his trim, blue suit and snowy-white tie, looked as handsome as he always did, save for the gash on his forehead where his head struck the tree. The wound, covered expertly with makeup, is small enough that no one else would notice.

But it cried out to me.

Gina has lost a husband. Her child has lost a father. And I have lost a good friend. We gather today to mourn the loss of a good, decent man.

"Joe looks fine," I say, "like he's in a deep, restful sleep."

She blows out a soft sigh. "I always told him he needed more sleep."

Her hands drift to the growing swell of her belly where she carries his baby, caressing it as if it was already in her arms. I shut my eyes against the intimacy of the gesture. I want to rail against this, to protect her from the sacrifices she has been asked to make. After all that has happened, after all Gina has been through, how will she find the heart to go on? This is so unfair.

So much of life is unfair.

Gina's eyes train on the gathering space. "Annelies is crying again. I should go to her."

She starts the long walk toward the coffin, followed by her mother and Donny. I turn away as they finally reach his sisters. There will be more tears shed today and in the days ahead. I head for the quiet the sacristy offers.

"Was that Gina's mother?"

Turning, I find my own mother framed in the doorway.

I nod. "Her mother and her brother."

"I'm glad they came. That poor child needs all the love and support she can get after what she's been through."

She clutches her rosary in her hand. "Gregory, I need to talk to you. I can't stop thinking about last night, and what you said about Raymond."

I swallow down a ragged surge of anger and frustration. I haven't got time to deal with this again. Mom made her position perfectly clear last night.

Her eyes are grave. "Those things you said about… well, about you-know-what."

It's Mom-speak for *let's not put a name to any unpleasantness. Let's not rock the boat. Let's pretend it isn't what it is and hope it goes away.* Her stinging commentary when I told her about Ray last night was harsh and unforgiving. Of all people, how could she stand in judgment against him? How could she condemn him? She's known Ray as long as I have, since my freshman year of high school seminary and the day she helped move me into the dorm.

How in the name of God, in the name of all that is good and holy, could my mother have turned her back on Ray?

How could she have admonished me for defending a friend? She was the one who taught me that you stand by your friends, no matter what.

How could she have forgotten?

I abandoned her in the living room and headed for bed before I said something I'd surely regret. A person can only take so much criticism before they lose heart.

Last night left me wondering if my mother even has a heart.

She trails me into the sacristy. "What will happen to Raymond now?"

"I don't know," I answer flatly and busy myself pulling liturgical vestments from long, lined drawers. Things aren't the way they used to be. I've picked up a variety of new jobs in the past month or two, now that both Cynthia and Lila are gone. And while I don't miss Cynthia, Lila is…

I give the drawer a hard shove.

"What you said about Raymond losing his parish, and about him being in seclusion…"

I close my eyes, cursing myself as I shut her out. It's the same sin I condemned her for last night when she shut Ray out. Am I not called to be better than that?

But why doesn't she understand how I feel? This news about Ray has left me broken and beaten. I have lost my friend. I am grieving. What does she expect? I'm only human.

I swallow hard. My mother is human, too.

"Do you think we'll see him again?"

"Maybe. Hopefully." I barely manage the words.

"Will this mean the end of him as a priest?"

"I don't know, Mom." She's voicing the same questions that have tormented me since Holden broke the news. "It depends on what they decide to do."

"Who? The lawyers?"

"I wish it were that simple." It's not the legal court that worries me, but the court of public opinion. The people in the pews dictate to the diocese. And knowing how quickly Holden banished Ray, I've got very little hope Holden will change his mind and decide to *stand by his man*.

The Catholic Church could use a few parishioners like Tammy Wynette.

"Bishop Holden and the Vatican will have the final say."

Her face turns a queer shade of gray. "And if they decide he's not fit?"

I close my eyes and think of my old friend, all bluster and bravado, stripped of his collar. It would destroy Ray.

"This is all so upsetting." Her hand drifts to her face, trembling. "I didn't sleep at all last night."

"Well, that makes two of us." I curse myself as I see the grief slide across her face. Her words last night were harsh and hurtful, but she spoke out of shock and surprise. I don't have the same excuse today. I've taken deliberate aim at her heart.

She bows her head, and suddenly I note how tiny she is. Her body is frail, her hair thin and white. She seems to have aged overnight and emerged an old woman. I have to cut her some slack. I have to let this go. If I don't, the anger and resentment will destroy me.

But what do I do with this ultimate sadness that will not leave me? It's like my heart has been battered with a two-by-four, my body punched and kicked by a bunch of thugs with their own idea of how life should work.

How could I have been so wrong?

With Ray gone, how do I go on?

With Joe gone, how will Gina go on?

The church bells begin to toll in the background. Like it or not, I have no choice. I have a job to do. Gina needs me. Joe needs me.

They all need me.

My mom clutches my arm. "Gregory, I want you to know that I'm…"

I can't bear it. My mother is a bigot, and now, merely to assuage her conscious, she wants to say she's sorry? What about last night? What about the day before? The weeks before? Does simply saying you're sorry suddenly make things all right?

I grab my vestments. "I've got to go."

"But, Gregory—"

There is no room inside me to help her. Not now. Not when I can barely help myself.

"I don't have time." I turn my back on her and walk away.

The congregation before me waits in silence as I walk across the altar to the podium. I bow my head at the sight of Joe's casket centered in the nave before me. A white funeral pall, placed there by Gina at the start of the liturgy, drapes the rich wood. I glance toward the front pew, where she sits surrounded by her mother and Donny and Joe's sisters. I think of the gospel I have just read aloud.

Well done, good and faithful servant.

Joe was certainly that: a good and faithful servant.

"We lost a good man today. A very good man."

Sweat pops on my forehead and I fumble under my chasuble for my handkerchief. When did the church get so hot? I wipe my forehead and mouth. I clutch my notes centered on the podium and scan them for any words that might make sense. The eulogy I scribbled last night isn't half what I wanted to say. Joe was an extraordinary man; the type of man who changed people's lives. He changed my life. The usual sentiments spoken at funerals just won't do. But what do I tell them?

Upturned faces watch me. People shift in the pews, waiting for me to speak. I gaze around, take in Gina, her mother, Joe's coworkers, Gina's friends from college. But one of the front pews is empty. My mother isn't in her usual space. My eyes scan the pews. And there, seated in the middle of the church on the far right-hand side, I spot the one person I never expected.

Lila.

My heart beat takes off, as do my notes. They flutter from my hand and float to the floor.

When did she get here? How could I have missed her? Is she back for good?

How in God's name will I get through this Mass, knowing that she's here in church, judging every word I say?

But that's exactly what I deserve. I will live with the guilt for the rest of my life for having caused her so much pain.

For not having had the courage to be the man she fell in love with.

But who is that man?

We've lost Joe. We've lost Ray.

And somewhere along the line, I lost me.

A hush grows over the church as I stoop to retrieve the notes scattered around the altar floor. My hand trembles as I shuffle the jumble of paper.

I thought you were the kind of man who stood up for something, but you're not like that at all. You take the easy, softer way every time... walking in fear, living in shadows.

Lila was right. I've lived my life in the shadows far too long. I cannot be afraid. Not any more. I need to let go and step into the light.

People cough. Bodies shift. Even Gina looks nervous. I cannot continue to stand here and say nothing.

I scan the congregation. "I had a eulogy prepared to give about Joe today, but obviously it wasn't meant to work out. And perhaps that's for the best. Because, quite frankly, it wasn't very good. Joe deserved better, and I knew it when I wrote it."

Gripping the podium, I whisper a silent prayer to Joe. *Help me through this.*

"I've never done this at a Funeral Mass, so I ask for your indulgence. Because today, just for Joe, I intend to wing it."

I open my hand and let my notes fly. A murmur ripples through the pews as they flutter around my feet and settle once again on the altar floor.

"Anyone that knew Joe well enough remembers he had a love for our language. But sometimes he got things a little mixed up. I'm sure if he had ever heard me say that someday I would give his funeral eulogy flying by the seat of my pants, Joe would have asked what, if anything, my pants had to do with his funeral."

Polite laughter washes through the front pews. Even Gina smiles.

"Joe might have gotten our language messed up sometimes, but he never messed up when it came to how he lived his life. Joe was an engineer. It's a precise science that requires analytical thinking. From what I understand, he was excellent at what he did and admired by his peers. Certainly, had he lived, his intelligence and skills would have led him to accomplish great things. Some people— many, I'm sure—will say that his life ended in tragedy. They'll say that Joe was taken much too soon, before he had a chance to do all the things he was put here to do. But who are we to say that his life was wasted and that he did not succeed in the one thing that matters most? For Joe was a master when it came to winging it. He knew that each day is all we have and that life holds no guarantees, save for God's love."

I grip the podium tighter and deliberately keep my gaze from straying anywhere near the right side of church and the middle set of pews.

"We gather today to celebrate the life of Johan VanBrabant, a man all of us were blessed to call our friend." I shake my head slightly. "And though it sounds odd, I can't help thinking how appropriate it is that we are brought here together to celebrate Joe's life during this holy season of Lent.

"Lent is a call into action. It is a call into service. It is a call for each of us to wing it, just as Joe did every day of his life. He went about each day being of service to others with grace and humor and a deep love for God. Who among us, when our lives come to an end, will be able to say we've done the same? Joe did his best, every day, to live the gospel message. I'm sure it wasn't easy at times… especially once he and Gina moved to James Bay."

The back of my neck prickles as I think of the two of them shunned as greeters in our church, of the racial slurs hurled from a passing car, of Cynthia's rudeness, and Gina's own father denying his child because of the color of her husband's skin.

"Joe certainly would have been justified in his anger. There must have been times when he felt resentful. Times when it would have been easier to give in to the fear and selfishness instead of going forward and trying to be the man God intended him to be. But Joe's life wasn't about prejudice. It was not about ignorance or hatred or resentment. It was about moving forward. He never complained. He never asked *why me*? Instead, he asked *why not me*? Then he picked up his cross and winged it every day of his life."

The church is silent, and suddenly I'm aware that I'm nearly shouting. Everyone's eyes are on me. Am I wrong? Do I continue? Do they understand?

I look to Gina. She is so small, so young, so solemn. Her dark eyes, locked on my own, burn with a fierce intensity. And then she smiles and nods.

And I have the courage to go on.

"Each one of us has our own cross to bear. Lent is a time for us to pick up that cross and go forward, just as Joe did. Without complaining. Without negotiation. Without seeking reward. I ask you today not to consider Joe's death, but to remember the way he lived his life. He set aside the petty resentments and frustrations and focused on being of service to others. Each of us needs to find our own way. We are called, just as Joe was, to be patient, tolerant, kind, understanding, and loving. Are you too busy to visit the sick? To comfort the dying? To call your mother?"

My gaze roams the church, coming to rest on my mother, seated alone in a pew near the back. How quick I was to brush her off today. I was not tolerant, or patient, or kind. I could have made time for her, given her a few moments. I could have handled things so much better than I did.

Help me, Joe, always to remember your message of love.

"We can go from here today saying that Joe's life was cut too short, that it was a tragedy. We can lament our loss and simply sink back into the routine of our everyday lives. But that would be the real tragedy. We must not allow ourselves to forget Joe."

Never, I make the silent vow. I will never forget him.

"Johan VanBrabant's life here on earth may have been short, but he was a man who considered himself blessed. He had a wife who loved him, sisters who cherished him, and friends that will miss him dearly."

I swallow over the sudden lump in the back of my throat. I will miss him dearly.

"He was a man with a magnificent sense of humor who lived a life of grace and quiet dignity. And in his own way, he showed us rather than told us the way to God's favor. Joe winged it, every day of his life. And that, my friends, is the legacy Joe leaves us. Each of us should be so lucky."

Then, like so many others seated in the congregation before me, I bow my head and finally begin to cry.

"Father Greg?" Gina slips through the sacristy door. She is alone. "I've come to say good-bye."

My heart slides sideways like the lengthening shadows moving across the floor. "You're leaving for the airport?"

She nods. "Annelies made the arrangements. Our plane leaves at seven."

I slip the clerical stole from my neck, fold it gently on the counter, then turn to face her. Her red-rimmed eyes hold a weary sadness that makes me want to weep. "What about your mother and Donny?"

"They've already left. Donny has school tomorrow."

The news surprises me. Seeing them here today had given me hope that Anita King had finally made up her mind to leave her husband.

"What about your mother? Has she made a decision about what she intends to do?"

"I don't know. Maybe she'll stay with him, maybe not."

Gina sighs. "I don't think Mama even knows. But one thing is certain. His days of bullying her are over. Things will be different now. The fact that she came here with Donny is proof enough of that." A wistful smile washes across her face. "I am so proud of her. I can't imagine how much courage it must have taken for her to do that."

She can speak of another's courage, despite all that has happened? Gina herself has suffered tremendous tragedy. Yet somehow, through it all, she has managed to flourish, to take heart and fly, to wing her way through life.

Joe has taught her well.

"Your mother is a brave woman. And I'm glad you were finally reunited. Though I wish the circumstances..."

My voice breaks.

"It's all right, Father." Gina reaches out and touches my hand. "I know what you mean. Joe always wanted to meet Mama and Donny. I know they would have loved him, too, if they'd had the chance."

I spy the sudden shimmer of tears mirrored against her pale face. But instead of crying, she bites her lower lip and swallows down the grief. I want to reach out, take her in my arms, and offer her a shoulder to cry on. But instead, all I can offer is a smile.

"Thank you for what you said about Joe today. It was perfect. He would have loved it."

"It was my honor. Just as it was my honor to call him my friend."

She bows her head, and for one brief moment, I think to add something else, but then decide against it. No other words are necessary. Both of us know how we feel about Joe.

She tilts her head, looks toward the parking lot, and I suddenly realize that this is good-bye.

"When are you coming back?"

"I haven't decided. Annelies and Annelore want me to stay with them in Belgium, at least until the baby is born. After that, I don't know." She shrugs. "I suppose eventually I might come back. I don't want to live so far away that I can't be close to Mama and Donny."

"But I meant…"

Soft understanding fills her eyes. "No, Father, I won't be coming back to James Bay."

Knowing she is about to leave fills me with a tremendous sadness, the kind of which I have never felt before. I love this young woman as if she were my very own. No longer is there any hesitation on my part or in my heart. I take Gina in my arms. And finally, I understand. This is what it feels like to say good-bye to a dearly loved child. This is what a father feels like when his daughter leaves home. This is what it feels like to be a parent, to realize you may never see your child again.

How in the world can I let her go? I hug her closer to me. If I let her see my hurt or my grief, it will only make things harder. "I'll miss you, Gina."

She doesn't reply, only buries her face in my shoulder. Her hair brushes against my cheek, leaving soft wet trails, and I suddenly realize why she isn't speaking. Gina is crying, too.

"If you need anything, just let me know," I whisper. "I'll always be here for you. Whatever you need, whatever you want." I stroke her hair, hug her tight. "I love you, dear child, and I'd do anything for you…"

Abruptly she pulls away.

I've gone too far. I've let her know how much I care and how much she means to me. How much I've come to cherish and love her.

"I'm sorry." The words spill out of me. "I had no right to say that."

"No, you're wrong, Father. If anyone has a right, it's you." She halts me with a look that twists my heart into little pieces. "Don't you know that I love you, too?"

My throat thickens. Even if I could talk, words are beyond me.

She wipes away a few tears. "Remember the first time we met? I stormed into your confessional late one Saturday afternoon, rattling on about my father, stuffy old priests, and the Catholic Church. It felt like my faith in everything I'd believed was gone, and I was ready to give up. But the things you said that day helped me start to find my faith again. You didn't judge, you weren't critical, you didn't tell me what to do. Rather, you said that if I couldn't love my father, I could pray for him instead. I started that day, and I still do it, every morning. Maybe I'll never know if it's made any difference in his life, but that doesn't matter, does it?"

Gina offers me a shy smile. "Because, thanks to you, it's made a difference in mine."

She looks at me with huge dark eyes. "Do me a favor?"

"Anything," I whisper in a ragged voice.

"Take care of yourself," she says softly. "You've made a difference in so many lives. So many people love you. Joe loved you, I love you. And we worry about you."

My heart is in free fall.

"Promise me?" she insists.

I barely manage a nod. "You take care of yourself, too… and that little one."

She gives me one final hug. It is time for her to go.

"Gina?"

She turns with an expectant look.

"Please don't forget us."

But what I really mean is don't forget me.

She offers a soft smile. "No worries, Father Greg. God put you in our lives for a reason, and you'll always be a part of us. In Joe's life, my own life, and the baby's life, too."

And then she is gone, leaving behind a hole in my heart I know will never mend.

CHAPTER EIGHTEEN

I stand at the sink and gulp the glass of water like I've been wandering lost in a desert for days. But the view from the rectory's kitchen window doesn't show sand, only dirty snowbanks and an empty parking lot. The hearse bearing Joe's body is long gone. Gina and his sisters must be at the airport by now.

Getting through the past few days and Joe's funeral Mass this afternoon has left me exhausted and sick to my stomach. Why Joe? Why now?

But who am I to question the ways of God? Joe's body and soul each have their own journey. Gina is moving on.

And so must I.

Somehow I need to learn to live in the now. To live in the love.

A gentle touch from behind caresses my shoulder, startling me.

"Son?"

I glance down at the wrinkled hand spotted with age. She taught me to hold a cup, to print the alphabet, to reach out to others in friendship and love. She helped when I was young.

But she can't help me now.

Her grip on my shoulder tightens. "Are you all right?"

"I'm fine," I answer, though I know it's a lie. Things will never be fine again.

"I'm sorry if I upset you last night, with all those things I said about Raymond. I never meant for that to happen."

I bow my head, close my eyes, struggle not to shrug off her hand. "Let's just forget it, Mom. It's over and done with."

"No, it's not," she says quietly. "Please hear me out."

I turn and stare at her with empty eyes. What does it matter? Everyone I cared about—Lila, Ray, Gina, Joe—all of them are gone now. Nothing she says can make any difference.

"What they did to Raymond was wrong," she says. "I want you to know that. And God help me, I was wrong, too. I'm embarrassed and ashamed of myself."

I blink. "What?"

"After you went to bed last night, I thought long and hard about all those things you said. *Hate the sin but love the sinner.* You were right, Gregory. What does it matter if Raymond is gay or not? He's still the same Raymond, the honorable, decent man we know and love. I forgot that for a few hours last night, but you never did. You stayed loyal to your friend, even when your own mother attacked you for doing so. When I think how I sat there, prattling on about Raymond, judging him for what he did, going on and on about the way people should live their lives…"

Her faded blue eyes fill with a wistful sadness. "You'd think I would know better, seeing how I call myself a Christian. The last thing I want is someone sitting in judgment of me." She shakes her head. "If they called me an old fool, I couldn't argue with them. After last night, there's no doubt in my mind that's exactly what I am: a stupid old fool."

"You're not stupid, Mom, and you're certainly no fool. You're one of the smartest women I know."

She shrugs off my words with a tiny smile. "Thank you, Gregory, but we both know that's not true. Meanwhile, Raymond is very lucky to have you for a friend. We should all be so lucky," she adds.

Her eyes light with a fierce determination, like from when she was still teaching and came home railing about an injustice done against one of her students.

"It's a rare man that finds the courage to put his convictions on the line and stand up for what he believes to be right. That's the kind of man you are, Gregory. You stood up to the bishop, and last night, you found the courage to stand up to me. And thank God you did, because it was the right thing to do. I am so sorry, Gregory. And I hope you will forgive me."

I'm sure my mouth must be hanging wide open, for I can barely believe what she's said. In little more than twelve hours, my mother has flipped her way of thinking. And from the tight clench of her jaw and firm tone in her voice, it's obvious she means every word.

Suddenly I am mightily ashamed of myself. Last night I lashed out at her in harsh judgment, when I had no business taking her inventory. She is a proud woman, but not too proud to humble herself and confess she believes she has made a mistake.

I could take a lesson from her.

"I'm the one who owes you the apology, Mom. I never should have walked out on you the way I did last night. And then to ignore you like I did before the funeral when I knew you wanted to talk?" It makes me cringe, remembering the hurt reflected in her eyes as I cut her off and turned my back on her. Every bit of anger and resentment I've felt since our fight has melted away sometime while we were speaking. And her compliment to me, so poignant and heartfelt, touches me deep inside. Somewhere so hidden, I cannot begin to name it.

"I can't imagine what Raymond must be going through," she says. "His parents are dead, his brothers have turned against him, and now the church has abandoned him, too. He needs to know that he's not alone. You need to find him, son. Find him, and tell him that we love him, that he is part of our family." Her voice is firm. "Tell Raymond that we will stand behind him, no matter what."

I have never been prouder of my mother than I am at this moment. She has opened her mind and heart to rally against prejudice, injustice, and ridicule. God alone knows what the diocese might try. The fight on Raymond's behalf will surely involve heartache, but my mother looks ready to march into battle.

Bishop Holden versus my mother? If I were a betting man, my money would be on Mom.

She has God on her side.

"I'll find Ray," I say. "We'll take it from there."

"Good. And if the bishop gives you any grief, you just let me know. He had no business cutting Raymond loose like he did. It was God Himself who said *woe to the shepherd who forsakes his flock.* That bishop of yours needs to brush up on his Bible verses. Who exactly does he think he is, a man of God, treating people like that?"

An odd sound catches in my throat, and abruptly I realize it's the sound of my own laughter. I'm chuckling for the first time in days. Suddenly I don't feel so alone anymore. If my mother can open up her mind and question the rules, maybe there's hope for us all.

"I love you." I open my arms and clutch her in a tight hug.

"And I love you, Gregory," she whispers fiercely. "I will always love you. Nothing will ever change that. You're a fine man and a fine son. No mother could be prouder."

I'd thought there were no more tears left inside me, but I was wrong. Standing there in the shelter of her arms, I suddenly begin to sob. I cry like when I was a child, and her words and hugs took away all the hurt.

"There's something I need to tell you," I finally say.

She pulls back slightly and searches my face.

"I'm thinking about going away for a while."

"Away, like on a vacation?"

I catch the fleeting glance of faith suddenly leap in her eyes, and curse myself for what I'm about to say, for dashing her hopes.

"No, Mom. It won't be a vacation."

For a long moment, she does not answer. A symphony of emotions—fear, apprehension, doubt, panic—plays across her face, finally crashing into a confusion of wrinkles lining her forehead. Then slowly she nods. "Maybe that is best."

Her response surprises me. As do her next words.

"Are you leaving the priesthood?"

I draw in a deep breath. No matter what I eventually choose to do, she'll have to know sooner or later. "I haven't made that decision yet."

Her lips move together in a silent whisper. It takes me a moment before I realize she must be praying. For me. Finally she offers a tiny smile. "All right, Gregory. I trust you know best."

"Are you saying it doesn't matter?" All this time I have been afraid to tell her, afraid of what she would say, what she would think. "It doesn't matter what I decide? You don't care what I do?"

She clucks her tongue. "Of course I care. I will always care. I'm your mother, Gregory, and I only want what's best for you."

"But I know how happy it made you when I decided to become a priest," I say slowly. "All those years you worked so hard, the prayers you offered, the sacrifices you made… the money you spent on my education, only now, perhaps to have it…" I swallow hard. "The last thing I want is for you to think that any of it has been wasted or that it was a mistake."

My voice clutches. How do I go on? Knowing I could cause her pain is nearly too much. "Because, above everything else, Mom, I never want to disappoint you—"

"Stop it." She presses a finger against my lips, silencing me. "I love you, Gregory. You could never disappoint me. All I want is your happiness. And this is not about me or what I think. This is about you."

Does she really believe that in her heart, or is she merely saying what she thinks I want to hear? And if so, how can I live with that kind of guilt hanging over my head for the rest of my life?

"What if I did decide to leave the priesthood?" I ask slowly. "How would you feel about that? I've been a priest for a long time."

"And I've been your mother even longer," she replies. "A mother knows when her child is unhappy. I think you've been unhappy for a very long time."

If the two of us are finally being honest, what's the point in hiding how I feel? "I am unhappy," I admit. "I've been unhappy for a while. And I don't know what to do."

"Oh, Gregory, I am so sorry." There is no triumph in her voice, only sadness, concern, and love. She embraces me gently. "This is a time for you to trust God. Turn to Him, son. He will show you the right thing to do."

I bow my head. "I know."

But I see the hesitation on her face. "What is it?"

"Just that, if you do decide... well, you know." Her voice falters. "Is this a decision you're making on your own, or does it have to do with someone else?"

There's no need to mention names. Both of us know exactly who she means. My thoughts stray to earlier, to Joe's funeral liturgy, and the one face I never expected to see in church today.

"She's a lovely woman, Gregory. Everyone would understand." One hand strays to her neck, where her fingers dance nervously. "And if that is what you want... if *she* is what you want, then I... well, I promise I will try my best to understand."

Tears well in her eyes and she blinks them back. "I loved your father deeply. How can I deny you the same happiness? It would be so selfish of me. Everyone needs to love... and be loved."

Guilt, sadness, and shame rushes through me. All my life, my mother has had only my happiness in mind, and today is no different. Though it would go against everything she believes, she is willing to open her mind and try to accept what I want for myself.

If that is what I choose.

"This has nothing to do with Lila. Perhaps it did once, but not now. Not anymore." And as I say the words, I realize they are the simple truth. "This is between me and God."

She nods. "Then everything will work out as it's meant to be. It always does when we put our trust in God. In all things... including this. He will lead you in the right direction."

I see the pain in her eyes. This concession has cost her

dearly. But she only wants what is best for me, even if that should mean me leaving the priesthood. Opening my arms, I hold her close. I have no idea what the future might hold, but one thing is certain.

I never need doubt my mother's love.

She pushes me away after a moment with a slight sniff. "All right, I suppose that's enough of that. There's no use getting maudlin about things." She glances at the stove clock. "Goodness, look at the time. How did it get to be so late? You must be hungry for dinner. I'll make us some eggs."

Without waiting for a reply, she bustles around the kitchen, opening cupboards, pulling out a frying pan. I lean against the counter and watch her, smiling to myself as she hunts through the refrigerator. Give her a reason to cook and my mother is content.

She sets a carton of eggs on the counter next to me, then suddenly stops and peers through the window. "The lights are on in church."

"I thought I turned them off." Turning, I glance through the window and see a light in the sacristy glowing through the twilight.

"Maybe the janitor came back to clean up." She returns to scrambling the eggs.

"I don't think so," I say, frowning. I saw Vince lock up and leave shortly after the hearse pulled away. "Maybe I'll take a walk over and have a look."

"Don't be long," she warns. "These eggs will only take a few minutes."

I head out the back door and trod through the snow. I find the sacristy door locked, just as Vince left it, just as it should be. Hauling out my keys, I unlock the door and slip into the empty room. The lights are on. Nothing looks disturbed.

Then from beyond the wall I hear a soft clink, followed by another, louder than the first.

My heart slams against the wall of my chest. Someone is in the church.

I snap off the lights. Unlike other parishes in the area, Our Lady's has been lucky not to be victimized by thieves... until now. I strain to listen, waiting to hear more sounds filtering through the darkness Finally comes a muffled thud, followed by a rhythmic clink-clink-chink, like glass tinkling against metal. I steal down the hallway behind the sacristy and slip onto the empty altar.

A lone figure hovers in the gloom of the side sanctuary. I hang back and watch as he begins to fumble with the money box attached underneath the votive stand.

"Stop right there!"

The figure freezes, caught in the shadows.

What if he has a gun? But it's too late now. I summon all my courage. "Turn around," I command. "Slowly."

"You think I'm going to rob the votive-light money?"

My knees nearly buckle as Lila steps into the light.

"I'm sorry, Greg. I didn't mean to startle you."

But she's done more than that. There was no time at the funeral for more than a hurried hello and a quick exchange of glances. Now, to suddenly find her in front of me, a mere few feet away, has reignited all my doubts, my fears...

And my desires.

I push down the feelings. This is neither the time nor the place.

"I was on my way to dinner and thought I'd stop in and refill the votive lights. I noticed this afternoon that they were nearly empty." She points at the bulky carton of candles on the floor near the stand. "I remember you told me when I started as sacristan that it was important to keep the candles stocked so people could offer up prayers." She bites her lower lip. "I guess I shouldn't have left town without making sure whoever replaced me knew what she was doing."

"*He*," I correct her. "And actually, he's pretty clueless."

Her eyebrows lift. "Oh?"

"I've been doing it myself."

"Oh." Her brows arch even higher. "I see."

No doubt she sees the entire picture. I should have asked someone to take over long before this. I should never have kept the job to myself. Did I do it because of some deep-rooted sense of guilt or frustration? Some anxious need to keep busy, to keep myself from thinking?

Or was it because I didn't want anyone trying to take her place?

Lila moves a few steps closer. Close enough to see the silent question in her eyes. Close enough to catch the faint scent of her perfume. Close enough for me, if I wanted, to reach out and stroke her hair, caress her cheek.

Close enough to remember everything I once felt for her.

Feelings and desires that have not gone away.

Her eyes are wary. "I'll stay and finish stocking the candles, if you want."

Who gives a damn about the candles? "What I really want is for you to take the job back."

Her face is guarded. "I can't. I'm leaving again tomorrow."

"You're going back," I say flatly. And why shouldn't she? There is nothing for her here.

"Lucy and I have taken a little house in the Caribbean. We have it for one more month."

I nod, remembering Max's words.

"Lucy talked me into it. I didn't want to go, but she

276

insisted. And once I got there, I fell in love with the place." Her face brightens for the first time since our conversation began. "The house sits on a cliff and has its own little beach. I spend every afternoon there. It's the perfect spot, private and secluded."

Obviously the warm weather suits her. Lila looks sun kissed and golden.

"The sea is the most beautiful blue you've ever seen. And at night, I fall asleep listening to the tide rushing in and the waves crashing upon the sand. It's like paradise on earth. I would stay there forever, if I had a choice."

But paradise is of our own making. It is what fills us inside. It is the serenity, the peace, the overwhelming sense that, no matter what happens, everything is right with the world.

Lila has found her paradise.

But where is mine?

"Excuse me, but I need to sit down." I stumble from the altar and grab the railing of the front pew. The wood is smooth and cool under my hand as I slide onto the bench.

Lila trails behind me. "Are you all right?"

Hell no, I'm not all right. I pinch my nose, close my eyes, try to shut her out. I think about the tasks needing my attention: the carton of votive candles that should be put away, the pile of soiled altar linens heaped in the sacristy. I try and concentrate on anything and everything except the scent of lilacs and roses drifting in the air between us. It is the same scent that has haunted my dreams since the day she left.

But this is no dream. Lila is right in front of me.

And tomorrow she will be leaving once again.

"Greg?"

I shake my head. "Sorry, I just need a moment. I'll be fine. It's been a long day."

She slips into the pew beside me, kneels and whispers a silent prayer, then blesses herself and sits. Her perfume mingles with a faint whiff of incense lingering from the funeral. A hush settles between us, and we sit there for some time without speaking. There is plenty of room between us.

Enough to fill a lifetime.

"Those things you said today at the funeral?" She finally breaks the silence. "I want you to know how much they helped us all. And then, when you began to cry…"

"No, stop. Please, just stop." Never in all my years as a priest have I broken down on the altar like I did today. I had no business allowing my personal emotions to get the best of me. If I never preach another eulogy, it will be too soon.

"Don't tell me you're ashamed?" Lila stares at me. "Or embarrassed."

I shake my head. The memory of Joe dying in my arms is too close, too painful to discuss.

"For God's sake, Greg, don't do this to yourself," she says quietly. "What happened to Joe was a terrible tragedy, and every one of us wondered how we would get through it. Then you stood there on the altar today and allowed us to see just how much you were hurting and how much you loved him. What a tremendous gift to us all, those things you said. And then, when you cried. You found the courage to stand there and openly grieve. Surely you must realize how much it helped us all. It touched everyone, and it meant so much. Even Gina herself told me so, just before she left."

Gina. By now, she and Joe's sisters must be somewhere high in the skies, accompanying Joe on his final journey home.

"It never should have happened," I say in a ragged whisper. "He should still be alive. None of this makes sense."

"It *doesn't* make sense," she agrees. "And you know that better than any of us."

I shift in the pew and turn to face her. "Why are you here?" Suddenly I have to know.

She frowns. "But I already told you. The votive lights needed replacing."

"No, I meant today," I insist. "Why did you come back? Was it because of the funeral?"

Surprise washes over her face, then softens. "But of course I had to come back. I didn't know if her mother would be here. I couldn't bear the thought of Gina being alone."

Slowly I absorb what she is saying and then I finally understand. Lila came back because of Gina. It is as it should be.

"I'm sorry, that's not fair," she says, "for there's something else, too. I wouldn't be honest and working my program if I didn't admit it," Lila says softly. "It's true that I came back because of Gina. But I also came back because of someone else. I came back for me."

I stare at her through empty eyes.

Lila clasps her hands and folds them in her lap. "When I left here, I was angry and afraid. I was angry with you, and afraid for myself. I blamed everything on you and I ran away. That was terribly wrong of me. And I am very, very sorry, Greg, for doing that to you."

She is not making sense.

Her eyes search my face. "Do you remember how I accused you of walking in fear and living in shadows?"

I nod slowly. How could I forget?

"Once I left town and had some time to think, I realized that was exactly what I'd done, too. I was angry and hurt that you wouldn't make a decision. I thought I knew what was best for both of us, and I was angry that you didn't agree. I spent a lot of time walking the beach, thinking about things. About you and me... and if there ever could have been a chance to be an *us*."

My mouth goes dry, hearing her confession. I am not the only one who wondered about the future, or thought about what might have been. All this time, Lila has carried the same doubts in her heart.

"I wanted to curse God after I left. I thought He was the one standing in the way, like a stumbling block to what you wanted for the rest of your life. But I don't feel that way anymore." Lila hesitates. "Both of us love God so much. And I've come to realize that it isn't fair that either of us should be forced to choose for or against Him. That's the other reason I came back today. I wanted to you tell that I've made a decision.

"I don't want to live my life in fear or shadows. But I also don't want to be alone. I know you've made your decision, Greg. You've chosen God. And if that's what you want, then who am I to say that's wrong? It's exactly as it should be." Her eyes search my own. "But I made a different decision, Greg. I choose both of you. I choose God *and* you."

A cold swell of panic fills my throat. Lila has no understanding of what she is saying or what it would mean. "Nothing has changed," I remind her. "I am still a priest."

"I know that," she says quietly. "And I am not asking you to give up your vocation for me. The last thing I want is to do is force you into making a decision you would later regret. That would be a real tragedy. And something you would hold against me for the rest of your life."

Her face softens. "Don't worry. I don't intend to make trouble. You don't have to be afraid. I promise I won't make a pest of myself. I won't phone or bother you. There will never be a hint of scandal. What happened between us is in the past. We can leave it there and go on. We can start fresh. Right here, right now... if you're willing."

She draws a deep breath. "But if you think it would be best for me to leave and never come back, then that's what I'll do." Her eyes fill with an age-old sadness, but her voice never falters. "I want you in my life, Greg. Even if that means you are the priest and I'm just one of your parishioners. It would be difficult, but I have to believe that it's better than the alternative. For that would mean living the rest of my life without you."

And there it is, no longer between us. In less than five minutes, Lila has bared her heart and soul and removed any impediment standing between us. She's offering me a way out. She's offering me the chance to experience a spiritual, platonic relationship with a woman. She's offering to shoulder all the guilt and blame.

But allowing her to carry that cross would be wrong. I wouldn't be the man she wants me to be. I wouldn't be the man God wants me to be.

I wouldn't be the man *I* want to be.

Quietly I share the news about Ray, about Holden, and my discussion with my mother. And finally, I tell her of my decision.

Lila hesitates. "Do you know where you're going?"

Shrugging, I pinch back a smile. "Nope."

But wherever I end up, one thing I'm certain of. There will be no shadows, no hiding in my future.

You can't hide from God.

"It sounds as if it is for the best," she says. "And I know you'll do the right thing."

"I wish I was as confident as you are. Sometimes, I think I don't know what the right thing is anymore."

"You will," she predicts. "You're a smart man, Greg. Everyone knows that. That's why we all trust and depend on you."

"I think you're all crazy," I warn, "seeing how I barely trust myself."

"Give yourself some credit," she says. "God has blessed you with a gift for helping others see themselves clearly. He's given you other gifts as well. Tremendous gifts: compassion, empathy and forgiveness."

"But it doesn't feel like a gift." I knot my hands together, stare at the carpeted floor beneath my feet. "Sometimes, like on the altar today, it seems empty, like I'm stumbling through a desert. I don't know if I can ever find my way out. I can't see anything. The mountain is gone, and I'm surrounded by an endless valley."

Her eyes pool with understanding. "Remember what they tell us at meetings? It is in the valley that all the growth takes place. And when you can't see above to the mountain, that is when you need to put your trust in others. Believe them and the things they tell you. God puts people in our lives for a reason, Greg. Believe us when we tell you that the mountain is still there."

Hot tears well up in my eyes. "Is it?" I whisper.

"Yes, it is." She reaches out and gently touches my hand. "And the view from the top is lovely."

We rest there another few moments. Neither of us speaks. Her words sitting between us are comfort enough. Even when she finally draws her hand from mine, I do not lose heart.

I have not lost her.

No matter what I choose, I will never lose Lila.

"It's late." She stands, slips from the pew. "I should go."

My knees creak as I join her in the aisle. I'm getting

older, but moving forward suddenly seems easier than it did just moments ago.

"Would you like to stay for dinner?" I'm surprised to hear the words tumble out of my mouth. "It's nothing fancy. Mom is making scrambled eggs."

A tiny light leaps into her eyes, only to be snuffed out like a precious candle stub to be saved for later. "Sorry, I can't. I'm meeting Max for dinner tonight." She pauses. "Perhaps another time?"

"The invitation is always open. And... I think my mother would be pleased." I remember our conversation and my mother's remorse at how she had acted, what she'd said and done. And how she would welcome Lila into our lives, if that should be part of my decision. "Mom will be sorry she missed you."

She searches my face for a quick moment. "Perhaps I'll stop by and say hello."

"I think she would like that. She's in the kitchen."

She starts toward the votive-light stand and the carton of candles, but I beat her to them. I shoulder the box, awkward and heavy in my arms. How the hell did Lila manage them herself?

"I'll put these away. You go ahead. Tell my mother I won't be too long."

Lila nods. "I'll be back in James Bay in another month or so, shortly after Easter. If you're not here, know that I'll be thinking of you and keeping you in my prayers. And, Greg?"

Our eyes catch in a long look that seems to hold forever.

"Remember what I said. Whatever you want..." The air hums between us. "Whatever you decide, I promise to honor your decision. You've nothing to fear from me."

She studies me in the flickering lights of the votive

candles and sanctuary lamp, as if she is committing something to memory that will be important to keep tucked close to her heart in the times ahead. "Take care of yourself, Greg."

Then she turns and walks away.

I stand there for some moments, alone on the altar, hear the click of the outer church door. For the second time in months, Lila has left me.

I head for the sacristy. The room is shrouded in darkness and I fumble for the light switch, only to lose my grip on the box. It crashes out of my hands and splits as it hits the floor. Candles spill and roll across the room.

Sinking to my knees, I crawl across the cold tiles, plucking candles from beneath the table, scrambling to reach those in faraway corners. I grab the last three and plunk them on the counter. And as I reach up, still on my knees, I catch sight of something gleaming high above me.

The small crucifix on the wall isn't more than four inches high. A simple crucifix, it is often overlooked, but it works a mighty power as it blesses this room and all the people who move and work and pray within this holy place. The wood is not rich, the Christ figure does not gleam of gold.

I stare up at the familiar image, remembering how He cried out to God at the end. Did He feel the sacrifice was worth it? Did He think He'd done enough? Or did He believe that His life here on earth had been spent in vain?

What do I believe? The room starts to spin, my heart pounds in my ears, and I grab the floor, still on my knees. All these years I have spent as a priest, I have tried my best to know and do God's will. But has it been enough? Is it enough? Can I ever give enough? Has my life been a waste?

How do I know? How do any of us know for certain?

But Joe knew.

Do not be afraid... I am with you always.

The words he left behind for Gina were simple and comforting. As I held Joe in my arms and forgave him his sins, I knew he had no doubts. Joe knew how much God loved him.

How can I have doubts? I know how much God loves me.

No matter what I eventually decide.

As Lila said, even when we find ourselves in the valley, we are never truly alone. God has given me a gift of loving abundance with the people in my life. I am not alone and I never will be. He will never abandon me. And no matter how the rest of my life plays out, it will not be in vain if I spend it searching to find every solution in the expression of love.

Rules, laws, the church hierarchy; all of it will eventually fade into nothing. For when I find myself taking my last few breaths, facing the end, facing God, love *will* be—love *must* be—the only thing that matters.

But what matters now? What do I need to do to make this right?

In my heart, I know. Somehow, I've always known.

There is no need for another priest. This is solely between God and me. Still on my knees, I bow my head and bless myself with the sign of the cross. Then, my voice edging out in a ragged whisper, I begin with the words that have always comforted, that will always heal.

"Bless me, Father, for I have sinned..."

Tears stream freely down my cheeks as I kneel in the sacristy and confess my heart freely to God. I voice my doubts, my fears, my loves, and I voice my sins. And when my confession is finally complete, I am left with a sense of surrender and peace I haven't felt in years. No longer is there the need to rush or hurry anymore.

Things are as they should be and will be, in time.

Not in my time, but in God's time.

My knees creak as I struggle to my feet. I snap off the sacristy lights and stand there an extra moment, watching and listening, allowing the quiet that fills the room to settle in my heart. Twilight filters through the small window before me, and I can see light glowing from the rectory kitchen window, where my mother and Lila stand together, talking. Two women, a generation apart, searching for some common ground.

Devoted women, each of whom loves God.

Each of whom loves me.

Both of whom love me enough to give me the freedom to make my own choice. It is a choice I thought I would struggle with for the rest of my life. It is a choice that has caused me turmoil, heartache, and the most dreadful self-doubt in the depths of my soul.

But not anymore.

Lila was right when she talked about refusing to live in the shadows. There is no longer a need for me to run and hide. I already know what I need to do.

It is the right thing to do.

It is the only thing to do.

Reaching up, I unsnap my Roman collar and free it from my neck. I stare at it a long moment. For the many years that I have worn it, this collar has set me apart from other men. From the first time I embraced it, I felt a part of something larger than myself, of something that was holy, of the greatness that is Rome. It defined me as a man of God.

But I no longer need this collar around my neck to define me or remind me who I am.

I am, and always will be, a man of God. That will never leave me.

Drawing the collar to my lips, I reverently kiss it one last time, then lay it on the counter.

No doubts. It is the right thing. In my heart, I know it is the right thing.

I lock the sacristy door behind me and step outside. Overhead, the stars begin to twinkle, and I shiver as icy fingers of the cold winter evening reach down to embrace me. The parking lot is shrouded in darkness as I head down the path layered with icy patches. But tonight, for once, my feet don't slip. I have never walked more securely in my life.

Keeping my eyes focused on the rectory kitchen window, I step toward the light.

ABOUT THE AUTHOR

Kathleen Irene Paterka is the author of numerous novels which embrace universal themes of home, family life and love, including *Fatty Patty, Home Fires, and Lotto Lucy* from the Women's Fiction series, "*The James Bay Novels*". Kathleen is the resident staff writer for Castle Farms, a world renowned castle listed on the National Historic Register, and co-author of the non-fiction book *For the Love of a Castle*, published in 2012. Having lived and studied abroad, Kathleen's educational background includes a Bachelor of Arts degree from Central Michigan University. She and her husband Steve live in the beautiful north country of Michigan's Lower Peninsula. Kathleen loves hearing from readers. You can contact her via her website at
http://www.kathleenirenepaterka.com
or follow her on Facebook at
http://www.facebook.com/KathleenIrenePaterka.

If you enjoyed **FOR I HAVE SINNED,**
check out these other titles in *The James Bay Novel*
series by Kathleen Irene Paterka:

The James Bay Novels
FATTY PATTY (#1 – available now!)
HOME FIRES (#2 – available now!)
LOTTO LUCY (#3 – available now!)
FOR I HAVE SINNED (#4 – available now!)

Non-Fiction:
FOR THE LOVE OF A CASTLE (available now!)

Coming in 2013:
ROYAL SECRETS

www.ingramcontent.com/pod-product-compliance
Lightning Source LLC
Chambersburg PA
CBHW030029180626
46810CB00001B/290